A Cold Season in
SHANGHAI

A Cold Season in
SHANGHAI

S.P. Hozy

RENDEZVOUS
PRESS

Toronto, Ontario, Canada

Cover painting by François Tisdale, cover design by Emma Dolan

Le Conseil des Arts | The Canada Council
du Canada | for the Arts

We acknowledge the support of the Canada Council for the Arts for our publishing program. We acknowledge the financial support of the Government of Canada through the Book Publishing Industry Development Program (BPIDP) for our publishing activities.

RendezVous Press
an imprint of Napoleon & Company
Toronto, Ontario, Canada
www.napoleonandcompany.com

Printed in Canada

13 12 11 10 09   5 4 3 2 1

Library and Archives Canada Cataloguing in Publication

Hozy, Penny, date-
          A cold season in Shanghai / S.P. Hozy.

ISBN 978-1-894917-79-7

          I. Title.

PS8615.O99C64 2009   C813'.6   C2009-904774-8

Acknowledgements

Many books and authors provided valuable information and insight during the writing of this book, among them: *The Search for Modern China* by Jonathan D. Spence, *Shanghai Diary* by Ursula Bacon, *The Woman Warrior* by Maxine Hong Kingston, *Four Sisters of Hofei* by Annping Chin, *Spring Moon* by Bette Bao Lord, and *The Lover* by Marguerite Duras, the inspiration for Annette's story.

Throughout the book, I have used the Wade-Giles system of spelling for Chinese names and places, since it is the one that was in use during the time of the story, rather than the current Pinyin that was adopted in 1977.

It is only when the cold season comes
that we know the pine and cyprus to be evergreens.

-Chinese proverb

In human relations
kindness and lies are worth a thousand truths.

-Graham Greene,
The Heart of the Matter [1948]

Prologue

It's winter in Canada, in Toronto, where I've been living for the past twenty years since my marriage ended. The snow is piling up outside my door, and I know I won't venture out for a few days. I will become even more melancholic, and perhaps I'll drink a little too much gin. But who will really care? My sister Olga will phone tomorrow to ask how I am, and I will tell her I'm fine. She'll choose to believe me because she's much more interested in her grandchildren these days than in me.

In Shanghai, where I grew up, the winters were miserable, damp and cold. I learned to hate the rain even more than the snow. In Malaya, where I lived with my husband on a rubber plantation, the winters were as hot and sunny as the summers. The climate suited me fairly well, but in the end I could no longer endure the monotony or the marriage. I chose to come to Canada, where Olga and Jean Paul had immigrated a year after the birth of their second child. By that time both Papa and Mother were gone, both too soon and within a year of each other. Now that I've passed my sixtieth birthday, I think about the dead more than I think about the living. Sometimes this frightens me and I dump all the gin down the sink and swear I won't drink again. But nothing changes, and I buy another bottle to ease the pain and the guilt.

Nowadays I'm preoccupied with the past. When I think back on myself as a young woman, I'm surprised at how naïve I was, but I realize it was a wilful naïveté, just another way of maintaining the pretence of my life. I was obsessed with keeping it interesting and exciting. But where did that desperation come from? The more I pose the question these days, the more I begin to understand that the problem had more to do with my own character than with any of the circumstances surrounding me. I had a good family that loved me. I lived in a place that was often dangerous, yet I felt safe and secure within my world. I was educated and read books. Why did I become so contrary?

Today I marvel at how I could observe and participate in one kind of life and yet follow a completely different narrative in my mind. I insisted on telling the story the way I wanted it to be, and then I made myself believe it. Nobody could persuade me that the other version—the one they saw—was real. Especially not Olga or my parents. Not even Lily, when she tried. Annette, experienced in the ways of the world, never tried. She kept telling her story, "*l'histoire de ma vie*", the way she wanted to hear it. But in Annette's case I could understand. There were circumstances. Circumstances that could lead one to want to alter, or soften, the harsher aspects of the narrative. In my case there were none. At least, not at first.

But everything changed after Daniel's murder. Because I was the one who identified his body, I got to see the ugly reality of his death up close. That reality reduced the beauty of his short life to the single image of a bloated corpse on a metal table. It is an image that can still wake me in the middle of the night, gasping for air. I feel responsible, even though I didn't fire the gun that put those bullets in his heart. Is the person who pulled the trigger the only one who is culpable? Surely I must bear some of the burden of guilt. I was, after all, the one who set the whole thing in motion.

Do we ever really forget? The dictionary says that to forget means not to remember, to cease thinking about. I forget. I have forgotten. But is forgetting an absolute? Or does memory simply drift away, evaporating like fog? Is there nothing that is active or aggressive about forgetting, no tossing away, no burning up the past so that only the ashes remain?

Even though I have tried to forget the events of 1927, especially as they happened to me and to my friends, I find myself remembering those events as if they happened yesterday. Shanghai and the smell of death and peonies. The stench was at once so harsh and acrid that I feel a bitterness burning my nose, even after thirty years. At the same time, there was a fragrance so sweet and delicious, I want to bury my face in it and inhale its loveliness again. To remember Shanghai is to remember my life between 1906 and 1927, to remember my childhood and growing up, and to remember Lily and Annette and Daniel.

Many things happened to the world in 1927. In Shanghai, there was turmoil and revolution. Then Daniel was murdered, and I left Shanghai forever.

Now, Lily's letter has brought it all back to me with such clarity. She says she's coming to Toronto and asks if she can stay with me for a few days when she arrives. Her youngest brother, the one we always called Number Three Brother, has sponsored her. I'm surprised to hear that he wants her to live with him and look after his grandchildren. I would have thought she'd bring too much bad luck, but maybe he's not as superstitious as he used to be. I wonder if we will talk about Daniel when she gets here. I wonder if she will finally tell me what really happened between them.

In the meantime, until she comes, I'll drink another bottle of gin and try again to put the puzzle together. As always, I'll go back to the beginning.

Shanghai, China
1906

Chapter One

They stood at the rail of the ship as it sailed up the Yangtze River and into the Whangpoo River toward the harbour of Shanghai. They were an attractive family, Sergei, Katarina, and their two daughters, Olga and Tatiana, and obviously a family of means. Sergei, a man of medium build, was handsome and well groomed even after the long ocean voyage. His dark brown hair had a natural wave and was carefully combed, as was his moustache and small, neatly trimmed beard. People often commented on his resemblance to the Tsar, to which he would reply, "It is the Tsar who bears a resemblance to me." In truth, they were related, although Sergei didn't always publicly lay claim to the relationship, for he disagreed with many of the Tsar's misguided policies.

Sergei's wife Katarina was nearly as tall as him and slender as a stalk of wheat. She was blonde and ivory-skinned and, unlike her husband, Katarina looked as if she had endured a long, hard sea voyage. Her clothes were wrinkled as if she had slept in them, although she hadn't; and her expression was uneasy, as if she might be seasick, which she wasn't.

Her eldest daughter Olga, who was nearly eleven, kept her eyes fixed on their destination, her expression serious but not fearful, curious but not impatient. She was shorter than her mother by several inches, and she stood very straight, possibly in an attempt to appear taller. She resembled her father more than her mother, although she had dark curly hair, tangled and unruly, which she had unsuccessfully attempted to stuff into a dark blue velvet cap.

Her sister Tatiana, younger by less than two years, was as different from Olga as two sisters could be. She was already an inch taller and had her mother's slender build. Her hair was blonde with soft waves like her father's, and her eyes were as blue as cornflowers. They were open wide with anticipation, filled with an eagerness her sister would not express, her mother did not feel, and her father revealed only in a smile and a wildly beating heart.

As they approached the harbour and the Bund, the area by the Whangpoo that had been rebuilt after a fire in 1894, it gradually came to life before their eyes. All kinds of junks and sampans floated shoulder to shoulder on the riverfront, bobbing and jostling each other like restless children forced to sleep in the same bed. The Relnikov family would later learn that people lived their entire lives on these vessels, often with as many as three generations living and working together on a junk or a sampan in this floating neighbourhood. Some of them survived by fishing, others transported goods along the river, either to sell them or to deliver them to the many warehouses that lined the wharf. Women gave birth on the boats and raised their children to live the very same life, the only life they knew.

The Bund was a place of constant motion, both in the muddy water and on the wide, equally muddy embankment, where rickshaws and pedicabs cut each other off in the scuttle to deliver their cargo, human and otherwise. Clattering sounds gradually increased in volume as the ship drew nearer. The clatter of wooden wheels hitting stones; of cases and trunks hitting the ground as they were unloaded from wagons or handcarts; of voices shouting in Chinese, a sound the Russian family's ears would eventually adjust to but never understand, except in the most rudimentary way. It was the clatter of the marketplace, of Chinese commerce, of life in a city that, as they would also learn, never slept.

They had come from Russia at the instigation of Sergei, who had one foot in the past and one foot in the future. How could he be otherwise? He claimed descent from Peter the Great, the tsar who had tried to bring Russia into the modern world. Because he was distantly related to Russian royalty, both of Sergei's daughters had been named after Romanov princesses. Olga had been named for the Tsar's first daughter, who had been born just weeks before her in 1895. Sergei's second daughter, called Tatiana after the second royal daughter, was born on the same day as her namesake, June 10, 1897. They could not have known that both Romanov princesses, along with their two sisters, one brother and both parents, would be imprisoned and slaughtered by Bolshevik revolutionaries two decades later in the summer of 1918. Sergei's decision to leave Russia in 1906 had been prophetic, but even he could not have imagined what was to come.

Sergei never missed an opportunity to quote his favourite author, Tolstoy. It was Tolstoy who said that happy families are all alike and every unhappy family is unhappy in its own way. The Relnikovs were a happy family, so they must have been much like other happy families. Katarina was a classically trained singer who taught her daughters to appreciate music and art. She spoke French to them because it was the language of nobility. They had lived a charmed life in Russia and believed they were special, even if they were just another happy family. It had been a life filled with family and servants and land, lots of land, belonging to Sergei's family for generations. There were treasures as well, art and books, jewellery and antiques, silver serving dishes and candlesticks, fine china rimmed with gold, crystal heavy with the weight of lead, clear and sparkling like diamonds in the sunlight. Most of it they left behind, as if not truly believing they'd never see it again. Nobody who comes from such splendour easily grasps the concept of never. Besides, it did not all belong to them. There were brothers and uncles and cousins who also had claims to the Relnikov wealth. Things had changed, however, for the Relnikovs after the Revolution of 1905, when the peasant workers had revolted and violence had entered their lives. Russia's war with Japan over Manchuria the previous year had proved disastrous. After "Bloody Sunday", when a crowd of workers that had assembled in front of the Winter Palace to petition the Tsar was fired on by soldiers, Nicholas, whom Sergei called Nicky, signed a manifesto promising the people representative government and even set up an elected Duma, but he would soon take back much of what he promised. No more representative government. No more civil liberties. When agitators began inciting the peasants to claim the land that was rightfully theirs, the Relnikovs began to fear for their safety. Sergei was a farseeing man, and by 1906, he knew their future was not in Russia.

In 1906, there were already a number of imposing buildings lining the far side of the Bund, mostly banks built of stone. They stood in stately contrast to the hustle-bustle of human activity on the muddy avenue. It had been just over sixty years since the Treaty of Nanking had been signed in 1842 between the British and Chinese, which had opened up the so-called Treaty Ports to foreign trade. The treaty allowed British merchants and their families to live on Chinese soil as if it were a little patch of Britain, a self-governing International Settlement that maintained its own police force, laws and courts. Soon the French and the Americans also came to participate in this unique social experiment that lasted for nearly a century. It was a capitalist paradise like no other. Sergei Relnikov was not the only one to catch the fever that turned so many Europeans into "Shanghailanders".

He had heard about exciting things happening in Shanghai,

China, where the British, the French and the Americans were investing heavily in the future, but at the same time China was also entering a period of revolution. The Chinese were attempting to define their own nationalism in response to the growing foreign presence in their country. Sergei refused to acknowledge the parallels between China and Russia, and this time he quoted Confucius to back up his position: "By nature, men are nearly alike; by practice, they get to be wide apart." He dismissed the Boxer Rebellion in 1900 as the work of amateurs.

"They're killing missionaries," he said, "and who can blame them? Those people want to steal the hearts and minds of the Chinese. That's a terrible thing. It's good for the country to engage in trade and commerce with foreigners. Leave God out of it." Sergei had heard of Dr. Sun Yat-sen and believed he had a plan for democracy in China that would work. "Russia is in chaos," he told Katarina. "She is going backwards. China is on a path to the future."

And so they arrived in Shanghai in 1906 to begin a new life. Sergei went into business and began manufacturing and selling bicycles and bicycle parts. He knew enough about business to know that the best way to make money, anywhere, was to sell a product that people either needed or wanted, or thought they needed or wanted. He recognized that the bicycle was a valuable commodity in that part of the world, and that people would pay for a bicycle and, later, would pay for the parts they needed to fix their bicycle and keep it going.

The Relnikovs were still a happy family, but Katarina's happiness was no longer as great. To take such a woman out of Russia, even a Russia that was becoming a frightening monster, and to move her to a place as far away and foreign as China, was to take a flower out of a garden full of beautiful flowers and put it in a pot of dirt. Katarina's garden was her family of seven sisters and brothers, cousins and second cousins, cousins once and twice removed, aunts and uncles, and even some great-aunts and great-uncles. Her garden was as vast as Russia, and its roots went deep. It had nourished her and renewed her, and she had woken up every morning with a hundred things to do. In Shanghai her world was much smaller. It consisted of Sergei, Olga and Tatiana. Even though the Relnikovs eventually acquired a social circle in Shanghai, it did not make up for Katarina's loss.

Tatiana was especially saddened by her mother's unhappiness. She would one day come to realize that her mother had made the best of her new and unwanted life in Shanghai. But what does a child know of her mother's unhappiness? For Olga and Tatiana, Shanghai was a beginning, the future their father had promised them. They could still make a game of life. They cried when they said goodbye to friends and cousins, but they had no concept of forever. Far away meant nothing to them. In Russia, everything was big and far away. They thought everybody would come and visit, just like before. Sergei had painted such a vibrant picture of the future for them in the months before they left that they thought they were going to the most exciting place in the world. Who wouldn't want to go to China?

To Tatiana, with her nine-year-old eyes, Shanghai was an adventure. If she saw the stinking poverty and the filth of dead rats and human excrement, she turned her head and looked elsewhere, at the hustle of the marketplace and the single-minded activity of pyjama-clad men pulling exotic ladies in rickshaws. If the buildings were black from the dirt and smoke of charcoal fires, if the paint was peeling and the wood was splitting, she didn't see it. Her eyes focused on the rich, jewel-coloured silks that rushed by in those ubiquitous rickshaws; she saw the yellow and pink of flowers and the orange and green of vegetables in the market stalls. Tatiana wanted Shanghai to be beautiful. She willed it to be beautiful. If not for her own sake, then certainly for her mother's.

From the moment they had stepped off the steamship in

Shanghai harbour, Katarina's face had become a mask. For her, the city was a dung heap, the end of nearly everything. She recoiled at the stench from pools of urine and piles of excrement, rotting vegetables and, worse, the not so occasional rotting corpse of a dog or an unwanted baby, and she recoiled at the incessant noise and activity that filled the harbour area and the city. It was as if she froze on the spot, her muscles refusing to move. Sergei had to take her by the arm and pull her along. Her expressionless face refused to reveal the intense jumble of emotions she must have been feeling.

There was nothing about Shanghai that could ease the pain of leaving her beloved home. Katarina no longer sang when she performed a task. Her family rarely heard her laugh, and they occasionally heard her cry, but only when she thought they weren't listening. Tatiana prayed every night that her mother would be happy and yet, even then, with her unformed emotions and her lack of experience, she knew it was futile. Deep in her heart, Tatiana felt an ache whenever she looked at her mother's blank, unchanging expression.

Sergei, on the other hand, refused to be anything but cheerful and positive. He was determined to succeed in China as a businessman. The country was ready, he said, to become a powerful and wealthy nation. The government was instituting reforms in education, sending young men versed only in Chinese classical literature and calligraphy to Japan to learn the ways of the world. If he knew about the young Chinese revolutionary students who were studying the writings of Marx and admired the Russian Narodniks who espoused violence and anarchism, he said nothing. If he encountered merchants who wanted to rid China of foreign capitalists and goods, he never spoke about it. He believed Dr. Sun Yat-sen wanted to oust the Manchus and establish democracy. When the infant Pu-yi succeeded the hated Dowager Empress in 1908, Sergei said that the doors to the new China were opening, that the monarchy was on its last legs. The revolution that was underway could only bring enlightenment and prosperity. China was not about politics, he said, it was about business and commerce. All the men Sergei knew in Shanghai wanted either to get rich or to stay rich.

"'Life consists in penetrating the unknown, and fashioning our actions in accord with the new knowledge thus acquired,'" he said, quoting Tolstoy once again. Even though Olga and Tatiana loved their irrepressible father, there were times when they looked at each other and rolled their eyes. Usually when he quoted Tolstoy for the umpteenth time in a day.

"Nothing is ever accomplished by writers and poets," said Olga in a world-weary tone. By the time she was eleven, Olga considered herself quite adult and therefore wise.

"Who said that?" her father asked, arching his eyebrow suspiciously.

"I did," said Olga.

Sergei laughed, which made Tatiana giggle, although she wasn't sure why. "I've spawned a philosopher," he said. "And what's worse, a female philosopher. 'Woman is more impressionable than man. Therefore in the Golden Age they were better than men. Now they are worse.' That's what Tolstoy said about women philosophers, and now I understand why."

"Oh, Papa," said Olga. "You're impossible."

"'It is by those who have suffered that the world has been advanced.' When you have suffered enough, Olushka, then perhaps you'll do something worthwhile. I am only trying to contribute to your future greatness."

"I don't want to be great," said Olga, importantly. "I only want to be happy."

"Ah," said her father. "Happiness can be even more elusive than greatness, Olushka. Our greatness is judged by others, whereas happiness we judge for ourselves. And who do you think is harder to please?" Olga frowned but didn't answer.

Sergei laughed, and she knew he must be teasing her. "As your father," he said, kissing the top of her head, "I shall do everything in my power to bring about your happiness." Satisfied, Olga curtsied and said, "Thank you, Papa."

"Papa," Tatiana said, lines of worry creasing her young forehead, "do you think Mother is suffering?"

Sergei's expression changed, and he looked at her sadly. "Yes, Tatushka, I think she's suffering. But her suffering is not the kind I can fix like a bicycle."

"She wants to go home, I think."

"This is our home now, Tatushka. We can't go back to Russia."

"I wish there was something I could do," she said. She wanted so badly to be able to fix whatever was wrong with her mother so they could be a happy family again.

"So do I, my child. So do I."

Chapter Two

Sergei enrolled his daughters in a convent school run by nuns.
Les Soeurs de Notre Dame were among the most devout, and
they taught the girls religion, catechism, French and mathematics
with a rigor that both scared and impressed them. A few of the
nuns didn't hesitate to use a whip-like willow branch if they
caught the students chattering or thought they were slow to
answer. Sister Thérèse was the worst. Although the girls went to
confession every day, Tatiana never confessed her evil thoughts
about Sister Thérèse and what she wanted God to do to her. She
was even more afraid of Sister Thérèse than she was of God.

The classrooms were situated at the front of the convent, a
two-storied wooden firetrap of a building with rickety stairs that
creaked and complained when the young students ran up and
down them. The private business of the nuns—their secret life
of silence and prayers that the students knew nothing about—
was conducted in the back of the building, at the end of a long
corridor the children were forbidden to enter. Every inch of
the convent had been scrubbed and polished over and over by
nuns past and present, until its floors and stairs and banisters
shone like their black leather boots from layers of linseed and
lemon oil and elbow grease. The wood had absorbed the smoky
odour of incense over the years that smelled, combined with the
fragrance of candle wax and the sharp citrus oil, the way Tatiana
imagined heaven must smell. She pictured God sitting on a solid
wooden throne that angel nuns, hunched over like black beetles,
had polished to the same ebony hue as their desks.

Olga and Tatiana had spoken French all their lives, so they had an advantage over the British, American and Chinese girls who attended the school. It was easy for them to pass the regular examinations the nuns thought so essential to learning. But most of the students were from the French concession. They had been born in France and could talk circles around the two Russian girls, who struggled with reading and writing the unfamiliar alphabet. It was harder for Olga, because she was in a more advanced class. Occasionally, they were able to persuade their mother to help them with their homework, and they were overjoyed when they caught a glimpse of her old self.

Choir practice was the highlight of their day, and in the evenings they would sing for their mother the songs they had learned. Usually Katarina would listen with a faraway look in her eyes, but every once in a while she would join in, and they would want to cry with happiness. "Sing 'Kalinka' for us, Mother, like you used to," they would beg. "You sing so beautifully." Katarina would sing the lyrics of the love song, and Olga and Tatiana would sing the ecstatic chorus—"*Kalinka, kalinka, kalinka moya*"—faster and faster until their mother would chime in once again with the slow, melodic verse to Lyuli, the goddess of the earth, of love and fertility. The song would bring tears to her eyes and, when her daughters realized it only made her sadder, they stopped asking.

Sergei decided Olga and Tatiana should also learn to speak English, so he sent them to Mrs. Wilkinson's English language class in the British district of the International Settlement. They attended these classes at her home every Saturday morning. Mrs. Wilkinson was a formidable woman but nothing like the nuns at Notre Dame. She was strict only because she had to be; otherwise her young students would have run roughshod over her. She was a tall woman who towered over them and spoke in a loud, resonant voice. In the style of the day, she wore long dresses with full mutton sleeves and a bustle that rode atop her rear end. She was like the prow of a ship and sailed around the room as if it were the ocean. Her students never once saw her slouch, and she constantly reminded them to sit up straight. "Good posture," she intoned, "is essential to speaking well. The voice must emanate from the solar plexus, not the throat. We must speak as an opera singer sings, with a full voice and round, robust tones." Her students had no idea what she was talking about, but words like emanate and solar plexus sounded important, so they nodded in agreement. When Mrs. Wilkinson rolled her r's around words like round and robust, they could only dream of doing the same.

Mrs. Wilkinson had a portrait of Queen Victoria in the makeshift classroom in her large drawing room, which was furnished in the English style with uncomfortable horsehair-stuffed chairs and sofas and solid, heavy-legged wooden tables laden with porcelain bric-à-brac and figurines. The students sat on low wooden stools and were forced to crane their necks to look up at Mrs. Wilkinson as she sailed by. By the end of class, their necks would ache. They imagined that the late queen had behaved and spoken just like Mrs. Wilkinson; they both had piercing eyes that could look right into the soul and spot the evil lurking there. When Mrs. Wilkinson wasn't looking, Tatiana would cross herself and recite the Hail Mary, just in case. Between Mrs. Wilkinson and Queen Victoria, it seemed there was no chance of escape. But every now and then, Mrs. Wilkinson would let down her guard, and they could relax for a bit. She passed around candies, or sweets as she called them, and they were allowed to be children, laughing and making mistakes.

Olga and Tatiana first met Lily when she joined Mrs. Wilkinson's English class a couple of months after them. Tatiana remembered seeing the girl a few times at Notre Dame, but they were in different classes and had not spoken. Lily was the daughter of Sergei's business partner, a wealthy Chinese man with many interests in Shanghai. Soong Li-tan and his brothers were involved in businesses in China from banking to publishing, shipping to textile manufacturing. Their wealth and influence, once based solely on land, had expanded into other areas of opportunity almost as soon as the first foreigner with money to invest had arrived in Shanghai. The Soong family did not socialize with their European business friends, not even the Relnikovs. Their daughters, however, were not constrained by their parents' social boundaries.

Lily was very shy and very pretty. Her black hair was cut in a perfect, straight line across the back of her neck and across her forehead. She had fair skin and a heart-shaped face that reminded Tatiana of the pictures of delicately beautiful Chinese ladies she had seen in books. When Lily first came to Mrs. Wilkinson's, she spoke no English at all, but she could speak French well enough for her and Tatiana to establish a friendship. Lily was so terrified of making a mistake that she refused to speak any English at all for the first month.

"*J'ai peur de Madame Weekeesoh*," she told Tatiana. "*Elle est trop grande*." Lily had never seen a woman as tall as Mrs. Wilkinson, whose ample bosom protruded like a shelf above her cinched waist.

Although Olga and Tatiana were sent to Mrs. Wilkinson's in a rickshaw (Sergei would haggle with the driver every time to get half the quoted price), the sisters usually conspired to walk back through the crowded but endlessly fascinating streets of the Chinese district. Lily was horrified that they would even consider walking through the city. She was disgusted by the filth and the smells and told them they were mad to even consider it. Lily was picked up by the same rickshaw driver every week, a family retainer, she told them. The girls had no idea how wealthy Lily's family was, but from the way she talked, in the Soong household there was a servant for everything. If Sergei had known his daughters were walking home from class, he would have been livid. He always sent a rickshaw to pick them up, but the girls would pay the driver and send him away, begging him not to tell their father. Sergei gave them a certain amount of pocket money, which they happily spent on candied fruit from the sweet shops along the way, with their dusty glass windows and dirt floors. The girls were always careful to clean the telltale mud off their shoes before they got back to the house.

Although they were warned about pickpockets, beggars and crooked shopkeepers, Olga and Tatiana took the street life of Shanghai in their stride. They were careful never to show their few coins outside of the sweet shop and they knew not to step in the puddles of urine, animal and human. They stayed well clear of the gutters with their slimy green contents and grew adept at avoiding the grasping hands of lepers and beggars. They found their courage in each other and dared to do together what they would never have done alone. It was as though they had a pact between them never to be afraid, and perhaps that was why nothing bad ever happened to them. They were confident—or at least they appeared confident—and even the angry curses of beggars to whom they refused to give money didn't frighten them.

~ ~

I can still close my eyes and see the streets of Shanghai as they were in my childhood, with rows of grubby wooden houses leaning into each other and looking like they were about to collapse like a row of dominoes, open storefronts that offered everything from straw brooms or baskets and several varieties of rice or tea or flour, all heaped in open cloth sacks that stood upright on the floor, to candy and sweet drinks in dusty glass bottles, and dried fish, beans, nuts and lentils. Everything was weighed on brass scales and the prices were calculated by nimble fingers that flew across an abacus with lightning speed. There was smelly litter everywhere and mangy dogs, often with only three legs, covered in sores yet managing, somehow, to survive.

~ ~

Shanghai was a busy place, full of traffic and noise and endless chatter. Children with dirty faces stared at the two Russian girls and giggled when they stared back. Women, sitting on small stools and smoking shaggy cigarettes, nursed babies, whose black eyes stared out of round faces, their sparse black hair standing straight up from their head as though they'd just had the fright of their life. Barbers cut men's hair right on the street and cleaned their ears with long toothpicks wrapped in cotton. There were countless food vendors selling fruits and vegetables, small shiny onions, stalks of curly cabbage, pear-shaped eggplants no bigger than a fist, and long green beans that were folded over into bundles. Carrots were as thick as broom handles or as thin as fingers. Lichee nuts still in their husks were sold by the stalk. Sometimes there were apples and pears. Hawkers huddled over charcoal fires, charring fish until the scales were white as ash, and cooking pieces of duck or chicken on smoking black iron grills. Coolies in wide cotton pants and flimsy sandals made of straw on their flat, splay-toed feet ran by, yoked with bamboo poles from which were suspended clay or brass pots and baskets laden with goods. What you could not find in the shops, you could find on the street. To Olga and Tatiana, it was the most exciting place in the world. Tatiana especially had caught Sergei's fever and saw only the endless possibilities of life in Shanghai.

They lived in the Concession *française*, right next to the British sector of the International Settlement, where handsome bearded and turbaned Sikhs directed traffic with authority, blowing whistles and waving their arms while everyone seemed to ignore them. What Russians there were in Shanghai clustered together near Avenue Joffre where Sergei had built his bicycle factory. The Concession was cleaner and more orderly than the International Settlement, and wealthy foreigners were building mansions in the west end.

Sergei had rented a three-storey house ten minutes by rickshaw from the factory. It was built of stone, not wood, and was surrounded by a high wall of the same pinkish grey stone, with shards of glass embedded in the top to discourage thieves and intruders. The house had a lot of rooms, including a separate room off the kitchen for the polished copper bathtub. In Russia, the bathtub had been brought into the large, heated kitchen on Saturday nights, and the girls would be scrubbed in soapy hot water that was warmed in a copper pot on the stove. In China, the water had to be carted in jugs from the kitchen into the bath room, which had a marble floor and a drain in the middle so the tub, shaped like a very large gravy boat with a pouring spout at one end, could be emptied there instead of outside.

Olga and Tatiana each had their own room, which Olga liked, but Tatiana didn't, because she was lonely. In Russia, they had both slept in the same room in a big feather bed with feather pillows and a comforter made of fine goose down. Even though Tatiana eventually got used to sleeping by herself, she continued to miss the intimacy and the secrecy of the whispered conversations that she and Olga once had in the dark, even when they had nothing to say. Tatiana had been allowed to choose her own room when they'd moved into the house and had chosen the smallest room because it had a tall, narrow window that looked out onto the street. She could always amuse herself by watching the human traffic that passed by in both directions. She told herself that each person, whether it was the fruit and vegetable vendor, the washerwoman or the knife sharpener, had a purpose and a story. It amazed her that they could do the same thing, day in and day out, whatever the weather. She didn't see it as the grinding poverty that it was. She saw only their valiant determination and steadfastness of purpose. This was Sergei's influence, she would later realize, his unwaveringly positive attitude.

~ ~

I can transport myself back, even today, to a bed piled high with pillows and quilts, a green painted wooden table where I did my schoolwork, a chest of drawers, also painted green, and a wooden rocking chair where my favourite doll sat, dressed in blue satin and lace, her rosebud mouth painted red, her blue eyes always wide in a glassy expression of surprise. The walls were painted yellow, my favourite colour, and hung with pictures of Jesus and the Virgin Mary that the nuns had given us at Christmas. In later years, when I started sneaking in and out of the house to go to the cabarets, I was glad I had my own room and that Mother and Papa's room was at the other end of the house. My awe of Jesus and Mary had faded by then, but their pictures remained on the walls.

~ ~

The girls were allowed to visit their father at work from time to time. The factory's output had grown quickly, no doubt because the bicycles it produced were sturdy and reliable. Sergei employed nearly a hundred people, including a foreman who made sure no one was sleeping or pretending to work. Sergei insisted on a production quota, although he sometimes confessed it was nearly impossible to maintain. He had to hire three people to do one job, because his employees had so many excuses for not coming to work. Usually, they would say a relative was getting married or had died, and they had to attend a wedding or a funeral. There seemed to be no shortage of relatives in Chinese families. After a while, Sergei stopped keeping track of the "Honourable Uncles, Cousins and Grandmothers" and accepted the inevitable.

Although the girls didn't understand it at the time, they were blessed with a childhood in which they felt secure enough to take risks, believing that their father would protect them, no matter what, and that their mother loved them, despite her sadness. Olga and Tatiana were taught to be watchful but not to fear. Perhaps because Sergei did not have sons, he passed on to his daughters the qualities he valued so highly in men: courage and an independent spirit.

Chapter Three

By the time China was declared a republic, a few months after Tatiana's fourteenth birthday in 1911, the Relnikovs were well-established Shanghailanders and she was slowly becoming aware of the turbulent underbelly of Chinese political life, if only as it affected what she saw. Men everywhere had begun to cut off their pigtails to disassociate themselves from the despised Manchu Dynasty that had ruled China since 1644. As a result of her friendship with Lily, Tatiana had been allowed to meet Lily's family and to visit her home for the past few years. Through Lily's brothers and her many cousins, several of whom were at university, Tatiana began to learn about the history of China and the plethora of revolutionary movements that were dedicated to bringing the country into the modern world. It seemed as if Sergei's predictions were coming true.

The first time Tatiana was invited to Lily's house, Sergei and Katarina had made a big fuss. Lily's father belonged to one of the most prosperous and powerful families in Shanghai. Tatiana didn't discover until many years later that he had been secretly financing Dr. Sun Yat-sen's movement to expel the Manchus and take power. Dr. Sun's plan was to control China through a strong central party with himself as its absolute leader. Once the people were educated in the ways of representative government, he believed, China would emerge as a democracy. Forced into exile several times, Dr. Sun would spend most of his time raising money so he could return to China and implement his plan. In 1912, he would form the National People's Party, the Kuomintang. In the first-ever elections in China, in 1913, the Kuomintang would win the majority of seats in parliament. In reality, China continued to be governed by local warlords whose interests were best served by keeping the country divided and preventing a strong central government from taking hold. When Dr. Sun died in 1925, he would be succeeded by his old friend Chiang Kai-shek, leader of the Kuomintang army, who continued the campaign to unite China. Chiang Kai-shek was a personal friend of Lily's father and, as Tatiana was to learn, he had also been a classmate of Lily's future husband.

On her first visit to the Soong's, Tatiana was invited to celebrate Lily's tenth birthday. She was scrubbed until she shone, dressed in her best clothes, and Katarina braided her long hair so tightly it hurt. It was a sweltering July day in Shanghai, where the summers were not just hot but steamy, wet and stinky hot. Tatiana complained loudly but to no avail. She was instructed to ignore the heat and to think snowy thoughts of cold Russian winters so she wouldn't perspire. She wore her best pink dress, which had a lace collar and cuffs, and white gloves and stockings that stuck to her hot feet inside her buttoned leather boots. She carried a small bouquet of flowers for Lily's mother and a beautifully wrapped silk box that contained a hand-painted fan she had chosen as a gift for Lily. She knew Lily probably already had hundreds of fans, but Tatiana had decided this one would be special.

"Do you remember what I told you, Tatiana?"

"Yes, Mother."

"Repeat it for me."

"Say please and thank you and only speak when spoken to."

"And don't complain about being hot and uncomfortable. A lady never complains."

"Yes, Mother. I won't complain."

"Promise?"

"I promise."

"Good girl," said Katarina. "Papa and I are very proud of you."

A rickshaw was sent to pick up Tatiana and deliver her to the large walled compound where Lily lived and which contained the households of her extended family. The compound contained several multi-storied wooden buildings arranged around a courtyard that had a large pond in the centre. The pond was like a carefully crafted work of art. The plants that were set around its perimeter had been chosen for their variety of textures, colours and styles of leaf, either broad and flat, tall and sharp, or feathered with delicate fronds. The water bubbled gently with a soothing gurgling sound. Several fat orange fish darted gracefully between lily pads upon which rested pink, yellow and white blooms, their fine long roots gently swaying like a young girl's silken tresses, right to the bottom of the pond. Each of the houses had wooden railed balconies on the upper floors, where the women of Lily's extended family usually sat and chatted as they watched the comings and goings of children and servants. The compound housed Lily's paternal grandparents, two of her father's unmarried sisters, three of his brothers and their wives and children, plus Lily, her parents and her three brothers. There were a couple of cousins and their families living there as well. The number of servants exceeded the number of family members by at least two to one.

The meal was lavish and consisted of many delicacies like bird's nest soup (which Tatiana later learned, to her dismay, included real birds' nests made from twigs and bird saliva), tiny steamed dumplings, smoked duck, delicately prepared vegetables carved in the shapes of flowers, a fish that was surrounded by more carved vegetables, tiny little spare ribs in black bean sauce, plus a few things she didn't recognize and, of course, the essential bowls of rice. All of it was washed down with great quantities of jasmine tea. The family ate with carved ivory chopsticks, but Tatiana was given heavy silver forks, knives and spoons because it was assumed she had not mastered the art of eating with sticks, which was true.

The Relnikovs had a French cook, and Katarina insisted that he follow the recipes her cook in Russia had used. Sometimes, when their cook had the afternoon off, his Chinese assistant would prepare a local delicacy such as shark fin soup or a whole fish steamed in broth and soy sauce. The family was often surprised to discover how tasty these dishes were. Tatiana had attempted to eat with chopsticks a few times, following his instructions, but was glad that she didn't have to rely on her inadequate skills in front of Lily's family.

Tatiana's parents had instructed her to be polite, above all. Even if she didn't like the food, she was to smile and say thank you for everything. To her young palate, most of the food tasted sour or salty, the texture either soft and slimy, sticky or brittle. Tatiana did her best to swallow small bits at a time, usually followed by a large quantity of rice, and to smile after every mouthful. She noticed that Lily's family ate noisily and spoke constantly to each other in Chinese. Occasionally, someone would address Tatiana in English.

"Did you make a good grade in school?" Lily's Number One Brother asked.

"Yes, thank you," she replied, smiling.

"Are you happy living Shanghai?" asked Number Two Brother.

"Oh, yes, thank you. Very happy."

"And honourable parents are also happy?"

"Very happy, thank you."

It was a bit of an ordeal but, once lunch was over, Lily and Tatiana were left alone to talk and look at picture books in Lily's spacious bedroom, which was decorated like something out of an English magazine, with ruffles and ribbons and furniture painted white. Lily's large canopied bed was at the far end of the room, and the area closest to the door was furnished as a sitting room with a small sofa and armchairs that were upholstered in soft green silk. In the corner was a narrow cot where Lily's amah, her nanny, slept. The amah rarely let Lily out of her sight, and for years they had slept in the same bed. But, as Lily matured, the amah became more of a personal maid who looked after her clothes and her belongings, helped her dress and do her hair, and generally picked up after her. Whatever Lily asked her to do, the amah did. However, she was not above nagging or complaining that Lily made her work too hard. Like the traditional Chinese nursemaid, she was Lily's greatest defender and she had a deep and unconditional love for her charge.

In Lily's bedroom after lunch, Tatiana gave her the fan. Lily was so happy she ran to show her mother right away. The woman came to thank Tatiana personally. She was small and slender and wore a dark blue silk dress with a long skirt, high neck and long, tight sleeves, in the latest European fashion. Her straight black hair was pulled back loosely into a bun so that it fell in flattering soft waves around her delicate face. She wore makeup, as did many Chinese women of her class. Powder to whiten her skin and rouge to redden her lips. Tatiana thought she was very beautiful. Whenever she saw her after that first visit, no matter what time of day, Lily's mother appeared to be wearing her best clothes, as if every day were a special occasion. She was elegant and gracious and spoke to Tatiana in halting French, which she said she had learned in Europe. Lily's mother had been to school in Switzerland for one year and was very modern by Chinese standards. She wanted Lily to be educated before she was married and to learn a bit about the world.

Tatiana didn't know it at the time, but Lily was already betrothed to Tang Wu-ling, a boy she had never met. They were to be married when he completed his university education in France and a period of service in the army. He also came from a prominent Shanghai family, and it would have been unthinkable for Lily to choose to marry anyone else. Their parents had arranged the marriage when Lily was born, and Wu-ling was ten years old. It was considered auspicious that their two families should be united. Love was irrelevant; dynasty was everything. Tatiana knew something of this tradition because of her Romanov cousins. Being princesses, they would not have been free to choose their own husbands.

As the youngest child and a girl, Lily had been sheltered from the life beyond the walls of the family compound and the convent school the girls attended. She and her brothers each had their own amah from birth who spoiled and protected their precious charges. As a result, Lily was as much a stranger to Shanghai as Tatiana had been when she'd arrived. Tatiana and Olga had an amah, too, but she was more like one of the maids who helped their mother and did household chores. More often than not, the amah was glad when the girls were not underfoot so she could get her work done or gossip with the other servants. But Tatiana had seen more of life in Shanghai than Lily ever would. When she talked about what she saw in her weekly excursions with Olga, Lily couldn't believe many of the things she heard.

"You're very brave," she once told Tatiana, "but also very foolish."

"No, I'm not," Tatiana said. "There's nothing to be afraid of, at least not in the daytime."

"You are wrong," Lily said. "There are many robbers and bandits who kidnap children and take them far away so they never see their families again." Tatiana was pretty sure this was not true. It sounded like something Lily's overprotective amah would tell her to keep her from venturing beyond the compound on her own, should she ever have such a notion.

After Tatiana's initial visit to Lily's home, Lily's parents had allowed her to visit Tatiana, but only on the weekends in the afternoon for no more than two hours, and never for a meal.

The girls accepted these restrictions on Lily's movements, because Tatiana was allowed to visit Lily whenever she wanted. Sometimes Olga would go with her, but she had begun to form her own friendships, especially with a French girl from her class at school.

"Will you ever be allowed to go out on your own?" Tatiana asked Lily on one of her rare visits to the Relnikov residence. They were in one of the upstairs sitting rooms, the one with the yellow silk sofa that Katarina called the sunroom because it faced south and was bright and sunny most of the day. She had hung there the heavy, hand-crocheted lace curtains she had brought from their home in Russia, and the sun streamed through the hundreds of tiny openings between the lacy stitches to send shimmering spears of light across the room.

"Perhaps if I go to Switzerland to school, like my mother. Then no one can stop me." Lily smiled at the thought of one day being able to do whatever she wanted. "Once I am married," she continued, "I will have to serve my husband's mother, because I will have to live in her house. But someday I will be mother-in-law to my son's wife, and she will have to obey me. It is tradition."

"That sounds awful," Tatiana said. "Besides, what if you don't have a son?"

"Of course, I will have a son," Lily chided. "My husband will insist."

Tatiana was so far away from thinking about husbands and children that she only half-believed what Lily said. It seemed preposterous that a husband could insist on a wife having sons. Later Tatiana would learn how precious sons were to a Chinese family and how undesirable daughters were thought to be. An ancient Chinese saying compared having daughters to finding maggots in the rice. Some unwanted baby girls in China were literally thrown out with the garbage, either strangled, smothered or simply left to die. Too many families could not afford to feed another hungry baby, especially if it were female. As well, in order to marry, a daughter needed a substantial dowry. She was considered a temporary guest in her family, because she would one day belong to her husband's family and be required to worship his ancestors. It was considered a waste to invest too much in a daughter. Baby boys, on the other hand, were highly prized and necessary to continue the family line. Boys and men had rights and privileges girls and women could never have. A rich man could have several wives, as well as concubines, but they did not have the right to make decisions for themselves. Households were complicated little fiefdoms filled with intrigue and conflict, hierarchies and political manoeuvring. Rarely were they happy and harmonious arrangements. There were many things about China that Tatiana would never understand.

Her father lived in a household of women and knew that to insist on certain things was pointless. Katarina argued with him if she disagreed and frequently got her way, especially when she cried or persuaded one or both of her daughters to agree with her. He would usually just walk away, muttering something from Tolstoy, until everybody cooled down. Although he was the nominal head of the family and made all the important decisions, he depended on his wife's approval and support. There was never talk of obedience between her parents. Tatiana knew they loved each other and that love was the foundation of their family, but sometimes she worried that love might have its limits. Once, when her parents had been arguing for days over plans to expand the summer kitchen at the back of the house (Katarina wanted it but Sergei knew he would be the one who would have the headache of supervising the workmen) Tatiana had gone to her father and asked him if this meant they would be getting a divorce.

"A divorce, Tatushka? Your mother and I? No, no, never, my child. You mustn't concern yourself about such things." Sergei knew his clever second daughter was prone to fret about some things. She was already developing fine worry lines on her forehead from trying to fathom the ways of adults. He would often catch her squinting into space, as some troubling thought absorbed her.

"Who would Olga and I live with if there was a divorce?" she asked. She still was not convinced. This had been a louder argument than most, and her mother hadn't cried, as she usually did to get her way. A bad sign.

"Tatushka, Tatushka, there will never be a divorce. I promise you." Why was she so insecure? Sergei wondered. He could see she wasn't reassured by his words. This child, he feared, would want to seek certainty through experience, a route that could lead down many roads, some of them dangerous.

"Go and tell your mother I agree to the summer kitchen," he said. It was a small price to pay for his family's happiness.

Lily's family, Tatiana knew, was very modern. Her father had only one wife and, as far as Tatiana knew, no concubines. Luckily, Lily's mother had borne him three sons, so the ancestors would be well taken care of. Lily was their only daughter.

Tatiana's friendship with Lily grew and transcended culture, race and language. They were able to talk using their two common languages, French and English, but they also communicated through laughter and gesture. They liked the same things and found humour in similar places. When they were younger, they would laugh until the tears came to their eyes. Anything could set them off. They would look at pictures and make up crazy stories about what was happening in them. If it was a picture of a warrior on horseback and the horse was rearing on its hind legs, one of them would say, "The stable master fed the horse hot chilli peppers so that he would run faster, but now the horse is running all over the battlefield looking for water, and the soldier can't control him." They thought this was hysterically funny and laughed until their sides hurt. Olga thought them infantile, but Olga didn't have a friend like Lily to laugh and be a fool with, so perhaps she was jealous. As the girls got older, they made up love stories about a beautiful Chinese girl forced to marry an older man, even though she was in love with a handsome young man whose heart was breaking with love for her.

Despite their different natures, Tatiana bold and adventurous, Lily sweet and passive, neither of them would be able to control the events that shaped their lives. Both of them would live to regret the choices they made.

Chapter Four

Olga came to visit me today. It has stopped snowing, so she had my niece Anastasia drive her over in the car. Once a week, weather permitting, Anastasia takes her mother out shopping in the car so she can buy her meat from the butcher, her fruit and vegetables from the greengrocer, and her bread from the baker. Olga says she will never shop in those grocery stores where they sell everything "from canned soup to canned nuts." She always buys the best and brings me some because I don't have a car. Anastasia, who has two children of her own now, is the perfect daughter and niece. She seems genuinely pleased to see me whenever she comes, and she takes the time to have a real conversation with me. Unlike her mother. Olga spends our time together grilling me about my bad habits. How many cigarettes have I smoked today? How much have I had to drink? Am I eating properly? She's still the older, wiser, and in her mind, more experienced sister.

"I had a letter from Lily today," I tell her.

"Lily Tang?"

"Yes. Lily Tang. From Shanghai."

"You're kidding," Olga said. "I thought she was dead."

"I didn't know she was still alive either. I haven't heard from her in years," I said. "But she is alive, and she's been living in a village, working in an orphanage. When the Communists took over, she was too old to be of much use, I suppose, except to look after children."

"But how can she afford to come here?"

"Her youngest brother has sponsored her. Apparently he owns a restaurant in Toronto. Isn't that amazing? And he's applied to have her come as a nursemaid for his grandchildren. She wants to stay with me for a few days before she goes to live with him."

"You mean Lily's going to be an amah?"

"Yes," I said. "Sad, isn't it?"

"So many terrible things," said Olga. "I mean, to have her child taken away from her and everything." Olga was putting away the groceries she'd brought me, even though I'm perfectly capable of doing it myself. It's her way of letting me know she thinks I'm incompetent. One of the ways, because there are many. Olga thinks that because I never had children, I don't know anything about keeping house. But she's wrong; I know enough to do what I have to do.

"I know. I don't imagine she ever got over that," I said, watching her.

"How could anyone?" my sister said. "And he was such a talented little boy."

"I know. I wonder whatever happened to him?"

"Maybe she'll be able to tell you. She must have had some contact with him." Olga sighs and looks around when she's done. "Everything's so shabby," she says. She's looking at my old sofa and matching chair, upholstered in green fabric with large cabbage roses on it. "It's depressing."

I've never cared much about domestic things. In Shanghai, I used to have a maid who came in every day to tidy up and do my laundry. Here a maid would be unthinkable, not to mention beyond my means. I live in an apartment over a hardware store on Gerrard Street in the east end of the city, and it suits me just fine. I have to climb a steep set of stairs to get up here, but for now that's not a problem. Someday I'll have to think about moving. Olga thinks it's low class.

"Only poor people live in apartments," she tells me. "Especially apartments over stores. Respectable people live in houses."

"Well, I'm not exactly rich," I remind her. I'm treading a fine line here, because Olga and Jean Paul have offered to give me money many times, and I have always refused. "And besides, the hardware store has a quiet clientele, it closes at five o'clock every afternoon, and there are no cooking smells or cockroaches, no screaming neighbours and plenty of hot water. I never have to cut the grass or shovel snow. I'm quite content with my three rooms and kitchen."

"For God's sake, Mother," Anastasia says in exasperation, "leave Aunt Tati alone. She doesn't come into your house and criticize everything." Olga gives me a look that says, You wouldn't dare. There's nothing in my house to criticize. But she remains silent. She knows she's crossed a line, and she's embarrassed that her daughter has seen it. It's a pattern that goes back a long way in our lives. I have never lived up to Olga's expectations.

"I'm sorry," she mutters finally, but I know the next time she visits, she'll find fault with something else. On her way out the door, Olga turns. "Did they ever find out who killed that young man, Daniel?"

"Not that I know of," I replied.

"Wasn't that brother of Lily's involved with the Green Gang? He was some kind of gangster, wasn't he?"

"You mean Number Two Brother," I said. "He wasn't really a gangster, but he had a lot of power. He had some kind of government position. And the Green Gang had a lot of political connections. They wanted to get the foreign business interests out of China."

"That's right," said Olga. "Now I remember. You don't think he had anything to do with it, do you?"

"I can't imagine why he would," I lied, "but I've always wondered." I don't tell her of my suspicion that Lily's brother and Lily's husband arranged to have Daniel murdered. And I also don't tell her there were things I knew about Daniel that I should have told the police and didn't.

"Hmph," Olga grunted as she made her way down the stairs in her heavy coat and fur-lined snow boots. "Ask Lily when she gets here."

After Olga and Anastasia leave, I settle into my shabby but comfortable armchair and read Lily's letter again. It's clumsily written, as if she's translated it badly from Chinese. I think back to all those English classes with Mrs. Wilkinson and realize Lily probably stopped speaking English after the Communists took over.

"*Dear Tatiana,*" she writes,

> *I am sure you never would think to hear from me again, but I have found you. I have stayed living in China all these years and looking after children in an orphanage that Chairman Mao himself has built. It is a fine place for children who have no parents. They learn to read and write so they can be the best Chinese people for our Fearless Leader.*
>
> *Now I find out my Number Three Brother has a restaurant in Toronto Canada. He has ask me to come and look after his grandchildren. Such an honour. The government has finally give me a passport so I can come. Now I will be able to see my old friend Tatiana if she will let me stay with her for a visit. The ship will come to Vancouver in February and then I will take the train to Toronto. There are many years to talk about. Many memories. So sorry not to write before but I am very busy with the children. I hope you look forward to seeing me.*
>
> *Your old friend, Lily Tang.*"

So many memories, I thought. Did I really want to relive those times?

Chapter Five

By the time Tatiana was fifteen, she was a regular visitor to Lily's home. Lily's three older brothers regarded her as a younger sister and treated her the same way they treated Lily. That meant they lectured the two girls, chided and teased them, and played tricks on them. Once, when the girls had dressed themselves in Lily's mother's cast-offs, including her French high heels, and had painted their lips red with a lipstick stolen from her dressing room, the brothers had charged into the room and tossed a bucketful of water from the fish pond at them, drenching them and leaving them covered in the tangled roots of the lily pads. Several large gold fish lay squirming on the carpet, gasping for air. Lily's brothers roared with laughter, their half-boy, half-man voices cracking with glee. Lily and Tatiana were furious and embarrassed at having been caught playing childish games. They screamed at the boys, and Tatiana picked up one of the fish and threw it at Number Two Brother.

"You're stupid, and I hate you!" she yelled, as Number Two Brother picked up the fish and threw it back at her.

"And you're a baby and ugly, just like my sister, only uglier because you have big feet!" he yelled back, still cackling as his brothers laughed like maniacs at the girls' fury. Lily started to cry, and that made the whole thing worse. Tatiana wanted her to behave like the women warriors she'd heard about in Chinese mythology, avenging angels who punished the evildoers who had wronged them. But Lily, perhaps because she was the youngest in the family and dominated by both tradition and three older brothers, could no more be a warrior than Tatiana could be a fairy princess. Lily needed protecting, but Tatiana had vowed she would never ask for protection from anyone. She would rather die.

The brothers were never punished, no matter how much of a mess they made. There was always someone to clean it up, usually one of the amahs, who would cackle and complain, but who was clearly amused by their antics. China belonged to men and boys, especially to privileged men and boys.

Lily's Number One Brother eventually went to France for a university education in business and philosophy. It was where the most privileged Chinese sent their eldest sons. He would be his father's successor in business and financial affairs. Number Two Brother would go to Japan to be educated. After 1906, China had abolished the Confucian system of education and moved toward Western-style learning. This meant students no longer had to memorize the Chinese classics and pass a series of examinations called *wen-chang* to obtain a position in the civil service. In Japan, university students learned history, geography, foreign languages, political economy and law. Number Two Brother would also be exposed to the secret societies that were forming among Chinese students in Japan, who wanted in time to take control of their country. When he eventually returned, he would be given a key position in government, reflecting the family's status. Number Three Brother's destiny was to attend a military academy and become an officer. Thus, Lily's family would be represented in all levels of Chinese society: financial, civil and military.

Luckily, because her parents were more modern, Lily had escaped the tradition of female foot binding that had been the fate of her grandmothers. It was a tradition that had persisted in China for nearly a thousand years, since an emperor had fallen in love with a concubine who had especially small feet. A man seeking a bride would examine her feet before he looked at her face. A married man would never see his wife's naked foot, but he might occasionally be given a glimpse of his concubine's. Young, wealthy Chinese women spent their time learning to embroider the delicate silk slippers that covered their grotesquely misshapen feet, the toes of which were folded under and tightly bound from the age of four. As the young girl's foot grew, the front portion would be pushed toward the heel and securely wrapped in cotton binding, increasing the instep to an extreme and agonizing degree. Walking was painful and nearly impossible, so women were transported in covered sedan chairs carried by four bearers. What little walking they did was thought to strengthen the muscles around a woman's private parts, enhancing sexual excitement in her partner. Even some country girls had their feet bound in an effort to attract a better class of husband. Unfortunately, these women were still required to work in the fields, so they developed a waddling walk by balancing on the outsides of their mangled feet. Tatiana saw many of these women hobbling on the streets of Shanghai, elderly and stooped, but wearing slippers that would fit a small child. It made her angry at what she saw as the unfairness of Chinese society.

Through her exposure to Lily and her family, especially her brothers, Tatiana became more familiar with Chinese ways and Chinese ways of thinking. Her interest did not, however, extend to language, the strange, singsong cacophony of sounds that encompassed many languages and even more dialects spoken by the Chinese. Both she and Olga resisted their father's attempts to persuade them to study one of the Mandarin dialects.

"Oh, Papa," they would say to their father, "we're never going to have to speak it properly. Everyone we know speaks either English or French. It's enough." But truth be told, the girls were not eager to study something they were sure they would never be able to master. The best they did was to pick up the vulgar Pidgin English used by Europeans and Chinese alike to bridge the wide gap between them.

Rather than being repelled by the strangeness of what she learned, Tatiana in time became more interested in the complexity of ancient Confucian tradition mixed with the emerging modernity of China as it entered the twentieth century. In a way, her father had been right. China was looking to the future in its own complicated way, while Russia was still mired in the nineteenth century of landowners and indentured peasants.

"'Governments need armies to protect them against their enslaved and oppressed subjects,'" said Sergei, again quoting his favourite author. "Russia," he said, "will not change until those who govern Russia change their thinking. Tolstoy said it best: 'Everyone thinks of changing the world, but no one thinks of changing himself.' Remember, Tatushka, never be afraid to embrace new ideas. Without them, your mind will cease to grow and your spirit will harden." Tatiana had taken to spending her study hours in her father's library, surrounded by the many leather-bound books he had brought from Russia. Sergei would often take the opportunity to talk to his daughter about the ideas he had gleaned from those books and that were always forming and re-forming in his mind. He hoped to inspire her to embrace a life of books and learning, as he had dreamed of doing before their life in Russia had been interrupted by politics. He knew she was the brighter of his two daughters, but he recognized that she had a stubborn streak that would cause her to resist if pushed too hard.

"I fear for poor Nicky and his family," Sergei told her. "They are living in the past and cannot see that Russia is changing for the worse. How long can they ignore what is happening in the streets?"

Although it sometimes took weeks, even months, for them to receive news from Russia, they knew of the terrible things that were happening there. The peasants were still virtual slaves under the autocratic rule of the nobles, who were under the autocratic rule of the Tsar. When Nicholas began to reverse the reforms he had promised after the first revolt in 1905, the level of discontent rose and spread. Unfortunately, the Tsar chose the route of greater repression, not understanding that he was, in fact, helping to create a political underclass that would gain its support from the oppressed workers and peasants who had nothing to lose. Tatiana would be twenty years old when the Bolsheviks murdered her Romanov cousins and took over her homeland. In the meantime, in the rapidly changing city of Shanghai, she was becoming a young woman and experiencing life on her own terms.

As Tatiana grew into womanhood, Shanghai was developing into a place that catered to the tastes of thrill seekers and the reckless. Anything could be had in Shanghai for a price—and the price was relatively low. Those looking for excitement, from gambling and drinking to uninhibited sex and drugs, were drawn to Shanghai. Nightclubs and cabarets began appearing in the International Settlement, and every hotel had a ballroom with a dance band that played all night.

When Tatiana was sixteen, she started going out with Olga and her French boyfriend, Jean Paul. In those early days, their parents thought there was no harm in it. People went out to have fun, not to indulge in depraved and lewd behaviour—and the girls were instructed to be home no later than ten o'clock. At first they would go to a restaurant or teahouse, then go dancing at one of the fashionable hotels. As soon as they left the house, Tatiana would put on red lipstick so that she looked older, and she began to cultivate what she thought was a sophisticated look. She pinned her hair up and when she sat down, she crossed her legs and exposed her ankles and part of her calf, which was very daring in 1913.

Olga was horrified and embarrassed that her younger sister was behaving this way in front of Jean Paul. "Tatiana," she whispered hoarsely in her sister's ear, "sit up straight and pull your skirt down. Do you want people to think you are a—"

Olga stopped, not wanting to say the word.

"A what," Tatiana said, loud enough for Jean Paul to hear. "A whore?"

Olga was mortified, but Jean Paul, who seemed to understand that Tatiana needed to be outrageous in order to test the limits and the patience of those who loved her, was more tolerant. He was older than Olga by a few years, the son of a good family from France that had prospered in the textile business in China, the land of silkworms and cheap labour. Jean Paul had been to university in France. He had seen young women behave far more outrageously than Tatiana. During those years, he had enjoyed hanging out with painters and poets—and their women. Jean Paul was neither handsome nor talented, but he was gentle and kind, qualities that appealed to Olga, who was neither as beautiful nor as bright as her younger sister. But Jean Paul, neither tall nor short, his hair thinning but not yet bald, fair and pale-skinned and needing to wear glasses to read, was attracted to the shorter, darker, more sensible sister, possibly because she reminded him of his mother, who was also short and dark and sensible. Her ancestors from generations back had come from the Basque region of Spain, where plain looks could hide a fiery temper and a passionate spirit. Jean Paul found that possibility appealing.

One night, when the three of them were at a cabaret, a young woman approached their table. She was a little wobbly on her feet, and she spoke to them in English with a heavy French accent. "'Allo, kids. Wanna buy me a drink and hear *l'histoire de ma vie?*"

"Sure," said Jean Paul and signalled for her to join them. Olga didn't look too pleased, but what did it hurt to talk to someone? He called to the waiter, "Catchee gin tonic, chop chop," and the waiter scurried off.

To Tatiana's inexperienced eyes, the woman was very beautiful. She was probably in her late twenties and had thick, curly red hair that she had piled on top of her head so that some of the curls cascaded over her forehead and ears. Her green eyes and milky skin were dramatically set off by the emerald green silk shawl she wore draped over her pale shoulders. Her full bosom was enhanced by the cut of her dress, but she was otherwise slender, with long legs and slim ankles. She wore startling red lipstick on her full lips that emphasized the paleness of her beautiful skin. She introduced herself as Annette and began to tell them her story.

She had been born in France but had grown up in Saigon, in Indo-China, where her father had owned a small textile factory. Her family had fallen on hard times, however, when her father had become ill, and she and her brothers were forced to leave school to find work. Annette and her mother had worked as seamstresses, but sewing bored Annette. "So I found myself a rich lover," she said. But he was Vietnamese and had been betrothed since childhood to the daughter of a wealthy Saigon family. "I knew he would never marry me, but what did I care about marriage? I was only sixteen."

On the day of his marriage, Annette discovered she was pregnant. "That's when I decided to leave Saigon and the whole mess behind. I came to Shanghai to have my baby." She lit a cigarette and inhaled deeply. "I know what you're thinking," she said. "Why didn't I try and get money from him? I could have had a comfortable life, right? And raised my son, who would be called a bastard and half-breed, in some backstreet in Saigon. No, thank you. Not the life I wanted." She indicated that her glass was empty, and Jean Paul ordered more drinks all round. When Tatiana, who had listened intently to every word, asked for a gin and tonic, Olga raised her eyebrows in annoyed surprise, but Tatiana ignored her and turned to Annette.

"*Qu'est-ce que vous avez voulu?*" she asked. What did you want?

"I wanted adventure. I wanted to be surprised by life, not to have every day the same."

"And what about your child?"

"My son, my Daniel, is six years old, and he's beautiful, the best part of my life."

"But how do you support him?" Olga asked.

Annette just laughed. "Shanghai is full of opportunities, if you know where to look. Maybe I'll show you someday, *chérie*."

Tatiana looked at Olga and laughed, but Olga frowned and shook her head. Tatiana was fascinated by Annette and wanted to know more—about everything.

They were to run into Annette often after that night. She was usually in the company of a man or with a party of men and women. The men were always in well-tailored evening clothes, mostly French but sometimes British. Occasionally she would be on the arm of an American businessman who wore cologne and smoked large, smelly cigars. Olga usually clucked her disapproval, but to Tatiana it was all very glamorous. To be out drinking champagne and dancing every night with rich men didn't seem so bad to her.

"You are so innocent," said Olga. "Can't you see she's a whore?"

"She is not. Do people call you a whore because you dance with Jean Paul?"

Olga was clearly annoyed. "I can't believe you're being so stupid."

"Oh, leave her alone," said Jean Paul. "She's just a kid."

But Tatiana wasn't a child any more, at least not in her own mind. She was almost seventeen and ready for life to surprise her, like Annette. Lily was going to leave for finishing school in Switzerland soon and would be away for a whole year. Tatiana wasn't sure what she was going to do without her friend. Read books and listen to her father's lectures? Hang around with Olga and Jean Paul? The prospect was not appealing.

Tatiana and Lily cried the whole afternoon before Lily left for Switzerland. They gave each other diaries to write all their thoughts in and promised, promised, promised to write letters every day. Tatiana had begged her father to let her go to Switzerland with Lily, but he said it was impossible. It would cost more money than he made in a year. The truth was, he was afraid to let Tatiana spend a year away from home, even if she went with Lily. He saw that Tatiana was becoming restless, a dangerous thing in a young girl. Boys, he knew, could take care of themselves. Restlessness was a good quality in a young man. It made him curious and adventurous. Young men needed to take risks, find out what they were made of, especially before they settled down to marriage and a family. They needed to get that energy out of their system so they could take on the responsibility of work and family. But young women were a different thing altogether. No man wanted to marry a restless girl, and Sergei wanted his daughters to be married to fine and responsible men who would take care of them and their children, his grandchildren. Olga he was not worried about. Tatiana, he could see, was going to be a problem.

Tatiana did not believe her father when he told her they weren't rich. She knew they were rich, especially when she compared how they lived to the way most of the Shanghai Chinese lived. She had no concept of real wealth, however, and assumed that because they lived in a large stone house and were well-dressed and well-fed and had servants, they must be very rich. Her mother, who remembered how wealthy they had been in Russia, smiled sadly when Tatiana complained to her about her father's decision not to let her go to Switzerland and said, "My darling Tatiana, you have no idea."

They had been in Shanghai for almost a decade, and with each passing year, Katarina missed Russia even more. They had made friends in Shanghai, of course, mostly through Sergei's business connections, and the few Russians who had left, like them, before the situation became critical and even dangerous for people of their class. But these were not people that Katarina ever felt close to. These were not the people who inhabited her soul the way her family did. She could never replace that feeling of profound connection that had nourished her every minute of her life. She loved her husband and daughters desperately, but they were a fragment of the broken bowl that had been her life, one that had once been filled to the brim with meaning and life, with people whose love and support went to the heart of who she was and where she had come from. Katarina needed this more than her husband and daughters did. They did not understand how bereft she was and why her world got smaller while theirs seemed to grow larger. Why can't I be like them? she often wondered. Why can't I let go of what I once had and can never have again?

~ ~

As I grew taller, my mother seemed to get smaller and smaller. I could practically touch fingertips when I put my hands around her waist. She rarely left the house and lived for news from home. I didn't understand how she could just let her life float away on a cloud of sadness. It seemed like such a waste to me. Wasn't life to be lived? To be experienced? Why couldn't she pull herself together and just get on with it? Sometimes I was angry with her because her sadness and melancholia made me unhappy.

~ ~

"It isn't fair," Tatiana complained to her father.

Sergei once again summoned Tolstoy. "'Happiness does not depend on outward things, but on the way we see them.' Unfortunately your mother does not see joy in Shanghai. She left her happiness behind in Russia."

"But, Papa," she protested, "it's been nine years. I don't understand how someone can be sad for nine years."

"Be patient, Tatushka. Someday you will understand. 'The strongest of all warriors are these two—Time and Patience.' Even though you are growing up in China, you were born with a Russian soul. This you cannot escape."

Riddles, she thought. *My father talks in riddles.* "Tolstoy is dead!" she shouted and flung herself from the room.

Sergei couldn't decide what to do with his second daughter. He wanted her to have an education because he believed she had a good mind. He had thought briefly about sending her to Paris but had immediately rejected the idea. He could see the danger of letting his headstrong daughter go off on her own, so far from his influence. Besides, he was hearing too much about political instability and threats of war in Europe, and it made him uncomfortable with the idea of sending the impressionable Tatiana off into the middle of it. He was leaning toward designing a schedule of study for her, based on his own library and readings, and hiring a tutor to supervise it. He hadn't yet discussed it with Tatiana; he wanted a plan that was appealing enough that she would at least consider it before rejecting it outright.

In the summer of 1914, war broke out in Europe. Many of the young men began leaving Shanghai to take up arms for their home countries. The lives of a generation of young men and women would be disrupted for four years by a conflagration whose extent none of them could have anticipated. By the time the conflict ended, Shanghai would be a very different place.

Sergei could see his youngest daughter already beginning to drift away from him, and he initiated a campaign to draw her back into the world of books and ideas he had hoped she would embrace. He saw that the window of opportunity was very small, and if he did not capture her imagination now, she might be lost to him forever.

~ ~

When I look back now, I understand how much I underestimated my father's wisdom. He had to work so much harder at raising me than he did Olga. He knew she would be all right. She was centred and uncomplicated, like a compass. True north was never a problem for her. She always knew where it was. I was different, however. I wasn't willing to settle for anything without exploring the possibilities, and I think, in this way I resembled him more than I realized. It was many years before I understood that taking on the responsibility of a family had anchored my father. He had accepted the yoke of family life because, quite simply, he loved us.

~ ~

Sergei's family had been wealthy landowners in Russia. He was the third son, so he had fewer obligations than his older brothers. This had allowed him to indulge to his heart's content his love of reading. He was fascinated by history and what he thought it could teach the world. He was a philosopher at heart and lived in a world of ideas. Because everything had been given to him, Sergei could afford to be the optimist he was by nature. He saw something in Tatiana that he recognized, perhaps the legacy of his own insatiable curiosity, but he could not fathom her capacity for sadness—perhaps she had got that from her mother. He did his best to encourage the side of his daughter that was imaginative and perceptive, but he could not control the part of her that grew sullen and angry.

Chapter Six

The next year passed quickly for Tatiana. The program of study her father planned for her proved a welcome distraction. He engaged the services of Dimitri Lischenko, a well-known Russian scholar living in Shanghai who agreed to come to the house every afternoon to discuss with Tatiana the books she was reading and to test her progress with a series of written essays and examinations. Together, Sergei and Lischenko designed a course of study for Tatiana that included world history, ancient and modern philosophy, Russian, French and English literature, as well as readings in physics, since Sergei believed it was so closely tied to philosophy as to be relevant to the rest of her studies. Ever since Einstein's Theory of Relativity had been published a decade earlier, Sergei had intuited that a major shift in scientific thinking was taking place. He wasn't sure where it would lead the world, but he believed it could be as profound as Copernicus's claim that the earth revolved around the sun. Tatiana drew the line at mathematics, however. She said she had learned all the mathematics at Notre Dame she needed for a lifetime. She would read about the scientists' findings but not how they calculated them.

Dimitri Lischenko had fled Russia after his brother was shot during the "Bloody Sunday" massacre of 1905, the same event that had prompted Sergei's decision to take his family out of Russia. Dimitri, a university professor, and his brother Vladimir, a doctor, had joined the Socialist Revolutionary party in 1901, shortly after it had been formed. As educated left-wing intellectuals in a country deeply split along class lines, they were despised by both the wealthy elite because they wanted to overthrow the monarchy, and by the peasants who saw them as opportunistic dilettantes who could always take refuge in privilege. Dimitri was now nearing forty, unmarried and desperately missing his motherland. He had debated going back to Russia, and many times had been on the verge of returning, but he had always backed down. Dimitri was a true intellectual, a man who lived the life of the mind. Physical courage was not part of his makeup. He was a small, nervous man with a tendency to drink, which led to occasional bouts of melancholia, during which he wrote copious amounts of solemn poetry. His eyesight was poor, his skin sallow, and his fine, light brown hair was slowly but surely receding further and further back on his wide forehead. But he had a brilliant and incisive mind, was a voracious reader and spoke excellent French and English. In other words, he was perfect for the job. Sergei knew the man could challenge Tatiana intellectually and always be ahead of her by several steps. He also knew that there was no danger that Tatiana would fall in love with Dimitri, a complication Sergei did not need.

Tatiana, however, grew very fond of Dimitri over time. Perhaps she recognized his vulnerability in the real world beyond the books he buried himself in. She felt affectionate toward him, the way she would feel about a kitten or a child. She also learned a great deal from him. Not so much factual information that she could read in books, but how to interpret the information, analyze it and decide for herself if she agreed. This was the part of the learning process she enjoyed most. It made her feel powerful, as if this were one area of life she could control, the realm of ideas. She especially enjoyed those times when her father joined in the discussions. Then things would get lively, because her father liked to play the role of devil's advocate.

"So," he said, looking Tatiana straight in the eye, "if God created Paradise on earth, why did he let Adam and Eve destroy it by eating the fruit from the Tree of Knowledge? Wasn't he powerful enough to stop them?"

Tatiana had been reading *Paradise Lost* and had anticipated this question. Dimitri had discussed with her the notion of good and evil and why Eve had succumbed to the serpent's seduction.

"God gave Adam and Eve the gifts of reason and free will," she said. "So they were free to choose to obey God or to obey Satan. They were free to choose sin."

"Then why obey Satan instead of God? Didn't they owe their obedience to God for placing them in Paradise?"

"I suppose they did, in a way," said Tatiana, pondering the question. "But God didn't demand obedience, and he didn't make them perfect. Eve was deceived by the serpent, but she didn't know he was trying to destroy her and Adam out of jealousy and revenge. She gave in to temptation because his words made sense to her." She quoted from Milton:

"… in her ears the sound
Yet rung of his persuasive words, impregned
With Reason, to her seeming, and with truth…

"And then she persuaded Adam to taste the fruit and he chose to join Eve in her disobedience of God. Adam's better judgment told him it was wrong to eat the fruit, because God had told them not to, but he allowed himself to be seduced by Eve because he loved her."

"And ever since," smiled Sergei, "men have been led into temptation by women."

"Papa," said Tatiana, "that's not fair. If Satan had chosen Adam instead of Eve to eat the fruit, he probably would have found a way to persuade him. Men are just as likely to succumb to temptation as women. Then Adam would have tempted Eve, and the whole world would be different."

Sergei laughed. "I think we are creating a suffragist, Dimitri. Your pupil is able to turn every argument into a defence of women's rights."

"I apologize, Mr. Relnikov. I had no idea I was dealing with someone who could use reason so effectively to exert her free will."

"Ah," said Sergei. "Perhaps you and God both made the same mistake."

Tatiana laughed. "You two like to think that men are superior to women and that women were created to serve men."

"Well," said Sergei, "weren't they? Doesn't the Bible say that Eve was created to serve Adam and God?"

"Yes. But Eve didn't want to be inferior. She wanted to be equal. She says:

'And render me more equal, and perhaps,
A thing not understandable, sometime
Superior; for inferior who is free?

"She wanted to be free, which is what everybody wants. If God didn't want Adam and Eve to sin, why did he put the Tree of Knowledge in Paradise? Why did he put free will and temptation on the same plate?"

"It's a good question, Tatushka." Sergei was genuinely pleased at his daughter's intellectual progress. "Why do you think he did this?"

"Perhaps God needed to provide the opportunity for mercy and forgiveness. How could he be seen as a benevolent God if nobody ever needed forgiving? Why does God even need to exist if everyone is perfect?"

"But if that is the case," said Dimitri, "then it was in God's divine plan all along that Adam and Eve would be expelled from Paradise for succumbing to temptation. So what your father said is true. God let Adam and Eve destroy Paradise. He was powerful enough."

Tatiana looked at Dimitri then at her father. They had brought the argument full circle, and she hadn't seen it coming.

Tatiana was still tied to Olga and Jean Paul by invisible strings, but they were beginning to chafe. Despite her interest in her studies, Sergei had begun to sense that Tatiana's desire for independence might get her into trouble, so he did not allow her to go out without a chaperone. He had even started searching for a possible husband for her, a prospect that made her nervous and irritable. She endured many lectures that year about her frequent bad moods and controlling her temper. Mostly, her family's efforts to rein her in just made Tatiana angrier and more determined to break away as soon as possible. Olga, on the other hand, could not wait to be married. Tatiana could muster no enthusiasm for such a future. She was not ready for a husband, marriage, or, God forbid, children. Her father often despaired, knowing that the day would come when he could no longer make decisions for her.

Tatiana was becoming a beautiful young woman. She was tall, like her maternal grandmother, with thick, honey-coloured hair and a fair complexion, which she enhanced by avoiding the sun and rubbing lemon juice on her skin. Tatiana had the kind of face that didn't need make-up, but she was vain about her appearance and liked to dress up and wear powder and lipstick to emphasize her features. Her grey eyes were deep-set, with slightly hooded lids, and she was learning to use them in a way that made people uncomfortable when she stared at them.

Olga resembled the women on Sergei's side of the family. She was a good five inches shorter than Tatiana, with a thick waist and sturdy legs. Her hair was darker than her father's, and so curly that it would tighten into a frizzy ball when the air was humid.

She had straight, no-nonsense eyebrows and brown eyes that were almost black. This, combined with her square jaw, gave her the appearance of matronly authority. All she needed was a nun's wimple and robes and she could have been Mother Superior. When she walked with her sister in the streets of the French Concession, the young men looked at Tatiana, not Olga. Fortunately, Jean Paul, who was shorter than Tatiana but taller than Olga, balding and underweight, was devoted to Olga, and they were planning to marry as soon as he completed his army service.

The war in Europe continued, and each year more young Frenchmen were shipped home to do their duty. The few who returned brought back grim stories of something called trench warfare that made Tatiana think of the slimy gutters of Shanghai. She couldn't imagine having to spend days in one of them while being shot at round the clock. Every day she thanked God that she had been born a woman. She had been studying the battles of the great commanders from Caesar to Napoleon, and was fascinated by their strategic and tactical abilities, but it was all in the realm of the imagination for her. She wasn't hearing about the horrors of those battles first hand. Many of the young men Tatiana had known didn't come back from the war, but she refused to believe they'd all been killed. They must have chosen to stay in Paris, she decided. Given the choice between Paris and Shanghai, why would they come back? Much as she loved Shanghai, Tatiana imagined Paris to be a city of stylish and elegant people, as far removed from the chattering masses of China as a swan was from a chicken.

Things became glum in the Relnikov household when Jean Paul left for France. Olga worried herself sick that he wouldn't return. Tatiana prayed daily that he would, mostly because she liked him and really wanted Olga to marry him and be happy, but also because she missed going out in the evenings to the cabarets. Her studies kept her occupied during the day, but at night she wanted to go dancing.

Soon it was June and Tatiana's eighteenth birthday. She had not changed her mind about marriage and children, as her parents had hoped she might. She was growing tired of reading and studying but decided it was the lesser of two evils and far more preferable than marriage.

Lily returned in September. It was apparent as soon as she was home that the plans for her wedding were about to be launched. She and Tatiana had a brief few weeks to themselves, during which Lily told her all about her experiences in Switzerland. Her letters had said a lot, but not everything. It wasn't until Tatiana watched Lily's face as she talked that she realized how much her friend had enjoyed her taste of freedom. Lily's eyes sparkled, and she chattered on and on about all the girls in her class, the friendships she had formed, the school, the teachers, the mountains, and the food, which she had hated. "So bad," she said. "Dairy, dairy, dairy. Too much cheese. Too much milk. Not healthy."

Tatiana laughed as Lily showed her how she had been taught to walk with a book on her head, sit with her ankles crossed and serve tea while making polite conversation. Lily's French had improved greatly, but she still couldn't make the throaty "r" sound that only the French seem able to do. And she had never mastered the rolling "r" that Mrs. Wilkinson had prized so highly. Neither, for that matter, had Tatiana.

Lily seemed to have developed a confidence and a charm that she had not possessed when she left. She had been transformed from a shy and awkward girl into a graceful young woman. Tatiana towered over her by about seven inches, and her feet and hands seemed huge compared to Lily's delicate, manicured fingers and toes. Tatiana envied the fragile Oriental beauty Lily had acquired, the gentle voice she spoke with and the still serenity she possessed. Tatiana felt like a giraffe next to her friend.

A wedding date had been set for Lily's marriage to Tang Wu-ling. It had been chosen as a lucky day, declared so by an astrologer because of an auspicious formation of the planets. It was to be a traditional Chinese wedding, and gifts had already begun to arrive. Lily was putting together a trousseau of beautiful clothes, all handmade by seamstresses who appeared to be working around the clock. She and Tatiana spent many hours poring over catalogues and drawings, choosing fabrics and selecting accessories. Her wedding dress and shoes would be the traditional red, in elaborately embroidered silk brocade. She would also wear a bride's headdress, which would cover her face completely with a curtain of beads so that she would see nothing bad on her wedding day. On the day of the wedding, the bridegroom's friends would come to the house and transport Lily to the groom's home in a sedan chair covered in ornately carved decorations and hung with tassels and baubles.

As Tatiana sat in Lily's room surrounded by the trappings of her friend's upcoming marriage, she asked Lily if she was nervous.

"Of course. I will be leaving my father's home to live with a strange family. And I will be expected to respect and obey my mother-in-law. I have not met my husband, and yet I will have to live with him for the rest of my life. Wouldn't you be nervous?"

"I'd be scared to death," Tatiana said. "I think I'd run away before my wedding day."

"But wouldn't you want to wait and see if maybe you liked your husband? Don't assume that all arranged marriages are unhappy. Many are successful and last a lifetime. The parents will not allow a marriage to take place if the horoscopes are not compatible."

"Then if I didn't like my husband, I'd run away the day after the wedding."

Lily laughed. "You can't tell in one day if you like someone or not. You have to give it some time. Get to know one another."

Tatiana thought of the Tolstoy quote Sergei seemed to repeat constantly until she wanted to scream: "The strongest of all warriors are these two—Time and Patience." Tatiana had neither time nor patience. She wanted something to happen *now*, not a year from now or even a month from now. Lily's acceptance of a fate that Tatiana considered worse than death was incomprehensible to her.

"But by then you'll be trapped," she protested, "and you'll probably 'catchee baby' as Amah would say."

"But that would be good," Lily said. "A baby would bring me status and would give me something to do. My husband and his mother will have to treat me with respect."

"Ah, but only if you have a son," Tatiana reminded her.

"Yes. I must have a son. But then I can have a daughter who will be my companion."

Lily seemed to have it all figured out.

Before the wedding, Lily and Tatiana were allowed to go shopping together on the Chinese Bund, the part of the city that was a maze of narrow crowded streets lined with every imaginable kind of shop and kiosk. There you could buy everything from fresh produce, ivory chopsticks, brass bowls and sandalwood-scented soap to fabrics made of cotton, or raw and rough or finely woven and embroidered silk. There were hundreds of handmade items for sale in each little specialty shop—clothing made to measure in a day, gold jewellery, jade carvings, straw baskets in every size and shape, figurines carved from porcelain, stone and wood, hand-painted fans, handbags, hats, and silk and leather shoes. From every shop and stall came the cries of vendors begging, cajoling and shouting at people to buy their wares. The din was thick with their high-pitched, nasal voices. Lily and Tatiana were virtually on their own, even though they were followed everywhere by an ancient servant who carried their purchases and made sure they weren't robbed or kidnapped. Every couple of hours they would stop at a teahouse for *cha* and sweets, just to give the poor man a rest.

Even though Lily had given Tatiana many presents over the years, that day she bought her an exquisite hand-embroidered, yellow silk shawl Tatiana would keep and treasure for the rest of her life. As a wedding gift, Tatiana bought Lily a platter from the Willow Pattern Tea House. They had been admiring the platter, marvelling at the beautiful hand-painted design, when the shopkeeper told them the story behind the highly prized blue and white willow pattern. The large pagoda-style dwelling painted on the right side of the pattern was the home of a wealthy mandarin who had a beautiful daughter, Koong-see. Koong-see had fallen in love with her father's secretary, Chang, who was also in love with her. Infuriated, her father arranged a marriage between Koong-see and Ta-jin, a wealthy viceroy, and forbade her to see Chang ever again. But the lovers would not be separated. They escaped during the wedding feast and ran across the bridge to elope. Koong-see's father saw them and chased after them, which was why there were three figures on the bridge. They hid in the small home of Koong-see's servants, depicted on the left side of the pattern, but were soon caught. Chang managed to escape and returned with a boat to rescue Koong-see. They went to live on an island but eventually were discovered by Ta-jin, who killed Chang. The distraught Koong-see set fire to the house and also perished. The gods turned the lovers into the two doves that were pictured at the top of the pattern.

~ ~

After Wu-ling's death, when Lily was sent away, I went to her house to see if I could find the platter. I wanted it to remind me of happier times, and also I didn't want it to end up in the hands of a stranger, either, where it would lose all meaning. I never found the platter. I assumed it had either been broken or pilfered by someone in the days after the fighting that erupted in Shanghai between Chiang Kai-shek's army and the warlords. I was devastated. The platter had come to represent, in my mind at least, much more than the material object itself was worth. The house, in the style of a pagoda with a willow tree beside it, the curved bridge over the river and the two doves in flight came to signify a special place for me where love and friendship were forever enshrined.

I would see Lily many times after her marriage, but the fact was I viewed it as a point of separation, like a wall being erected between us. Lily was going to a place I would never know and could not share. I did not yet know where I was going, but I felt instinctively I would be going there alone.

~ ~

At eighteen Tatiana was standing on a precipice, her toes curled over the edge, preparing to jump. Within three years, the war in Europe would be over, the Armistice declared exactly a year after the Bolshevik revolution in Russia. Shanghai would soon be filling up with White Russians fleeing the purge of the Reds. Many arrived starving and indigent. The most beautiful among the women saw their opportunity for survival in the growing number of clubs and cabarets in the International Settlement. They became "dancing hostesses," offering companionship and more to any man with a gold watch and a new pair of shoes. They even consorted with the wealthy Chinese who frequented the cabarets, usually in groups and always with an assortment of beautifully groomed and dressed Chinese girls. Tatiana admired those exotic-looking Chinese girls with their masks of make-up so expertly applied. They were elegant in their tight silk dresses with high collars and slits up to their waists, or wrapped in satin-lined furs and satin gloves in winter.

To her eye, the Russian women paled in comparison to

these slender, porcelain-skinned beauties but, to the Chinese, the White Russians were fascinating and unfettered. They had nothing to lose, so far from home, so far from the life they would never see again. No amount of champagne could fill the empty place that had once been connected to a home and family, but enough could dull the pain and bring on the kind of laughter that only rang hollow the next morning, when the sun rose once again to reveal the filth and stench and noise that was Shanghai in the daytime.

Chapter Seven

Chinese tradition demanded that the bride go into seclusion with her closest friends and her sisters in the days leading up to her wedding. It represented a time of lamentation and tears, because the bride would be leaving her home and family and going to live with her husband's family. In the past, returning to her family's home often involved a journey of several days, and a bride knew she might never see her family again. In Lily's case, she would not be leaving Shanghai. In fact, Wu-ling's family lived within five miles of Lily's parents, so she could visit frequently. Her time of seclusion was more like a sleepover where Lily and her friends did each other's hair, painted their nails and generally indulged that part of themselves that was truly vain and shallow.

Tatiana was invited to assist in the pre-nuptial preparations because she was Lily's best friend and because Lily had insisted that she be there. Because Lily had no sisters, she also invited Olga and two other friends who had been with her at Les Soeurs de Notre Dame, and Wu-ling's sister, who was called Daisy. The six of them spent hours talking, laughing, listening to phonograph records and pampering themselves. They ate from an endless supply of food, including chocolate, and drank sweet drinks until they were giddy from too much sugar. The two other girls from Notre Dame, Hester, an American with long legs, and Sabina, a shy, bookish girl from Belgium, kept prodding Daisy for information about her brother. Lily pretended she didn't want to know. "No, no, I want to be surprised on my wedding day," she kept insisting, but they knew she was secretly dying to find out anything she could about her future husband. Daisy loved being the centre of attention and would feed them bits and pieces about Wu-ling as a child and then as an adolescent. He was a whole decade older than Lily and the other girls, but they weren't interested in him as an adult. They wanted to know what kind of boy he'd been.

"Well," said Daisy, coyly, "he was already almost a teenager when I was born, but my amah used to tell me stories about him. My amah's sister was Wu-ling's amah, so they were very close. They both absolutely adored him because he was so smart and so handsome." She threw back her head and laughed. "Handsome!" she shrieked. "He looks like a donkey. Lily, there's still time. You can still change your mind. Tell your parents you can't go through with the wedding. You can't marry a donkey!" They had great fun teasing Lily and planning her escape from Wu-ling and the marriage. They conjured up boats and trains and secret routes to Europe and hiding places where she would never be found.

But Lily remained firm. "I'm not backing out until I see for myself," she said. She knew Wu-ling didn't look like a donkey. She'd seen a single, faded photograph of him when he'd been at military college. He was, in fact, quite handsome, in a solemn, austere way.

"No, no," groaned Daisy. "He doesn't look like that any more. His nose has grown to twice that size, and his teeth are so big he can't cover them with his mouth. Please, Lily. Save yourself while there's still time."

Of course, the girls did not believe for a minute that Lily would be unhappy with Wu-ling. They were still at an age when their romantic notions far exceeded their experience of life. They imagined that Lily and Wu-ling would make a handsome couple and would produce beautiful children. They would love each other forever, and their marriage would be perfect. Even Tatiana believed it. Olga, who hoped soon to be planning her own wedding, felt a mix of emotions and half wished she hadn't agreed to come. Jean Paul had not yet returned from the war in Europe, and there was a part of her that lived with the constant fear that she would never see him again. Another part of her dreamed of their life together and the children they would have, and that part of Olga left no room for doubt to creep in. Having fun with other young women before Lily's wedding provided a temporary distraction and Olga tried hard to be a part of things, but somewhere, in another corner of her being, she felt guilty, knowing Jean Paul might at that very moment be suffering terribly or even be dead. It was a terrible time for Olga, one of the worst in her life but, when asked, she told everyone she was fine, and they believed her.

Tatiana wanted to be part of her best friend's wedding but would not be permitted to attend; only the parents were present at the ceremony, and family members would attend the reception that followed. Lily did her best to explain the rituals surrounding the marriage. She told Tatiana and the others about the traditional "six etiquettes" that were observed before the wedding ceremony. The first was the proposal. If the groom's parents decided a girl might be a suitable match for their son, they called on a matchmaker to present a proposal to the bride's parents. In Lily's case, this had been done while she was still a small child. Then came the astrological matching of the birthdays to make sure the couple's horoscopes were auspicious and compatible. Once it was determined that the birthdays matched, the proposal was accepted, the betrothal became official, and the groom's parents had the matchmaker present the betrothal gifts to the bride's parents. When the betrothal gifts were accepted, the groom's family then sent a series of wedding gifts to the bride's family. Next, an astrologer picked an auspicious wedding date. Lily's wedding day had been selected before she had left for Europe. Finally, the wedding ceremony took place after the groom arrived in a noisy procession at the bride's house to escort her to his family home.

As Lily had already told Tatiana, when a woman married, she went to live with her husband's family, and was required to worship his ancestors. Once she had married, she would forever be a guest in her own parents' house.

On the morning of her wedding, Lily took a bath in water that had some grapefruit essence in it. Then a special "good-luck woman" arrived to do Lily's hair and say a lot of auspicious things about the marriage. As she would no longer be a girl after her marriage, Lily now had to have a woman's hairstyle. Traditionally, this meant pinning up a girl's long hair for the first time. Lily's hair was not that long, but she had been letting it grow for several months. The hairdresser found clever ways to pin Lily's straight black hair into elaborate knots so that it was swept up from her neck. The others saw that even as simple an act as changing her hairstyle would take Lily away from them and their schoolgirl ways. She would become a woman before their eyes, and by the end of the day, she would be a married woman, lying beside her husband in the marriage bed.

By the time they had helped Lily into her elaborately embroidered red wedding dress and her red satin shoes, Tatiana was feeling stifled by the almost overwhelming weight of ritual. Lily had tried to prepare her for what would happen, but for Tatiana everything seemed to be sending Lily into the past instead of the future. She saw her friend's life as pre-ordained. Where was the free will that she had so recently debated and had grown to believe was an inherent right of the human soul? Her father had told her that China was the future, but the rituals of Lily's wedding and marriage seemed to say that, for women at least, it was the past that mattered, that determined destiny. Tatiana watched the hairdresser arrange the headdress on Lily's newly styled hair so that her white-powdered face was hidden by a curtain of beads. So much depended on correctly performing these ancient rituals.

It seemed to Tatiana a precarious way to start a marriage. Wasn't this the time for a bride to have her eyes wide open? To know what she was getting into? Instead, everything was wrapped in ritual and secrecy, hidden behind curtains of mystery. After their days of carefree laughter and fun, the six young women were now suddenly subdued. Tatiana was at a loss for something to say to Lily before she embarked on her life's journey.

"Good luck, Lily," she whispered, taking her friend's hand. She could think of nothing wiser or more appropriate. What was there to say except, good luck? Luck was very important in China. All the traditions were being observed to ensure as much luck as possible befell the married couple. There could be no ill omens or mismatched horoscopes or inauspicious solar configurations on the day of the wedding.

The two people whose fate had been decided for them were expected to walk in the pre-ordained footsteps left by centuries of other brides and grooms. Who had decided that this was the best way to do things? Tatiana pictured a committee of white-haired and bearded old men nodding their heads in approval at the most superstitious-laden and inhumane suggestions they could come up with. The six etiquettes—why only six? Why not ten or a hundred? Because, in fact, hidden within those six etiquettes, were a thousand little rules, and each of those rules had a rule master or mistress who made sure they were obeyed. It was suffocating, just like the elaborate costume Lily was forced to wear on the day she met her husband for the first time.

When they could hear the clanging and trumpeting of Wu-ling's procession in the distance, the five attendants, as the bride's closest friends, were told to block the door and not let Wu-ling and his groomsmen enter until they had negotiated and haggled with them for the privilege of receiving the bride. In the spirit of tradition, the groomsmen handed over packets of money wrapped in red paper, and as they did so, Tatiana saw Wu-ling for the first time. He was slim and tall and looked even taller in his traditional black silk cap and long silk gown. He had a stiff military bearing and a sternly handsome face that seemed unaccustomed to all the laughter and good cheer that was required of a bridegroom negotiating for his bride.

Would Lily be happy with this man, Tatiana wondered? Wu-ling seemed so much older and more serious than the rest of them. Would he make Lily laugh and appreciate her sense of humour? Tatiana thought of all the times they had been silly together, the stories they had made up. She thought of the world they had created with their friendship, where they could be themselves and not care what anybody else thought. She resented Wu-ling, she realized, for taking Lily away from her. She almost hated him for putting an end to their precious childhood.

When Lily's attendants released her, the good-luck woman led her to the elaborate sedan chair that would take her to Wu-ling's family. Daisy held a red parasol over Lily's head, and Tatiana was given a handful of rice to throw at the chair. Once Lily was settled in the heavily curtained sedan, firecrackers were lit to frighten off evil spirits. The young women covered their ears and watched the noisy procession take Lily away.

When the noise and the excitement had subsided, they turned and walked back into the house, now so empty and silent. The whole ceremony had been geared toward sending Lily into the world of her husband's family, so it was only natural that they should feel a sense of loss. For the Chinese bride, her wedding day was one of sorrow and apprehension rather than joy and anticipation. Tatiana wondered what Lily was feeling at that moment, and whether she would allow doubt or regret to enter her thoughts. Just before she walked out the door of her parents' house, Lily had said to her, "Don't worry, Tatiana. It will be all right. I'm not afraid." It had seemed to Tatiana an odd thing for a bride to say. But then again, marriage was an unknown territory for all of them. Maybe fear was a legitimate emotion for a wedding day.

Chapter Eight

After Lily's marriage, Tatiana tried to pretend that life was still normal and that not much had changed, but everywhere she looked, things had changed, and not always for the better. Jean Paul finally returned to Shanghai, but without his left leg, and he was even thinner than he had been when he left. He seemed like the old Jean Paul, but sometimes when he smiled, it was only with his mouth and not his eyes. As she looked around at the other soldiers coming back from the war in Europe, Tatiana realized that he was one of the lucky ones. Many were blind or shell-shocked and withdrawn, with a haunted look in their eyes that frightened her. Several were missing more than one limb. They were thin and stooped, old before their time. It filled her with rage to see them. Whenever she passed a healthy-looking man on the street, she wanted to shout, "It's not fair! Nothing in this world is fair!"

Sergei was still mourning the death of their Romanov cousins who had been shot by the Bolsheviks, a bunch of madmen with an insane ideology.

"The lunatics are running the asylum," he said. "After a thousand years of history, nothing has changed. Nothing has improved. 'The greater the state, the more wrong and cruel its patriotism, and the greater is the sum of suffering upon which its power is founded.'"

Tatiana wasn't sure whether he quoted Tolstoy to condemn the Bolsheviks or the Romanovs. For once she remembered something from Tolstoy she agreed with: "War is so unjust

and ugly that all who wage it must try to stifle the voice of
conscience within themselves."

"That's right, Tatushka. Unfortunately, conscience is much
too pliable a mechanism. While we stifle its goodness, we are
able to make it believe whatever we choose. We become deaf to
its voice and immune to its message. God gave us free will, and
we have used it to run roughshod over truth and mercy."

For the first time, Tatiana noticed that her father was getting old.

Olga's wedding to Jean Paul was the first major social event in
the Relnikovs' Shanghai life, and it was filled with celebration,
in contrast to Lily's recent, more subdued wedding. As a
family, and as Russians, they were still in mourning, but
they could not resist the opportunity to celebrate love and
the future. Olga's wedding would adhere to tradition also,
but Sergei and Katarina wanted it to be a grand and joyous
occasion, even though Olga and Jean Paul, especially Olga,
would have preferred to draw less attention to themselves.
Katarina organized a cohort of women to prepare more
Russian food than they had seen in all their years in Shanghai.
Everybody pitched in because, although there were many
cooks in Shanghai, there were not many Russian ones.
Tatiana personally shredded a dozen cabbages and peeled a
hundred potatoes and was happy to do it. Sergei had been
hoarding caviar for months, and the cook had smoked kilos
of salmon, carp and herring. He had pickled cucumbers,
cranberries, mushrooms and apples according to Katarina's
recipes. He and his Chinese assistant had scoured the city,
buying every quail and pheasant for miles around. There were
baskets of strawberries and boxes of chocolate. Cherries that
had been soaking in brandy for months were sampled and
declared ready. Jean Paul's family supplied vodka, wine and
champagne, cheese and pastries made with real cream.

On the day before her wedding, Olga had been caught slicing onions, which irritated Tatiana and her mother. It was almost as if she were sabotaging her own wedding. "Your hands will smell like a peasant's," Katarina told her. She really didn't understand this daughter of hers, who was almost a princess, for heaven's sake. If they had been in Russia, Katarina believed, this wouldn't be happening; there would be a hundred servants doing the work and knowing what had to be done. But in Shanghai, the only way to be sure it was done right was to do most of it yourself. If you couldn't behave like a princess before your wedding, she told her daughter, when could you? "Do you think Jean Paul wants to marry someone who stinks of onions on her wedding day? Let Natasha slice the onions—she already has a husband." She made Olga rub her hands with fresh lemons and soak her fingers in the juice.

"What were you thinking?" Tatiana asked Olga as she braided her sister's hair with ribbons. This was the one thing Tatiana did well, and Katarina had told her to take Olga upstairs and do it as slowly as possible to keep her out of the kitchen. "Slicing onions!"

"I don't know," Olga said. Tatiana had never seen her sister so restless and fidgety. "I suppose I'm a little nervous. Everybody's watching me. I'm trying to pretend it's just like any other day, but nobody will let me."

"Why would you do that?" Tatiana said, trying to understand. "It's not like any other day. You only have one wedding day, and it should be special. Besides, you never slice onions, and I never peel potatoes, so you're not behaving in a very normal fashion, anyway."

"I know," Olga said. "But wait till it happens to you. Everybody fussing and carrying on, telling you it will be the happiest day of your life. I don't want it to be the happiest day of my life. I want lots of happier days before I die. Not just this one." Tatiana concluded it was just like Olga to grumble on her wedding day.

"Are you afraid?" she asked, remembering Lily's words on her wedding day.

"Afraid?" Olga said. "Why would I be afraid? I'm marrying the best man in the world." And she was, thought Tatiana. Anyone who would marry her sister had to be a saint. She would have to chalk it up to wedding jitters. Nobody was behaving normally over this wedding. Her parents had never been so excited; they were constantly in motion, checking lists, coordinating servants and helpers, scheduling meetings with each other to make sure they had not forgotten anything. Katarina, especially, was a constant source of surprise. It was as if she had rallied all her inner forces for this one event, like Napoleon at Austerlitz, at the peak of her strategic and tactical abilities. This was what she had been born to do. Tatiana did not want to think about what life would be like after the wedding. Would the momentum continue, or would there be a Waterloo, the decline then defeat?

Sergei had given Jean Paul a job in his factory, keeping the accounts and effectively running the business in his absence. As a father without sons, he now had a successor. He had worked hard to build his business in Shanghai and, even though he had a Chinese partner so essential to greasing the wheels of industry, Sergei considered the business his creation and his finest achievement.

Olga and Jean Paul were a good match. Jean Paul came from an excellent family and, more important, he loved their daughter. The wedding was a chance for the Relnikovs to show their Shanghai friends and Sergei's business associates that they had done well and were prospering. No expense would be spared.

Olga's dress was made from cream-coloured French lace that fell in tiers from a tight bodice and waist. It was surprisingly slimming, given her rather sturdy build, although from behind she looked a bit like a wedding cake. Katarina wore pale green silk that complemented her porcelain skin, with a long strand of pearls and pearl earrings that were the exact same colour as Olga's dress. Tatiana and the five other attendants, who included Jean Paul's three sisters and two of Olga's friends from Notre Dame, wore the softest shade of pink with a darker pink satin sash around the waist that trailed down the back to the bottom of the skirt. The identical dresses had a scalloped neckline and sleeves that ended at the elbows. Olga and her attendants wore ivory silk stockings and satin shoes, but Olga's shoes had a pearl buckle, and her bridesmaids' shoes had pink rosebuds at the instep. Sergei wore tails with a grey striped waistcoat and a grey silk tie with a pearl stickpin in the centre. Tatiana thought they had never looked better as a family. Every time she looked at Sergei, he was beaming. Even Katarina smiled and laughed the whole day.

The ceremony took place at eleven o'clock in the morning at St. Ignatius Cathedral, the largest Catholic church in Shanghai. Sergei was solemn as he led his daughter into the church. Olga, her face partially hidden by a lace veil, took small steps and, much to her mother's relief, resisted the urge to march rapidly and unceremoniously down the aisle. This was a moment Katarina and Sergei wanted to prolong and appreciate. It was a moment that should have told them that all things were right in the world and in their family. Although Katarina wished the church could have been filled with their relatives, it was not to be. In the midst of her contentment was the sorrow that often attends celebration, the knowledge of loss, the perception of grief. Yet there was also the sense of beginning again, the understanding that life went on and that hope existed. Someday there would be grandchildren, and perhaps even Tatiana might find a husband.

As Olga and Jean Paul exchanged their vows, Tatiana, for the briefest moment, wondered what it would be like to be standing in her sister's place. But by the time Jean Paul slipped the gold wedding band on Olga's finger, Tatiana knew it would be a long time before she would willingly take on the challenge of marriage and a husband.

After the ceremony, the three hundred invited guests proceeded to the elegant Peacock Hall of the Astor House Hotel to drink the five hundred bottles of French champagne and sit at tables covered in white linen, where they would be served the many courses of food prepared by the Russians, by waiters wearing white gloves. The meal was magnificent and used up almost a quarter of Sergei's savings. From that day on, the Relnikovs would talk in terms of "before Olga's wedding" and "after Olga's wedding". It was a defining moment in their lives.

Sergei had hired twenty musicians, and the guests danced the traditional Russian dances like the kadril and the polka, something called the foxtrot from America, and even the tango. Jean Paul demonstrated the triumph of will over adversity when he hopped around the dance floor with a crutch under one arm and his new bride under the other. Everyone cheered and applauded their clumsy dance and the strength of their love.

For Tatiana, the dancing was the best part. The orchestra was good, and they could play anything. She was never off her feet but did manage to have one dance with her father. She was so tall in her two-inch heels that she could almost look him straight in the eye.

"So, Tatushka," he said, waltzing her across the floor, "what do you think? Is it a good party?"

"Yes, Papa," she said, gazing up at the magnificent stained-glass ceiling. "It's an excellent party."

"I agree. I think we have given your sister a good send-off."

"Send-off, Papa? Why do you call it a send-off?"

"Well," he said, "she's leaving us and going off to live with Jean Paul. We're sending her off to her new life."

"She's not really leaving us, though, is she? I mean, she'll still be in Shanghai. She'll still be part of our family, won't she?"

"Of course she will. I was speaking figuratively, of course. Her life will be different from now on, that's all. She won't just be a daughter and a sister, she'll be a wife and someday a mother."

"When Lily got married, they really did send her away. She is now part of her husband's family, and she doesn't belong to her parents any more." Tatiana could see Lily and Wu-ling sitting off to the side with Lily's parents and her brothers. She noticed the other Chinese guests had, one by one, deferentially approached Lily's father and paid their respects to him.

Lily looked very elegant, like her mother. Her hair had been professionally waved, and she wore an emerald green silk dress with hand-sewn beading on the collar and bodice. She looked much older and more sophisticated than she had on her wedding day. Tatiana had barely had time to speak to her, except to tell her how beautiful her dress was and to admire her new hairstyle.

"Yes," said Sergei as he waltzed Tatiana around the floor, "with the Chinese, marriage is all tied up with ancestor worship and dynasties. For us it's about bringing families together, not pulling them apart."

"I don't think I want to get married, Papa."

Sergei looked at her with amusement. "That's nonsense, Tatiana. Of course you want to get married."

"No, I don't think I do," she said.

"And what do you propose to do with your life instead, may I ask?"

"I'm not sure, but I see nothing appealing about marriage."

"What do you mean, Tati?"

"Well, marriage always seems to be about somebody else, especially if you're a woman. Suddenly you're expected to take care of your husband and live where he wants and do things for him. And then, when you have children, you have to take care of more people. I don't want to care for anybody but myself."

Sergei laughed. "You have a point, Tati, but marriage is about more than taking care of people. It's about having a home and companionship and never being alone. Nobody wants to be all alone in this world. A husband and wife take care of each other. I go to work and manage the business while your mother manages the household. It's a fair exchange. What kind of a world would it be if everybody lived alone in one room and never got together?"

"Papa," she said, "you're teasing me. You never take me seriously."

He kissed her forehead. "I *do* take you seriously, Tatushka. I know you're not like Olga, and it will be hard for you to find contentment. You have a restless soul. I can see that. But you're searching for something that might not be out there. You must learn to curb your restlessness, Tati. You must figure out how to be content with an ordinary life. Otherwise, you may end up with nothing. Life will pass you by. No father wants his daughter to be a lonely old maid."

The music stopped, and they stood in the middle of the dance floor looking at each other. "Promise me, Tati, that you won't throw your life away. Promise me you won't break an old man's heart." Tatiana suddenly felt sad, because she had taken Sergei away from the celebration of his eldest daughter's marriage and handed him something to worry about.

She wanted to promise, but she still had her doubts. Sergei thought she would eventually see that he was right, but Tatiana wasn't so sure. Why had he brought them to Shanghai if he hadn't been searching for something himself? If he hadn't believed that a different life could be a better life? If he hadn't had a restless soul? But to make him happy, she nodded and said, "I'll try."

Much later that night, after Olga and Jean Paul and all the guests had left, Tatiana and her mother sat with their feet up, drinking tea and surveying the empty dance floor.

"Do you remember how we used to go out mushroom picking every fall in Russia?" Katarina said. "You and me and Olushka?" Tatiana nodded and smiled as her mother reached over and touched her arm. "You always complained because we went in the rain, but that was the best time to pick mushrooms. Then we would come home, soaked to the skin. Our cook would make us mushrooms stewed in cream, my favourite, and you and Olga would beg him to make those crispy little cutlets." Katarina became quite animated as she relived their mushroom-picking adventures. "And remember how you hated the mushroom gravy that I had him make especially for Papa, saying it was too slimy?"

Tatiana threw back her head and laughed. "Yes, and cook used to chase us with a wooden spoon and threaten to make us eat a whole bowl of it if we didn't behave." By this time they were both laughing so hard, the tears were running down their cheeks. Tatiana wanted this moment between them to last forever but, just like the steamy vapour from their tea, it quickly vanished. Yet, for the rest of her life, when she remembered the mushroom-picking story, Tatiana would remember her mother telling it after Olga's wedding.

Once Olga was married, Sergei turned his attention back to Tatiana. He continued to introduce her to young men he thought would make suitable husbands. Tatiana agreed to see them a second time only if they would agree, without Sergei's knowledge, to take her to a cabaret. She had fallen under the spell of these places that were proliferating like dandelions all over the International Settlement. It seemed as if everybody went there, at least, everybody who wanted to have a good time. Every night Shanghai transformed itself from a place of business and commerce into one big party that spilled into the streets and lasted until dawn, when the night soil collectors came around with their pushcarts and emptied the honey pots.

Tatiana began to see more of Annette in the cabarets and

at the Shanghai Club on the Bund, where she and her friends
occasionally dropped by for a drink. A private club for the
British, it boasted the longest bar in the world. In order to
enjoy the privileges of the Shanghai Club for a few weeks, a
man had only to be recommended by a couple of members,
and they were in. One of Tatiana's Russian boyfriends, Ivan,
a handsome but dull young man, worked at the Hongkong
and Shanghai Bank and had several British friends. Although
Tatiana had heard the British were terrible snobs, she thought
they had a wonderful sense of fun, much more so than the
snooty French or the self-satisfied Americans. They loved to go
to the racetrack on Saturdays and never lost their temper when
the horse they bet on came in second or last. They were great
talkers, and the women—at least the unmarried ones—loved to
kick up their heels on the dance floor. Tatiana silently thanked
her father for sending her to Mrs. Wilkinson's English language
classes all those years ago.

She found herself spending more and more time with
Annette, who was nearly a decade older but seemed to have
lived two lives to Tatiana's one. They began to meet for tea
in the afternoons after Tatiana's sessions with Dimitri were
over, but before her father came home from work. Annette told
her more about her favourite subject, "*l'histoire de ma vie*".
Annette seemed to be most alive when she was talking about
her past, as if with each telling she defined herself more clearly.
She was like a painter adding brush strokes to a masterpiece.
Would it ever be complete? Or would it someday be yanked
away from her and declared finished, left to hang in a forgotten
corner of a forgotten room in a gallery? Was it that knowledge
that impelled her to keep telling the story to so many people, so
that at least a few would remember it, and she would achieve a
kind of immortality?

Annette spoke often of her Vietnamese lover, the father
of her beloved son Daniel. She described him as she would

describe a painting or an *objet d'art*. She talked about the perfect shape of his face and his skin that was the colour of creamy coffee and exuded a faint scent of almonds. "He had an exquisite body," she said, "slender and tall for an Oriental. I was often sullen, as teenage girls are, but he was fascinated by my sexuality. I was so skinny, I had no breasts or hips, but I had something, I tell you. I had a fire inside me."

"Did you love him?" Tatiana asked.

"Love?" she repeated. "I knew nothing of love until my son Daniel was born. What I felt for Tran was not love but a connection, a demand. We couldn't get enough of each other. And yet we were so unlikely."

"What do you mean, unlikely?"

"Our coming together was an accident, like a head-on collision that happens because two people are in the wrong place at the wrong time. It should never have happened, yet, at the same time, it had an inevitability about it. Two people in the universe, meeting on that day in Saigon, and their fate is sealed."

Annette spoke in such large, almost mythological, terms about the relationship that Tatiana could imagine all the tragic love affairs of the ages, in art and in history, coming together in those two "unlikely" people. They were Tristan and Iseult, Romeo and Juliet, Dante and Beatrice.

"You must have been furious when he married someone else."

"Marriage," Annette said, as if she'd just bitten into something sour. "Marriage is for ordinary people. We could not have sustained what we had in a marriage. Marriage is about getting up every morning and eating breakfast and reading the newspaper. It would have been over in six months. *Bien sûr*, at the time I was sad, upset, but not angry. Even at sixteen, I knew that it wasn't meant to last."

"But weren't your parents scandalized?"

"Oh, they were. Until I brought home money that Tran had

given me. Hard cash. Then my mother suddenly decided it
was all right. I don't think she told my father about the money,
though. When I look back, I realize how deeply ashamed my
father was. After all, it was his responsibility to look after me,
and he couldn't do it. He was a failure at everything. It must be
a terrible thing to define your life in the language of failure."

Failure was something Tatiana didn't think about, at least not
when she pondered life. You could fail an examination or fail to
show up on time for an appointment, but so what? You made an
excuse, forgave yourself and moved on. But could you forgive
yourself for failing at life? And what, really, did that mean?
And who decided? At least with an examination, there was a
clear line, or mark, above which you passed and below which
you failed. If you were late for an appointment, the clock was
the judge and there was no arguing with time, but a life was
different. Who was the ultimate judge? God? Your mother and
father? Your friends?

If the opposite of failure was success, then what defined
success? Were the rich bankers Tatiana met at the Shanghai
Club successful? Absolutely. Was her father successful? Yes,
of course. Unlike Annette's father, Sergei had been able to take
care of his family. But then Tatiana thought of her mother and
realized he had not been able to take away her sadness. Did that
mean he was a failure as a husband, but not as a businessman
and a father? Were all the poor people of China failures? And
all the rich people in Shanghai successful? Could you be a
failure and be happy? Or a success and unhappy?

"My head aches because I'm thinking too much," she told
Annette. "It's your fault. I was never like this before I met you."

"Are you sure?" Annette said. "Or were you just waiting for
the opportunity?"

"My father always tries to make me think," Tatiana said,
"but I'm starting to resist. I use it as an opportunity to be bad-
tempered and irritable." It was true. She was becoming bored

with reading books and discussing them with Dimitri and her father. Where was it all going to lead anyway? It was not as if she would be allowed to take a job (not that she wanted to), and she certainly had no intention of joining a nunnery. So what was the point?

Annette laughed and offered her a cigarette. "It's time for you to start smoking," she said. "If you have a cigarette in your hand, you have to think about the cigarette, or it will be gone before you notice it burning. And, with the cigarette, you have a glass of champagne or a gin and tonic in the other hand. Then there is absolutely no room for thinking about anything else. The minute you have an empty hand, you must try to fill it. It will focus the mind and force out useless thinking. That's my philosophy, and it serves me well."

It seemed like an excellent philosophy to Tatiana.

Chapter Nine

So here I sit, a philosopher with a gin and tonic in one hand and a cigarette in the other. Remembering where so many things began. Lily's marriage, Olga's marriage. Even my own brief marriage, so unlikely, so inauspicious, which took place so far away, without family and friends.

My thoughts are interrupted by the telephone ringing. It's Olga, reminding me that her son Nicholas's birthday is coming up. She wants to know if I have his address so I can send him a card.

"Of course I have his address," I tell her. "I send him a card every year."

"No need to get huffy," she says. "I was just checking."

I thank her and hang up. Some things, at least, do not change.

It has begun to snow again, big, shapeless flakes that hit the window and slide wetly down the glass to pile on the sill. As I think back, I realize that most of the conversations I had with my father after Olga was married were about his trying to get me onto some track that would make me happy, or at least content. He saw that I was searching for something— anything—and he was afraid that I probably wouldn't find it.

It's a terrible thing to have regrets. I regret that I didn't pay more attention to my father, that I didn't recognize, until it was too late, just how much he could teach me. I suppose I thought there would be more time, or maybe I'm just making excuses for myself. My father always did his best, turning every obstacle into a positive opportunity, but I gave in to defeat too easily, seizing the negative because it required no effort.

Recently I asked Olga if she thought Papa had been disappointed in me.

"In what way?" she asked.

"In the choices I made, the way I lived my life."

"If you mean, was he fooled into believing the excuses you made for yourself, he wasn't. He knew what you were really up to. You didn't fool him for a minute."

"That's not what I meant, Olga."

"I think it's exactly what you meant," she said. "If you want a simple answer, then, yes, he was disappointed. But not in the way you think. He was disappointed that you underestimated him and his capacity for understanding. You had it in your power to hurt him deeply, and you didn't even realize it. You made him believe for a while that you were interested in the things that he loved—the books, the studying—but all you thought about was yourself and the way you looked, the clothes you wore and your latest hairstyle. Papa wanted so badly to save you from yourself and to help you see beyond your own blindness. He knew you better than you think."

I was astonished and stung by Olga's outburst. Besides, it wasn't entirely true. I had loved the books and the studying for a while. But to me it wasn't a life. It was a pastime. "Did you two have conversations about me?"

"Only once or twice," she said. "Near the end of his life, when you wouldn't come and see him."

That, of course, is my other great regret. But how could I explain to Olga that by that time, I was incapable of dealing with the pain of watching Papa die. I had become an emotional coward of the first order, avoiding any situation that involved confronting who I was and what mattered to me. I had convinced myself that nothing mattered, but Papa's death mattered immensely. By then I had lost the ability to connect.

~ ~

Within a year of her marriage, Lily produced a son and named him Leonard. Both she and her husband agreed he should have an English name as well as a Chinese name, because someday he would be entering the world of international business, and it would be advantageous to have a name his colleagues could pronounce and remember.

He was a beautiful baby, tiny and perfect, with a round face and chubby cheeks. He had a sunny disposition, despite having inherited his father's serious forehead and eyebrows. And Lily, who had been beautiful before, was luminous after the birth of her child. She had been right; having a son changed everything. She had proved her worth and earned the respect of her husband and his family. Now her life had purpose.

"What's it like," Tatiana asked her, "to know who you are and what you're meant to be when you're only twenty years old?"

Lily laughed. "You make it sound as if I've reached the top of the mountain, that there's nothing left to achieve." They were drinking tea in the garden of her new home. Lily now lived in a house in the Tang family compound, which wasn't as large as the one she had grown up in. Wu-ling had an elder brother who did not live in Shanghai, and only his grandmother and an elderly aunt remained of the older generation. Daisy lived with her parents within the compound, but she would be married within the year and would move to Nanking. The house Lily and Wu-ling lived in was three storeys high and very old, but it had many large rooms, including separate sitting rooms for Lily and Wu-ling and several rooms that weren't occupied but were probably designated as bedrooms for future children. The central courtyard was much quieter than the one in the Soong household, and Lily and Tatiana could sit outdoors on bamboo lounges and enjoy the late spring weather. The pond, full of plants and fat, orange koi, babbled beside them.

"Far from it," Lily continued. "I still have to raise my son and make sure he's the kind of man his father expects him to be."

"Which is what?" Tatiana asked.

"Which is someone with a respectable, I should say, honourable, position, who will manage the family's wealth with integrity. Who will respect his parents and his ancestors and who will honour his family, including his own wife and children."

"So much honouring and respecting," Tatiana said. "He's just a baby."

"Yes, and he can be a baby for a few more years. But then he will be the boy becoming the man. His education will be the priority. He will have to learn discipline and…"

"I know, I know…and honour and respect."

"Yes," said Lily. "And respect."

Tatiana sighed. It was all too much for her. What if this poor child was unable to shoulder all that responsibility? Part of her hoped that Lily would have more sons, just in case the first one faltered. Tatiana thought of Lily's three brothers and how they were becoming established in Chinese society as planned, in business, government and the military. So far, not one of them had faltered, but she had heard rumours that Number Two Brother had connections to one of Shanghai's secret societies, a political organization intent on ridding the country of all foreign elements. Her British friends referred to him as "someone to watch". In the next few years, the Russians would be added to the list of unwelcome foreign elements, when the Kuomintang began looking to the Communists as allies against the powerful warlords in the north.

~ ~

I can see now, as I look back on events with the perspective of more than thirty years, how the individual pieces of the puzzle were forming and gradually moving into place, but at the time, the combination of my youth and a wilful blindness kept me from seeing what was probably right under my nose. As the historians would later say, the storm clouds were gathering, but most of us chose not to acknowledge them. After all, we had just seen the end of "the war to end all wars", and life was beginning to return to a more familiar routine, one where bread was baked and eaten every day, people met and fell in love and babies were born. The future looked rosier.

We didn't want to know that the world would never be the same again. We wanted to believe that we could forget, not simply cease to remember, but truly forget in the absolute sense, what had just happened to all of us. But the genie of world war was out of the bottle, and it was already sowing the seeds for its next appearance. And, who knows, maybe the one after that. The sleeping giants of China and Russia were waking up, preparing to embrace the rigid ideologies of intellectuals and madmen who, with their combined forces, would nearly drive their respective homelands into the ground.

How could a twenty-year-old girl imagine, even in her worst nightmare, that politics and ideology would combine to put the final nail in the coffin of her dearest friend? But, before politics and ideology could finish the job, the ancient bugaboo of morality, of right and wrong, would set the wheels in motion.

~ ~

Tatiana began to go out several nights a week and occasionally stay out until dawn. Sergei tried to reason with her, and Katarina wept. Sergei was at one point so frustrated that he threatened to cut off Tatiana's allowance and lock her out of the house, but she knew he would not. A servant was always waiting, asleep at the gate, posted there to unlock it and let her in whenever she returned. Because she slept until early afternoon, she rarely saw her parents at breakfast and spent her afternoons with Dimitri in a sleepy stupor or in sullen silence.

Dimitri finally spoke to Sergei. "She's changed," he told Sergei, for lack of anything more insightful to say. Dimitri was not experienced in the ways of young women and had no idea how to deal with Tatiana's lack of interest in her studies. "I don't know what to do, sir."

Sergei was equally baffled. He saw his plan of introducing his daughter to eligible young men backfiring in his face. She never left the house alone, so perhaps it was these bachelors— he cringed when he thought how he had trusted them—that maybe these bachelors were leading her astray. Even as he thought this, Sergei wondered if it wasn't the other way around. He had no way of knowing the deal Tatiana had struck with each of these young men, that she would go out with them if they agreed to take her to a cabaret. There were three regulars: Ivan, the handsome dullard, Arkady, who drank too much and flirted with other women, and Vanya, who was homosexual.

Tatiana had no compassion for the scope of her parents' fears for her. She had the arrogance of youth on her side and had not yet acquired the burden of experience. They tried everything to force her to see reason. One afternoon, they sent Olga and Jean Paul to her room with a breakfast tray.

"What are you doing to yourself? To your life?" her sister asked in a voice filled with every parental tone imaginable, rage, indignation, horror, self-pity, sadness, bewilderment and, finally, desperation. "Don't you know how you're hurting Mother and Papa? And what about me? I lie awake at night worrying that you'll be raped and murdered."

"Oh, Olga, you're overreacting. Worse, you're being melodramatic, like an hysterical old fishwife."

"I'm not hysterical. You're my sister, and I'm forced to stand by and watch you ruin your life."

"I'm not ruining my life. I'm just having a little fun while I'm still young."

"A little fun! You call staying out all night with strangers having a little fun? It's dangerous what you're doing. You don't know what these people are capable of. Especially when they're drunk or smoking opium. You're being irresponsible."

"I am responsible for my own life. No one else is responsible for me. I'm not a child any longer, and I can look after myself."

"No, you can't!" Olga was shouting at her. "You can't look after yourself. Certainly not in Shanghai. Not unless you have a gun and know how to use it."

"For heaven's sake, Olga, what are you talking about? Shanghai is not that dangerous. I go to the clubs with my friends and we dance and have a few drinks. That's all. Why would I need a gun?"

Jean Paul, who hadn't said a word, gently took hold of Olga's arm and started leading her out of the room. She was sobbing into a handkerchief, shaking her head and blowing her nose loudly. He turned to Tatiana.

"Please be careful, Tati," was all he said.

Of course I'll be careful, she thought. *Do they think I'm stupid?* It annoyed her that they still treated her like a child. She could hear them speaking to her parents downstairs, Olga's hysteria piercing the air like a soprano's aria, Jean Paul trying to soothe her, and Katarina, caught up in Olga's anger, adding her voice to the general din. Then Sergei's sad baritone filled the air. "Enough. I can't stand all this wailing and carrying on. We'll try again another time."

But Tatiana knew it was hopeless. They could never bring back the old Tati. She felt alive for the first time in her life. She wasn't waiting for something to happen; she believed it was finally happening. She was living her life at a pitch she hadn't known was possible, and she was dancing faster and laughing harder than she had ever done. Like Annette, she kept a cigarette in one hand and a glass of champagne in the other. Her hands were never empty, her feet never still. This was living as she had dreamed it would be.

She began to make new friends: Ben and George, Iris, Roger, Ernest and Betty, François and Leo. And Annette, of course. They would meet up at different times, at different hotels or cabarets, in a different combination every night. Sometimes it would be Ernest and George and Betty, other times Leo and Ben and Iris. Tatiana would show up with one of her "three Hussars", as she called them, and they would blend in with the crowd at the table. Annette would bring a different new man every week. If she saw someone more than a few times, it was because he had a lot of money, and she hadn't grown tired of him yet. Or, at least, that's what Tatiana thought.

One afternoon, as they were having tea, Annette asked her if she wanted to meet Daniel. They lived in a small house off Avenue Joffre, but in the opposite direction from the Relnikovs' home. It was in a working-class part of the French Concession, where the houses were built in blocks that faced onto a common courtyard. There was a pond made of grey stone in the middle of the courtyard, overgrown with weeds, the fish long gone. The concrete paths were cracked and had heaved in the cold weather. "Be careful," Annette told her. "You can break your ankle walking through here, especially if it's dark."

Annette's narrow, two-storey wooden house was charming in a shabby, old-fashioned way. The furniture was ancient and tired-looking, like someone's great-grandmother dressed in velvet and lace from another era. The colours were sombre, but there were accents in odd places, as if someone had pointed a finger and said, "There, there and there." In a corner behind a small covered stool stood a tall ceramic vase with three shimmering peacock feathers exploding from it. A mirror was draped on one side with a dazzling shawl of yellow silk embroidered with vermilion and blue thread. A single cushion

on an ebony rocking chair was a puff of purple satin with a
shiny glass button in the centre. Tatiana had never been in such
a house before, one that looked, when you first entered it, as
if it had been abandoned then, slowly, as you looked around,
clearly revealed in bits and pieces the personality of its owner.
Because Annette, when you first met her, had a world-weary
appearance that belied, as you looked closer, the vanity of a
silver bracelet around her wrist, or a tortoiseshell clip in her
hair, or a red lipstick so dark it looked almost black on her lips.

They had not been in the house more than a few minutes
when Tatiana heard the scurrying of feet on the stairs, and an
explosion of energy bounced into the room, shouting, "*Maman!
Maman!*" This was Daniel, Annette's beloved son, followed
closely by a Chinese amah of indeterminate age who never let
him out of her sight.

"*Mon chou, mon chou,*" cried Annette, wrapping her arms
around the small force of nature and squeezing him tight. "Have
you been a good boy for Amah? Did you have your supper?"
All the while, Amah was bobbing and nodding her head,
smiling at her little charge, whom she clearly adored. "Massah
vely goo," she said, "vely goo."

Tatiana had never seen such joy on Annette's face before.
Like Lily, she glowed with love when she looked at her child.
Tatiana remembered the time not long after they'd met when
Annette had told her that she had never known love until her son
was born. He was an exquisite boy, almost nine years old when
Tatiana first met him. He was delicately built, with the coffee and
cream skin and black hair of his father, and the green eyes, long
legs and graceful physique of his mother. He had already been
playing the piano for four years and had shown extraordinary
ability from the beginning. Annette introduced Tatiana as her
very good friend and asked Daniel to play something for her.
He chose Beethoven's "Für Elise" and performed the lovely,
cascading piece with skill and tenderness, his long, shapely

fingers moving as gracefully as an octopus's tentacles over the keys. Tatiana was astonished, not just at his ease and agility, but because his performance brought tears to her eyes.

Annette had found a Russian music teacher for the boy who came once a day and spent two hours leading him through the works of the European composers and drilling him in finger exercises. She dreamed of sending him to Europe to study. She saved every penny she could in a silk stocking hidden inside the stuffing of the sofa. Annette referred to her gentlemen friends as "patrons", and Tatiana chose to believe they willingly contributed to Daniel's musical future.

Chapter Ten

In her early twenties, Tatiana's life in Shanghai began to follow a routine. She would sleep till noon, or later, perhaps have some coffee or a bit of lunch then, two days a week, spend two or three hours in the library with Dimitri until it was time to bathe and get ready to go out for the evening. She had told her father she no longer wanted to study, that she felt it was going nowhere. He insisted she continue. Unless she was prepared to consider marriage, which she was not, she would have to pursue some activity that demanded discipline. Sergei was adamant that while she was living under his roof, she would comply with his wishes. When she had a husband, she would no longer be his responsibility. So they compromised, and she agreed to two days a week.

The afternoons she did not spend with Dimitri she often spent with Annette. Occasionally they would go shopping or stop for tea in a café, but mostly they would spend the time at Annette's house, chatting or listening to music and waiting for Daniel to finish his lessons. Then they would take him to the park so he could play with other children. Annette was constantly worried he would hurt one of his hands and put an end to the musical career she dreamed of for him. He was precocious and fearless with other children, almost too fearless, as if he were testing himself. Tatiana could see that he badly wanted to be like the other boys, rough and rambunctious, but he was not. He was sensitive and wary and, in his unguarded moments, she saw the look in his eyes that told her he knew he was different and that he was lonely.

"Aunt Tati," he said to her one time, "do you have any children?"

"No, Daniel," she said, "I'm not married."

"Will you have children when you get married?"

"I don't know, Daniel. No one knows for sure until it happens." These were odd questions for a young boy to be asking. "Why do you want to know whether I'll have children?"

"Because," he said, as if he'd thought about this a lot, "if you have children, they can be my friends. I'll be able to play with them."

Tatiana wasn't sure how to respond. He was such a sensitive child, she didn't think it was fair to promise him something that might never happen. "I'll be your friend," she said. "I'll always be your friend."

Before she went out in the evening, Tatiana would spend an hour or two deciding what to wear, doing her hair and makeup, and listening to records on her gramophone. Fashions had changed since the war. Skirts were shorter, dresses were skimpier and made from thin, sheer fabrics that clung to the body and emphasized the hips and legs. Bosoms were out of fashion and, if you had one, you bound it tightly and flattened it. She often thought of Mrs. Wilkinson and her magnificent shelf of a bosom and wondered if the teacher had adopted the new style of dress.

It was not just a new style of dress people were adopting but a new style of living. It was as though they had thrown off the shackles of the nineteenth century and finally decided that the new era would be entirely different. The war had been the final break with the past; the old ways had proved unworkable, the old solutions unsuccessful. Young people wanted to reinvent everything, to stop listening to the voices of their elders and to create their own language. It was the age of jazz, or, as the French called it, *le jazz hot*. Hot music, hot dancing, hot everything. There was no past, no future, only the present.

And Shanghai had everything to offer the modern young men and women who chose to reject the past. It was a lawless frontier with all the amenities. Luxury was available for a pittance. Anyone could live the high life, although Tatiana knew a few of her friends had to count their pennies. Betty, who was from London and had a thin, pale face that looked weary when she wasn't smiling, worked in a shop that catered to wealthy American women. She rented a flat with two other girls. They mended their stockings and shared their clothes but, in the dim lights of the cabarets, no one could tell. A few sequins provided enough glitter to distract the eye. Leo was a bookkeeper and wore the same suit and shoes every night. He never talked about money, but Tatiana knew he gambled. Sometimes they wouldn't see him for days, then he would turn up, in need of a haircut and with his shirt cuffs frayed, and buy drinks for everyone. To Tatiana, however, Betty and Leo were admirable, because they defied convention and chased a dream.

Tatiana, on the other hand, received a generous allowance from Sergei, but she had no sense of the value of money. She knew she could buy clothes, shoes and silk stockings whenever she wanted, or the latest jazz recording from America. Sometimes she would buy sheet music for Daniel, not because she was generous, but because she wanted to appear that way. Tatiana quite readily accepted appearance as reality and believed it was authentic. From time to time she offered Betty her cast-offs, dismissing her gratitude with a wave of the hand. If Betty was offended, Tatiana didn't know it. If her gratitude was insincere, Tatiana didn't care. Betty once asked her if she knew how lucky she was. They were at the Golden Dragon Cabaret, one of their favourites. It had a large dance floor, and the orchestra was particularly good, the music very loud. A shimmering globe covered in tiny mirrors hung from the ceiling, sending rainbows of coloured light around the room.

There were six at the table that night. Tatiana was not sure she'd heard Betty correctly.

"Lucky?" she asked, shouting across the table at Betty. "What do you mean?"

"I mean," Betty said, cupping her hands around her mouth like a megaphone, "that you're lucky you don't have to work. You don't have to pay rent. You can do anything you want."

Tatiana just stared at her, not knowing what to say. What Betty considered lucky, Tatiana took for granted. She didn't think of herself as particularly lucky. In fact, she thought she was rather unlucky because, unlike the rest of them, she still lived with her parents and had to listen to them complaining about her late hours and frivolous lifestyle. And not just her parents, but Olga, too. She told Betty she thought everyone else was luckier than her because they didn't have to put up with the constant carping of their family. How lucky they were to be free of the heaviness of that burden. She loved her family, but she saw them as baggage she was obliged to carry around all the time. She couldn't identify it then, but it was the burden of morality that Tatiana found so onerous.

Morality was something Lily understood and accepted with every cell in her body. There was no question of living anything but a moral life, which was why she was disturbed and even angered by Tatiana's attitude and the rumours she had heard about her friend's behaviour.

"Tatiana!" she said in exasperation. "Why are you being so bad? I hear about you going out every night, dancing and drinking. How will you find a husband if you behave in such a way?"

"A husband?" Tatiana laughed, but when Lily looked offended, she tried to stifle her laughter. The notion of finding a husband seemed hysterically funny to Tatiana, like the silly scenarios they used to imagine as children. "I don't want a husband," she said. "Some stuffy old bugger who'll make me stay home and read the newspaper. To hell with that." Tatiana had recently taken up swearing in the manner of her English friends and took great pleasure in watching people's reactions.

"You'll be an old maid soon," Lily warned, choosing to ignore her friend's bad language, "and then it will be too late. Even if you change your mind."

"Too late" was a concept that Tatiana couldn't grasp. Ben, who had been in the war, was always saying, "Life's too short, you know. Too short. Need to grab it by the balls while you can." In a world where life was short, too late would never happen. All that mattered was now. Tatiana changed the subject and asked Lily how Leonard was doing. Lily told her that at three years old, he was already showing extraordinary musical ability. He was drawn to sounds of all kinds and would stop whatever he was doing to listen to the tinkling of bells or the warbling of songbirds. They had bought him half a dozen canaries in delicate bamboo cages and all manner of toys to develop his sense of rhythm. His favourite was a xylophone with a small mallet. He never tired of hitting the notes and singing along to his own accompaniment. This thrilled his mother.

"I think we will buy him a piano soon," she said. "But I think he is still too young."

Tatiana wanted to tell her about Daniel but knew Lily disapproved of Annette, so she merely mentioned that she knew of a Russian music teacher if Lily was ever interested.

Daniel, meanwhile, continued to practice his finger exercises and astonish them all with his playing. His teacher had begun telling Annette that it would not be long before he would have nothing more to teach the boy. It would soon be time to send him to Paris or Vienna. Annette kept putting money into the silk stocking, but there never seemed to be enough. Tatiana thought about asking Sergei for a large sum of money but she knew he would not give it to her without demanding something in return.

It was around this time that he began threatening to reduce her allowance if she didn't start behaving more responsibly. He still thought quoting Tolstoy would bring Tatiana to her senses.

"'The more is given, the less the people will work for themselves, and the less they work, the more their poverty will increase,'" he called out to her once when she was leaving the house.

"Yes, Papa," she said and blew him a kiss. Tatiana knew that if she had been Sergei, she would have spanked her bottom and locked her in her room for such impertinence. She avoided her parents even more, so that the subject could not be discussed.

Tatiana knew Lily had heard from Number Two Brother about her frequenting the nightclubs. She would see him from time to time with a group of young, smartly dressed Chinese men who smoked cigarettes in long ivory holders. There were always at least three or four women in the group, stunning Chinese girls with pale skin and bright red lips, wearing tight silk *cheongsams*. Tatiana knew Number Two Brother was married, but he was never accompanied by his wife on these occasions. He had some position in the government to do with finance or the treasury and he had an air of importance about him already. She noticed his companions laughed extra hard at his jokes and deferred to him whenever he spoke. Tatiana's English friends told her he was well-connected and they did not trust him as far as a camel could spit. Why they didn't trust him she had no idea, except that it was prudent to be suspicious of anyone connected to the government. Number Two Brother was always accompanied by bodyguards, either tall, fierce-looking Mongolians or bulky White Russians, who were plentiful in Shanghai since the Bolshevik revolution.

One night, Number Two Brother sent a bottle of champagne over to Tatiana's table. George, who reminded Tatiana of a

donkey with his long face and braying laugh, thought this was
"a bit of all right", and made it the joke of the evening that
she had been sleeping with some "right high mucky-muck
of a Chinaman". Tatiana liked being the centre of attention
and didn't bother to mention that she had known him since
childhood, and that he was, in fact, the older brother of her best
friend. Why spoil the fun?

A few weeks later, Number Two Brother stopped by on the
way to his table and said hello. His English was impeccable,
spoken with a sort of clipped British accent, as if he had
learned it from a private tutor. It was not at all the way Tatiana
remembered him speaking as a teenager, when he and his
brothers used to torment her and Lily. Annette happened to be
with them that night, with her latest friend, an American she
had introduced as Mr. O'Sullivan, a distinguished man in his
sixties who claimed to be a friend of Teddy Roosevelt.

"Ooh, *chérie*," she said to Tatiana, "have you been keeping
secrets from your old friend?"

"Maybe," Tatiana replied, and laughed at the shocked looks
around the table.

"I say," said Roger, who affected the look of a British
aristocrat by always wearing gold pince-nez. "You want to
watch out for him, you know. He's got a bit of a reputation as a
ladies' man. Bit of a heartbreaker, I hear."

"I heard he breaks more than hearts," said Leo. "They say
it's all a front to hide what he really does. Secret societies and
all that, you know." Leo was a former boxer who was deaf in
one ear but listened extra hard with the other.

"Oh, do tell," said Betty. "You mean he's some sort of spy or
something?"

"Well," said Leo, leaning forward and lowering his voice,
"it's all very hush-hush. But they say he runs some sort of cadre
or something that's planning to take over the government when
old Dr. Sun pops off." He pronounced it "cawdray".

"Oh, for heaven's sake, Leo," Tatiana said. "Who are 'they'? You make it sound like there's some sort of conspiracy happening."

"Well, there is, old tart, there is. This country's full of conspiracies," Leo said, offended that she'd questioned his credibility. "Loaded with them."

"You've got that right," said Roger. "They're a scheming lot, these Chinamen. Always plotting. They'll bugger the whole country if they're not careful. I mean, you don't know from one day to the next who's in charge. Like a game of musical chairs."

"Well," Tatiana said, remembering her father's words, "it's a revolution of sorts, isn't it? There's bound to be a certain amount of instability for a while."

"Absolutely right," chimed in George. "But don't you think twenty-five years is enough instability? I mean, that Boxer Rebellion thing's ancient history now."

"I heard old Sun's been to Moscow and signed some sort of agreement with the Communists." This was Ben, who had been to war and was generally believed to be the most politically savvy of the group. "Seems the Kuomintang thinks getting into bed with the Reds will solve the problem of the warlords."

"I can tell you, the Bank's pretty upset about that," said George. "Can't trust the Reds. Open one door, and they'll all come pouring in through it. Take over the whole country before you can say 'bloody Bolsheviks'."

"Can't we talk about something else?" Tatiana pleaded. "This is getting boring."

"Oh, boo hoo," said George, making a face. "The baby's bored. Why don't you go ask your Chinaman friend if he wants to dance?" Everybody thought this was hilarious and laughed as if they'd never heard anything so funny.

Chapter Eleven

The rumours about Number Two Brother were true. He was deeply involved in the Green Gang, one of the most powerful secret societies in Shanghai, and had been since his university days in Japan. It was both anti-imperialist and anti-communist, which meant it was at odds with the Kuomintang's policy of forging an alliance with the Communists to eliminate the warlords. The Green Gang was bent on eliminating any and all leftist tendencies in the Chinese government.

It was impossible not to be aware of the turmoil in Chinese politics after the war. Even Tatiana knew about the May Fourth Movement that had begun as the result of a student protest held in 1919 in Peking to protest the terms of the Treaty of Versailles. In their wisdom, the British and French had awarded Germany's rights in Shantung to the Japanese. Years later, she would understand the role student radicals played in China and how the tradition of Chinese intellectualism gradually led to the growth of communism in that country. While Tatiana was dancing her life away in cabarets, Chinese students her own age and younger were immersing themselves in long and wordy debates about the future of their country. China was rife with competing elements of democracy, socialism, communism, warlordism, landlordism, an international stranglehold on trade and commerce, feudalism, and a system of taxation that had produced an enormous underclass.

On the rare occasions she spent any time with him, Sergei would regale her with some editorial that had appeared in the newspaper that week. Once, on a beautiful, sunny day that wasn't too humid for a change, they were having coffee in the garden. Tatiana was up earlier than usual because she was going to have her hair done. Feeling a little hung over from the night before, she was not in the mood for conversation, but when her father folded his newspaper and looked up at her expectantly, she had no energy to protest.

"These Chinese," he began, "are just like Russians. They talk and talk about a problem, name it and rename it until they have added a new word to the language, then they congratulate themselves because they think they are creating solutions, when all they have done is create another theory. The world has enough theories, Tatushka. What it needs is solutions, solutions to poverty and opium addiction, to ignorance and war, to filth and disease."

"But, Papa," she said, beginning to revive after her first cup of coffee, "you once told me that China was the future and Russia was the past. Have you changed your mind?"

"No, my dear, I have not. I still believe China is the future. She has resilience and a willingness to open her eyes to new things. But things are not as rosy as I would like them to be. I know, I know, there are many problems here. There is corruption and factionalism, and the whole country is fragmented by politics, but there is also art and literature and a love of knowledge that goes back thousands of years." He held up a book he had been reading about something called Social Darwinism. "You see this book? It applies the theory of evolution to the development of human society. Don't you see, Tatushka," he said, "it is not just as a species that we must evolve. In the struggle between social groups, the fittest and most able must survive to lead mankind to a better world. In this struggle, the Chinese are way ahead of the Russians. They are steeped in moral philosophy, but they are beginning to recognize the need to find practical applications. Their children now study science and technology as they do in Europe and America." He paused only long enough to take another sip of his coffee. "In Russia, the Communist intellectuals think they can control the peasants and manipulate them to their own ends. 'Unite the workers,' they say. 'Destroy the aristocracy.' Destroy, destroy. It is all they think about. Mark my words, Tatushka, their social experiment will never work."

~ ~

When my father spoke like this, there was a fire in his eyes. He became animated in the world of ideas, but I saw that his excitement fell mostly on deaf ears. Olga was least interested in what he had to say, and my mother only pretended to listen. I felt a tug at my heart for the Tatiana I knew he wanted me to be. I felt his frustration and knew there was nothing that could replace that loss for him. In me he had placed his dreams. I knew he had hoped I would shine and do something worthwhile with my life. Instead, I realize, again with the wisdom of hindsight, I had chosen to be frivolous and uncaring. I refused to continue my sessions with Dimitri, saying I was too old to be in school, when in fact I was simply bored. I resented the time and the discipline. I saw it as unnecessary and irrelevant to my life.

I suppose I can make excuses for myself. Perhaps I had been disappointed by life or my inability to feel the kind of passion my father felt, or the depth of sorrow my mother felt. Or maybe life had just been too easy for me, nothing insurmountable in my path, nothing to challenge me and bring out the best in me. I believed there was no consequence to my taking classes with Dimitri and there was no consequence to my ending them. Instead, I buried myself in indifference and played my life like a game. I see now how truly shallow I was, expecting things to be handed to me and then, when they were, rejecting them as insignificant. I had proven that if the game became too demanding, I could just run away from it.

~ ~

Four years after her marriage, Olga gave birth to a daughter they named Anastasia, which pleased Sergei and Katarina greatly. After two miscarriages, the baby's safe arrival seemed to give them renewed vitality. Now they could place their hopes for the future in a grandchild with blue eyes and a beautiful name. They were overjoyed and, for the first time in years, Katarina sang because she was happy. Little Ana slept the sleep of the angels when her grandmother sang her a lullaby. Everyone laughed when Tatiana told her mother to stop singing because they wanted the baby to wake up so they could play with her.

It's the old Tatiana, they were thinking, *back in the family*. But they were wrong. It was a brief interlude, this novelty of having a niece. In reality, Tatiana was about to step over a threshold into a place from which it would take her years to return.

As China's turmoil deepened, Tatiana refused to acknowledge the changes around her. She had long avoided asking Annette about her men friends and why she seemed to attract them then discard them like the scraps from a dinner plate. Finally, when the two of them were sipping tea in Annette's tiny sitting room with the sound of Daniel's music lesson in the background, she brought up the subject.

"Oh, *chérie*," Annette told her, "we discard each other. When you have nothing to say to each other between hello and goodbye, what's the point? They would only tire of me as quickly as I would tire of them. Once the transaction is complete and we both have got what we want, then it's back to the party for something different. That's the way it works in

Shanghai. We all know the bubble will burst some day, so we can't waste a minute."

Tatiana was puzzled by her use of the word "transaction", but, instead of asking Annette to clarify it, she put it down to her being French. The French liked to talk in abstractions, she told herself, taking the simple and making it complicated.

"Would you like to meet some gentlemen?" Annette asked her. "They're very generous. Not like these English working boys you hang around with."

"Why not?" Tatiana replied. "Maybe it's time for a change."

~ ~

So I walked through a door with both eyes shut. How was I to know? I've asked myself that question a thousand times over the years. How was I to know? What in my experience had taught me about such things? I knew nothing about what existed beneath the shiny surface of Shanghai's nightlife. I had always accepted what I saw at face value. The surface was the reality for me, and it was enough. The dancing, the laughter and joking, the shallow friendships. The champagne was in the bubbles. We watched ourselves dance in our reflections in the mirrors that lined the walls. Look at us, we said. We're dancing. We're laughing. We're having the time of our lives.

Did Betty and Leo and George and Ben know something I didn't know? Of course they did. They lived in the real world. The world where you received money for the things you did, not for what you didn't do. They knew the definition of "transaction". They were versed in the rules of exchange. Nobody got something for nothing.

~ ~

At first it was just gifts, trinkets given in exchange for an evening of laughter and dance. This evening was worth a bracelet or a necklace. In appreciation for a good time. I accept, she said. Thank you. I had a good time, too. If Tatiana endured some groping, a hand on her breast or between her legs, the bracelet was heavier or the necklace came with a matching pair of earrings. Not so bad, she thought. A fair exchange. She was getting better at laughing with someone's fingers probing her. As long as the champagne had bubbles, she was still having a good time, and Annette was always there, keeping an eye on her, making sure she was enjoying the party.

One night the party was in a suite at the Metropole Hotel. Six of them, or eight, or ten. The champagne had the tiniest bubbles she had ever seen. She later remembered a long table covered with a white cloth. Platters of food. Whole fish poached in wine. Small pieces of meat skewered on sticks with slices of onion and pineapple. Caviar in bowls sitting in silver buckets of crushed ice. Smoked duck cut into pieces you could pick up with your fingers. She remembered sitting on someone's lap and feeding him pieces of duck while he licked her fingers then licked her breasts. His face got very red when he laughed, and his teeth were even and square, like a horse's. She remembered thinking she was enjoying herself. Remembered thinking he was almost handsome and he was very definitely funny. She remembered laughing.

Then it was dawn, a cold, grey Shanghai dawn, and she was in a taxi, sobbing on Annette's shoulder, remembering something else that had happened. Something that wasn't so much fun, that in fact had been painful and unpleasant. So unpleasant that she had screamed and cried and begged him to stop. But he had liked that game, the kicking, the fighting. "A wild one," he kept saying. "You're a wild one." And, in the end, of course, he had his way. Then she understood what the word "transaction" meant, and why it was such a hard word that sounded like someone swinging an axe into a tree.

Chapter Twelve

After Tatiana had reached the safety of her own room, she found a fistful of American dollars stuffed into her little evening bag. Somewhere in the back of her mind, she realized she wouldn't have to depend on Sergei's generosity forever. If he chose to withdraw her allowance, she could look after herself. She had begun to twist the threads of shame and pride together into a tight little knot, so that soon she wouldn't know the difference between them. Tatiana had not yet picked up the thread of fear, but she soon would.

The year 1925 would introduce her to things she had long hoped did not exist. She had grown so accustomed to shielding her eyes from unpleasantness that it wasn't until Olga pointed it out to her that she began to notice Sergei's failing health. He looked tired, and there were dark circles under his eyes. His skin, which seemed to hang from his bones, had taken on a yellowish cast.

"It's just the light," she told Olga. "He reads too much and doesn't spend enough time outside." She was trying to convince herself that there was nothing unusual about it.

"I'm worried, Tati. He refuses to see a doctor, and if I mention it to Mother, she waves her hand in front of her face and changes the subject. I saw him wince in pain one time when he didn't know I was there. He doesn't even have the strength to pick up Ana any more."

Tatiana wanted to wave her hand in front of her face, too, and change the subject the way her mother did, but she knew

Olga wouldn't tolerate it. She begged Tatiana to try to convince their father to see a doctor. She had tried everything, and Tatiana was her last hope. "You used to be able to talk to him, Tati. Can't you try again? Before it's too late?" But the last thing Tatiana wanted to do was confront him. Even though she was still living under his roof, Tatiana had lost the ability to have a civil conversation with him. How was she going to speak to him as a concerned daughter to an unwell father? He had tried cutting back her allowance, but she hadn't changed her habits. Sergei was not stupid, and he knew she must be getting money from somewhere, although she didn't imagine that he suspected the truth. The thought that she might be sponging off her friends, letting them pay her way and buy her drinks, was shameful enough. What Olga wanted her to do was impossible.

Tatiana could not explain why she had allowed herself to slip into a way of life that usually only desperately poor girls chose. She didn't need the money or the gifts of jewellery. She had a home and a family that she believed would always be there. She was not like Annette, who had no one she could count on but herself. There was something else driving Tatiana, something she had never felt before. She liked the element of danger that was attached to it, and the danger somehow outweighed the shame. Maybe it wasn't so much a sense of danger she was experiencing, but the feeling of triumph that she could do such a thing and get away with it. Because Tatiana didn't really know what danger was; she only knew what she thought it was. And she was quite wrong.

The increasing violence in the streets of Shanghai was becoming apparent to even its most protected citizens. Tatiana experienced it while riding in a taxi on Nanking Road with her "date" (the word she had begun using to refer to her escorts). He was a man named Ian McCaffrey, whom she had met one night at the Shanghai Club. He told her he was a customs agent in Bombay, and he was in Shanghai for a brief vacation. Ian was easy company, the sort that didn't need a lot of prompting to carry on a conversation. The chatty type, but not bad-looking. Tall, broad-shouldered, with a square jaw, thin mustache and wavy blond hair. He and Tatiana made a striking couple, so she had enjoyed being on his arm for a few days.

They were on their way to the Pagoda Bar for a drink when the taxi was forced to stop by a throng of students and workers carrying placards that said "Kill the foreigners" and "Give China back to the Chinese". The car was barely crawling as people swarmed around it and began slapping their hands on the hood. Ian locked the doors of the car and instructed the driver to back up. When they began to hear popping sounds somewhere ahead of them, he yelled, "Christ!" and pushed her down onto the floor of the car.

Suddenly there was panic all around them as people ran in every direction. Tatiana could hear screaming and shouting and the sound of shoes against pavement like rain hitting a wooden roof. The car rocked from side to side as people pushed and shoved to get around it. The engine was still running, but the terrified driver didn't know which way to go. "Back! Back!" Ian shouted. "Chop-chop! Now!"

The car backed away to the sound of gunshots. It was a sound Tatiana had never heard before, but it was one she would never forget. A sound like small hands beating on a metal drum. And she would never forget the colour of the blood staining the clothes and running down the faces of the ones lucky enough to get away. It was the colour of poppies she remembered from her childhood in Russia. And it was the colour of the lipstick the Chinese whores wore. It was also the colour of the lipstick in her own handbag, a bright, hot, vivid red.

What she felt that day was beyond fear; it was a mortal terror. A proximity to death, her own death, that she had not planned on experiencing for many years. If she was confronting her own mortality, only her soul was aware of it. Her brain felt like it was exploding in her head, and her heart was somewhere in the pit of her stomach. She should have been rejoicing because she was finally experiencing the thrill of life on the edge, something she had been trying to achieve for years. Instead, she was rolled up like a ball, with her hands over her ears and her eyes squeezed shut, praying to God for it to be over.

When they were safely out of range of the rioting students and the gunfire, Ian, a bit red in the face, took a deep breath and wiped his forehead with a silk handkerchief.

"Are you all right?" he said. "That was a close call, by God."

Tatiana brushed the dust from her skirt and nodded her head. She was still shaking and badly needed a drink. They continued on to the Pagoda, where she quickly downed two brandies and Ian put back a large Scotch. She had no desire to go anywhere else and asked him to take her home. He agreed that it was not a good night to be out on the town.

"Bloody hell," he said. "Makes Bombay look like a bloody paradise. Won't say there isn't a spot of trouble now and then, but nothing like this. Haven't been shot at since the bloody war."

She was glad to say goodnight to him and be by herself. The last thing she wanted to do was listen to him prattling on about his life. She went up to her room without a word to her parents and closed the door. Ian left Shanghai the next day.

According to the papers, a total of forty-four shots were fired into the crowd on the orders of the British police inspector. Eleven of the demonstrators were killed, and twenty more were wounded. Tatiana didn't know how close they had come to being hit. They could have driven right into the centre of the mayhem.

~ ~

Did I experience some kind of miraculous conversion, curled

up on the floor of that automobile? Was I meeting my Maker
and praying for His forgiveness? Promising to be good and
never, ever to disobey my parents again? No. Of course not. But
something in me changed after my so-called brush with death.
If anything, I danced faster and lived harder, but now there was
an edginess that hadn't been there before. I began to wake up
in the middle of the night, covered in sweat. Sometimes, even
in broad daylight, I found myself gasping for air, as if I were
suffocating or trying to breathe through a wet blanket. I started
applying more make-up when my friends began commenting
on how tired I looked. But I wasn't tired. If anything, I was too
alert. I couldn't relax, couldn't let up or let go for a minute.
Some voice kept telling me, Don't stop. Don't stop. Don't stop.

I realize now that I was obsessed with death. My own and
everybody else's. I avoided my father when I should have
been spending more time with him. He reminded me of the
very thing I was fleeing: the knowledge that death was near,
inevitable, beyond my control. Annette's old advice to keep
both hands full, a glass of champagne in one and a cigarette
in the other, wasn't working. The relief was only temporary.
The fear was pervasive; it never rested. And so, I stepped over
another threshold one night, the threshold of an opium den.

~ ~

There were just four of them, Tatiana and three others: her
"date", Simon, a tall, thin, nervous young man with more money
than sense, and his friend Albert, a sloppy man with features
to match, including large, fleshy ears, droopy eyes, and lips
that seemed swollen, as if he'd been stung by a bee. Albert had
picked up a Russian taxi dancer somewhere. She was very drunk
and was giggling from too much champagne. Her lipstick was
smeared all over Albert's collar and she kept adding layers of it
to her lips in an attempt to be more alluring. Her dress and shoes

were cheap, not just inexpensive, but in bad taste. She made
Tatiana feel dirty. "I'm Nadia," she kept saying. "Nah-dee-ya."
She wanted them to remember her. Tatiana kept thinking of
Annette, whom she hadn't seen for days, endlessly repeating her
"*histoire de ma vie.*" Was she also afraid of being forgotten?
What's wrong with being consigned to oblivion? she
wondered. *Who cares if people remember you or not?*

The taxi brought them to a nondescript, narrow wooden
building several storeys high, with balconies on every floor,
part of a row of similar buildings in the Chinese district.
Inside, the lights were dim and the air was pungent and stale,
as though someone had been burning incense the day before.
They were taken to a private room, where they reclined on
comfortable sofas upholstered in some dark velvet fabric and
watched a thin old man in a long black coat prepare the pipe.
The floors were richly carpeted, as were the walls, so that all
sounds fell gently into nothingness, along with all thoughts.
There was nothing to know, nothing to fear, nothing to care
about. Life was a dark velvet sofa that you could sink into and
forget that the world outside was in chaos, that your life had no
meaning and never would. Forget that your father was dying
and that you desperately wanted not to care.

Chapter Thirteen

It was around this time that Tatiana began to seek out Lily's company more and more. Lily became her island of solace in a sea of despair. For the past two years, she had been visiting Lily once a month out of a sense of obligation to their long friendship. Lily was so completely absorbed in Leonard and his remarkable musical talent that Tatiana had become bored with their conversations. It was always "Leonard did this" or "Leonard did that. Leonard, play something for Aunt Tatiana. Leonard, sing. Leonard, dance. Leonard, stand on your head for us."

But now Tatiana found comfort in the banality of their visits. It was as if she needed very badly to cling to something that was solidly anchored in the earth, or she would float away into the ether and never find her way back. She could not express this to Lily, but she suspected her friend knew she was adrift.

Because Lily was neither introspective nor probing, she did not attempt to talk to Tatiana about it, except to scold her when she looked particularly bad. Lily knew better than to lecture Tatiana about her lifestyle, about which she actually knew very little, and would resort to saying things like, "You should eat more vegetables, or drink more green tea. It will clean your blood." There were times when Tatiana wanted very badly to believe that eating more vegetables and drinking green tea would solve her problems, but she knew she had gone far beyond such remedies. On the one hand, Annette exhorted her to forget her troubles and enjoy her good fortune and, on the other side was Lily, suggesting home remedies as a cure for the incurable.

Sometimes Tatiana wanted to shout at both of them. "There is nothing to enjoy! There is no disease; there is nothing to cure! There is only death, which is an end to everything." There was only sensation for her now, no emotion. She could feel emptiness. She could feel tiredness. The opium brought about a feeling of nothingness that lasted sometimes for hours. It was like a deliverance, a place to go that demanded nothing and offered nothingness. It was oblivion on demand. Tatiana liked it and hated it at the same time. She wanted it more, but she also wanted not to want it. She was torn by her own conflicting desires but had trained herself well not to notice.

Lily would have given anything to "fix" Tatiana. Her own contentment, which she considered to be her good fortune, or, as she called it, luck, was not earned, she believed, but was the result of a series of auspicious events occurring at the right time. How could Tatiana be blamed for having a character that burned like a fire and consumed itself? How was she responsible for her father's illness? Things were the way they were, and it did no good to question them. From Lily, Tatiana felt a kind of acceptance that she did not receive from anyone else. It was strangely liberating. She didn't have to pretend, didn't have to dance faster or laugh harder. She could just be.

By the time Leonard was six years old, it was clear that he was a prodigy. He had been receiving piano lessons for over a year from an elderly British woman who had been something of a prodigy herself many years before. She had been a concert pianist, touring Europe and America during the last century until, in an unfortunate accident, she had broken her elbow. It had not set properly, and she was no longer able to practice the gruelling number of hours a day that were necessary to maintain her touring schedule. She married a wealthy textile manufacturer and moved to Shanghai, where she took on the occasional promising student. She saw great promise in Leonard.

"Mrs. Mackenzie says we need to find someone who can tutor Leonard every day," Lily told her. She and Tatiana had just finished a lunch of vegetables and rice and were sitting in the garden drinking green tea. An idea began to form in Tatiana's head, and she decided it was worth a try.

"Annette's son Daniel is a brilliant pianist," she said. "He's a wonderful young man and might be an ideal tutor for Leonard, at least at this stage of his development. Would you consider giving him a try?"

Tatiana knew Lily was never going to think favourably of Annette. Lily believed that Annette had led her friend astray. Tatiana had been a mere child, an innocent, in Lily's opinion, when Annette had started exerting her influence. She believed Tatiana's life would have been very different if she had never met Annette, and she was probably right. But Tatiana hoped that Lily might at least give Daniel a chance. He was now nearly eighteen years old and an accomplished musician.

Annette had been unable to save enough money to send him to Europe. As fast as she was able to put money into the silk stocking, there was always a reason to take it out. It had nothing to do with a lack of devotion to her son's musical career. At one point, she had needed an operation when her appendix was infected. Then, a couple of years later, one of her brothers had turned up, broke and dissolute.

"*Mon Dieu, chérie,*" she said. "What am I supposed to do? I can't just leave him to die when I have the money to save him."

It was a terrible dilemma for her, because nothing mattered more to her than Daniel's future. How many chances would there be for him? And yet, her brother was a part of her, too. There had been a time, when they were very young, when they had been close. Then, when life had become hard, she and her family had grown cold toward one another. They were all competing for the same piece of bread, in a way, and they became no better than hungry animals, eyeing each other suspiciously, and losing their trust. But now one of them was on her doorstep, begging her for help. It changed everything.

Her brother was a hopeless addict and was soon sucking up her savings like a bottom feeder in a fish tank. He had an endless supply of excuses and absolutely no limit to the depths he would plunge to extort money from her. Tatiana had been very careful about what she said to Annette during that period of their friendship. Annette was a woman of great loyalty to those she loved and to those who needed her, but she often confused the two. Between her brother and her son, she was torn beyond reason by her conflicting loyalties, and it had blinded her. So great was her need to be needed, that by the time she realized her brother was never going to change his ways, she had sacrificed her son's future. She would never be able to make back the money she had given away.

And why, Tatiana asked herself, had she not offered to help? She had watched the boy grow into a young man. She believed in his talent, as much as it was possible for her to believe in anything in those days. And she had some money.

~ ~

My "patrons", mostly Americans, were generous. I was a glamorous companion who listened patiently to their puffed-up boasting, laughed at their silly jokes and occasionally submitted to their hasty lovemaking. I accepted their gifts and their money and thought it was a fair transaction. Whatever I lost of myself, I made up for it by filling my closets and my jewellery boxes. I had become thin and sharp as a knife, and there was a certain kind of man who was attracted to that. I could always put on a good show with my silk dresses and lacquered nails. The sparkle came from real diamonds. The polish was all silk and pearls.

So why didn't I become a patron of sorts myself? Had I sunk to such depths of selfishness that I couldn't extend a hand to a friend? Or had I felt the rebuff before I even tried? I'm not trying to exonerate myself by laying the blame on Annette. I simply do not know why I didn't give her money. Maybe by suggesting Daniel to Lily as a tutor for Leonard, I was trying to expiate some kind of guilt that I had buried as deep as all my other guilts. And there were many.

My neglect of my father in his last months is something I will have to live with to the end of my own life. If there is a Heaven, and we both should happen to meet there, then maybe I'll be able to make it up to him. I'll be able to say, "Papa, I should have been there. I shouldn't have let you go so easily." But I know now that "should" never happens. It's just a word we made up a long time ago to punish ourselves, or maybe to comfort ourselves by at least acknowledging that we know what's right and what's wrong. We know the difference, but we act badly anyway.

Chapter Fourteen

L ily agreed to meet Daniel, much to Tatiana's relief and
delight. She would hire him, she said, only if Leonard
liked him and was willing to take instruction from him. Tatiana
crossed her fingers and told Daniel and Annette. They were
thrilled. Here was a chance for Daniel to earn some money
and also a chance for his reputation to spread. Lily and Wu-
ling were well connected. Wu-ling was an aide to Chiang
Kai-shek. When Dr. Sun Yat-sen had asked Chiang to lead the
Kuomintang's military academy at Whampoa and to build a
Nationalist army, Wu-ling had been one of Chiang's advisors.
Now Chiang had rewarded Wu-ling with a government
position. This meant that Lily and her husband were among
the elite. Wu-ling opposed Chiang's association with the
Communists, as did Lily's Number Two Brother, but only in
private, behind closed doors. Unlike his brother-in-law, Wu-
ling did not want to contradict Chiang. He was prepared to wait
and see what would happen. But all this had nothing to do with
Daniel becoming Leonard's tutor, or so Tatiana thought. She
and Annette saw it as a big, wide door opening for Daniel, one
that could lead only to good things.

Tatiana brought Daniel over to meet Lily on a day that had
threatened rain since early morning. The sky was the colour
of gun metal, and people went about their business quickly,
expecting the rain to fall any minute. None of this diminished
Daniel's excitement at having a job that involved music and the
possibility of performing for influential people.

"Don't get your hopes up too high," Tatiana warned him. "I don't want you to be disappointed if this doesn't work out."

"It'll work out, Aunt Tatiana. Don't worry," he said. "Think positively, and good things will happen."

"Who told you that?" she asked. Surely not Annette.

"Nobody told me," he said. "I just think it's a good thing to believe in. You have to believe in something."

Tatiana looked at the handsome young man beside her in the taxi and wondered anew at his optimism. His suit was nearly threadbare, the sleeves and pant legs half an inch too short. But his shoes were polished, and the knot in his tie was exactly right. He shone with confidence and the eagerness that defies disappointment. She touched the back of his hand with her fingertips.

"You're right," she said.

The first heavy drops of rain were falling as they entered the Tang compound. Tatiana huddled under the umbrella held by a servant, but Daniel laughed and refused to run for shelter. "It's only water," he said. "We're not going to drown."

Lily was waiting for them in her sitting room. As soon as they arrived, she ordered tea, making a fuss over them as if they'd been out in the rain for hours.

"It's all right, Lily," said Tatiana. "It's only a little rain." Daniel laughed, and she had to smile. He always managed to put her in a good mood. He was the innocent one, the boy, yet he had the grace of wisdom, if not wisdom itself. When he was around, she trusted in the rightness of things.

Lily did not look once at Daniel's shabby suit or even his shiny shoes and perfectly knotted tie. She looked at his face, which she thought was beautiful, and into his eyes, which caused her to smile because they were warm, laughing eyes, and at his hands, which were so exquisitely shaped, and she knew Tatiana was right. He would be a wonderful music teacher for her son.

Leonard took to Daniel immediately, perhaps because Daniel was still a child himself in many ways. He was playful and easy to like. He had a gentle nature that communicated itself in the softness of his voice and the gracefulness of his mannerisms. Yet when he played the piano, he showed a maturity beyond his years. He did not have to ask for your attention; it was given willingly, surrendering to the pleasure of the music. He was also a very handsome young man. He was tall and slender, but not thin in an angular, bony way. He was all soft lines and curves, as if he'd been sculpted by Michelangelo.

"How did you ever create such an exquisite creature?" Tatiana once teased Annette while they drank sherry and listened to Daniel play the piano.

"With a lot of passion and a little bit of luck," she told her. "His father was also very beautiful. He made your heart beat a little faster every time you saw him. Women couldn't take their eyes off him. I learned a lot about desire from watching them undress him with their eyes." She chuckled, and there was a note of triumph in her voice. "And now I have his son, who has given me more joy than anything else in my life, including his father. That's because I can look at Daniel and say to myself, I created this magnificent creature. I gave him life and that has made everything worthwhile. You cannot know, *chérie*, what that feels like until it happens to you."

The lessons began almost immediately. Daniel arrived at Lily's house at one o'clock in the afternoon, five days a week, and tutored Leonard until three o'clock, when Lily would have tea served. Then they would talk for half an hour or so. They would talk about Leonard and music, but they often talked about themselves. Daniel confided his dreams to Lily about wanting to be a concert pianist who travelled the world, and Lily told Daniel about her year in Switzerland and how she wanted to go back to Europe someday, perhaps when her

children were grown up. She told him she looked forward
to having more children, because so far it had been the most
rewarding experience of her life.

"Your mother must be very proud of you," she told him one
time. When he blushed, she said, "No. I mean it. A mother's
greatest dream is for her children to be unique and special. You
are gifted, Daniel, and your gift gives pleasure to those who
hear you play. How many can say that?"

"Thank you, Madame Tang," he said. "You honour both me
and my mother."

Lily laughed. "And you honour me," she said, to tease him.
She remembered Tatiana's words about Leonard from a long
time ago: "So much honouring and respecting. He's just a baby."

His new schedule meant that Daniel had to get up extra early
on the mornings he tutored so he could do his own practicing,
but it was worthwhile, because after a few months, Lily began
to arrange concerts for him in her home, which became a kind
of salon. She invited close friends and family members, and
sometimes Wu-ling's associates. On those occasions, guests
wore formal dress, drank cocktails and were served food from a
sumptuous buffet. It was clear that Lily had taken Daniel under
her wing and was introducing him to Shanghai society.

Annette was thrilled, and so was Tatiana. Finally, she had
done something worthwhile for another human being. It was
a relief to know she was capable of making a connection with
someone that had nothing to do with money, champagne, opium
or sex. This was a human connection, strictly from the heart.
Just as Annette took pride in "creating" Daniel, Tatiana took
some pride in knowing that she'd had a hand in introducing him
to what could be the most significant period of his life. Perhaps
she overestimated her own importance.

At home, though, matters had taken a turn for the worse.
She was in trouble with Olga because she had so obviously
been avoiding their father. Tatiana couldn't make her sister

understand how she felt, how much it distressed her to see him. Olga only saw Tatiana's absence, but she could not see how her sister was suffering. She told Tatiana that she was a coward, and after a while Tatiana came to believe that her sister was right, that she was the worst kind of coward. She thought only of herself and her own comfort and nothing of the pain she was causing others.

"He's going to die," Olga said, "and then you'll cry only for yourself because you will be filled with regret. You disgust me," she went on, looking at Tatiana with contempt. "My own sister. I'm ashamed of you and I'm angry and I'm sad, all at the same time."

Olga was pregnant with her second child by this time, and it was not an easy pregnancy. Most mornings she was sick to her stomach, and the sight of food often made her nauseous. Although she had an amah for Anastasia and servants who did the cooking and cleaning, she was trying to run her own full household and take care of her parents' needs at the same time. Tatiana appeared to be avoiding all responsibility for anything to do with her family. She told herself Olga was exaggerating, and that things were not so bad. Olga liked to be dramatic; it was her way of getting attention. Tatiana thought that once the new baby came, Olga would be preoccupied and would leave her alone. Maybe they could hire another servant to look after Mother and Papa. But for now, arguments seemed to take place every day.

When she could stand it no longer, Tatiana took an apartment on Bubbling Well Road near the racecourse. She couldn't face any of it. Mother, Papa, Olga. She told herself she was doing everyone a favour by moving out. She was only in the way and upset her parents by coming and going at odd hours. It was time she started paying her own way in life. But, in reality, she knew she was escaping. When she had refused to take lessons from Dimitri, she had felt guilty—she wasn't entirely without conscience, she told herself—and now she wanted to leave it all behind and begin life on her own terms. It was not right that she should sacrifice her life when her parents could afford servants. Olga was being a martyr.

As for Katarina and Sergei, they felt helpless. They had known for some time that their second daughter was lost to them. "She's a child of the twentieth century," Sergei told Katarina. "What can we do?" It was the only explanation he could think of. He did his best to hide his despair from his wife, whose confusion saddened him even more. He tried to tell himself that Tatiana would find her way, that the world was being re-made by her generation, and she would know what was best. He wanted very badly to believe it.

Then one day, Jean Paul came to her apartment. "Tati," he said, "please come to your parents' house with me. Olga is not there this afternoon, and your mother is sleeping. Come and spend some time with your father. He's not so bad today. He's even reading the newspaper. I think he would like to see you."

"Did he ask you to come?" she said.

"No. I came because I didn't want to have my own regrets. Because he's been so good to me, and because I'm a father now with a daughter of my own. And because I know how much he loves you."

"Ah, Tatushka. There you are," Sergei said when she walked into the room. He tried to behave as if she had never left, hoping to recapture something precious from the past. "I've been thinking about so many things now that I'm an old man."

"You're not an old man," she said, willing herself not to cry when she saw him. He was so thin, the bones in his wrists were like knobs. The backs of his hands were covered in large brown spots. *You're too young to die*, she thought.

"Without knowing what I am and why I am here, life is impossible," he said as she kissed his forehead. His skin was cool and damp against her lips. She remembered that it used to be warm and dry.

"Is that Tolstoy or you?" she asked, pulling a chair close to the bed. He was sitting on top of the covers, his legs straight out in front of him, crossed at the ankles. He had on leather slippers and a dressing gown over his pyjamas.

"Does it make a difference?"

"Yes," she replied without thinking.

"Why?"

"Because if it's Tolstoy, it's boring. If it's you, I want to know why you said it."

"Then it's me," he said. She pretended to believe him but knew he was lying just to engage her in some sort of dialogue.

"So," she said, playing along. "Why did you say it? What does it mean?"

He folded the newspaper he had been reading and took off his glasses. "Well," he said, "I think it's a universal truth. Human beings cannot live a life without purpose. We are always asking, What is the meaning of life? Who am I and why am I here? It's human nature to seek answers to the fundamental questions of existence. Philosophers and writers since the invention of language have asked these questions."

"I don't want to know about the questions," Tatiana said peevishly. "I want to know the answers."

"Ah, the answers," replied Sergei. "Therein lies the dilemma. Because for every questioner, there is a different answer. You and I are not the same, nor do we have the same purpose, except perhaps to serve humanity."

"Serve humanity," she snorted. "Why would I want to serve humanity? I don't want to serve anybody."

"That's because you are still in the selfish, immature part of your life. Wisdom only comes with experience. And when you start to look around you and see what's wrong with the world, as well as what's right with it, then you'll begin to define the meaning of the word 'serve'. It doesn't have to mean cleaning up someone else's mess in the literal sense. But, in the much larger context of humanity, we all have a responsibility to, first of all, not make a mess, but second, clean up the mess we see around us. To make the world a better place for our children, for example."

"I see a lot of mess in Shanghai," she said, "but I only see the very poorest people picking it up off the streets."

"But Tatushka," he protested, "you're still thinking in a literal way. Yes, it's important to pick up the garbage on the streets, and you're right, it's usually the poorest in a society who pick it up. But you must think in a larger context."

"Like what?"

"Like religion, politics, art, philosophy. The context of ideas. This is where change begins. You know that. In the exchange of ideas we invent new ways to do things. We plan. We experiment. Life is an ongoing experiment. A work in progress, if you will. As we evolve, society evolves. And as society evolves, we must change or be left behind."

Sergei seemed to find new energy as he talked to her about his two favourite subjects, history and philosophy. She could see that he missed the discussions they used to have with Dimitri. Jean Paul had been right to bring her to see him; it was as if he had been waiting to tell her these things.

"Why do you think they referred to the Middle Ages in Europe as the Dark Ages?" he asked.

"I don't know," she said. "Because it rained a lot?"

"No," he replied, trying to make his frail body laugh at her joke. "It had nothing to do with the weather. After the fall of the Roman Empire, Europe was in chaos. It was a time when literacy declined, and there were very few written records. The church was the dominant institution in the land, but it had its hands full trying to maintain its own power and convert pagans. Society was ruled by warriors, knights and feudal lords. Very little in the way of new ideas emerged from this time, and so, no change."

"Then what happened?" She was humouring him, basking in the warmth of a voice that she hadn't realized she'd missed so much.

"Then came the Renaissance," Sergei continued, "the rebirth of culture and learning in Europe. It started in Northern Italy, where the trade routes from the east brought goods for the wealthy, which in turn made the traders themselves wealthy and led to a greater demand for goods. Along with all this wealth came leisure and an increased interest in the classics from the Greek and early Roman civilizations. The Renaissance gave us Petrarch and Boccaccio, Michelangelo and Leonardo da Vinci. Then came the printing press, so everybody had access to books and ideas. People began to ask questions again. Civilization began to move forward after the stagnation of the Dark Ages."

"Are we still in the Renaissance?" she asked. "Or is it over?"

He shrugged and seemed to lose some of his vitality. Tatiana propped the pillow up behind his head, and he leaned back into it. "We are still questioning things. We are in an age of science, where everything is open to question. When Galileo said the earth revolved around the sun, he was punished by the church for holding beliefs that contradicted the Bible. But now, since Charles Darwin, many people question whether God created the universe. These are dangerous questions, Tatushka, because when you begin to question faith in God, you begin to ask, who am I and why am I here?" She began to see where he was going, and a familiar sense of impatience began to creep into her chest. She didn't want to go down the road he was taking. "Once you open that door, you are walking into an empty room where anything is possible. This takes courage. The kind of courage to understand that your need to know is greater than your need to be safe. Do you understand?"

If she had said yes, she knew that her father would have taken her hand and said, "Then come back to me, and I will teach you what I know. We will explore the nature of the universe together." She knew nothing would have given him greater joy, but she did not say yes. She merely shook her head and said, "Oh, Papa. You make me tired with all this thinking."

~ ~

At that point in my life, my ritual with the opium pipe became my best friend, my family. It was the meaning and purpose of my life. I was smoking every day now, but only one or two pipes. I was in control, I told myself. Opium was not my master but my ally. At the time, I couldn't see the irony of it. I was trying to escape from the life I had created, the one I thought I wanted so badly and had sacrificed everything for.

~ ~

Sergei died near the end of 1926. The last time Tatiana saw him, he was so weak he could barely keep his eyes open. He weighed less than she did, and his skin was so yellow, he looked like he had fallen into a vat of dye.

"Tatushka," he whispered. "Tatushka." He smiled, and she saw there were great gaps between his teeth. She wanted to beg his forgiveness, but Olga had warned her that if she dared to upset him, she would beat her with a broom handle until she was black and blue. Jean Paul barely spoke. Tatiana thought he was so worried about upsetting Olga, whose baby was due in a few months, that he hoped he could influence her mood by maintaining a calm silence.

But it was the sight of her mother that really broke Tatiana's heart. She was like a skeleton, so thin and frail, she looked a hundred years old. It was as if every day of Sergei's dying had taken the toll of two or three on her own life. Her vitality had been seeping away ever since they had arrived in Shanghai twenty years earlier, but lately there had been little to sustain her. Tatiana didn't like to think about how much of Katarina's sadness she had been responsible for. Sergei was the only one who had been able to lift her spirits, with his indomitable nature that filled a room with promise. He made you believe that life would get better, that for every valley there was a hill that would lead you out of it. As Tatiana looked at his face, almost unrecognizable now, she wondered when and why she had stopped believing him. Had he worn her out with his history lessons and his interminable Tolstoy quotes? Or had she become afraid that all his talk would force her to examine her life and discover who she really was?

Chapter Fifteen

Anastasia came with the children this morning. They'd been to the library, and Ana, as usual, picked up a couple of books for me. This time she brought Dickens, *Our Mutual Friend*, and Graham Greene, *The Quiet American*. One old, one new. Rarely does she bring me a book I don't enjoy. She is sensitive, like her father, and picks up things that others don't notice. Ana knows right away if something is troubling you or if you have good news. She is observant, always watching, always listening. She is a good mother, too, and gives her children room to develop into themselves, knowing instinctively when to discipline and when to instruct. Ana married a Canadian whose name is Keith. He's an architect, and his company is working on some big planned community in the suburbs. It's a very exciting project, and he and Ana are planning to move into one of the houses as soon as it's finished. It seems everybody wants to move to the suburbs these days. I don't understand it, but then, I'm not raising children. People are always talking about more room and better schools. Everything bigger and better. Give me a crowded city any day.

The children were quietly reading their books on the living room carpet. Andrew and Heather—such Scottish names my niece has given her children—are both readers, although Andrew usually grows restless after fifteen or twenty minutes.

"Your friend from China will be coming soon, won't she?" Ana asked.

"Yes. In a couple of weeks."

"If there's anything you need, just let me know. I can take you in the car."

"Thank you, Ana. I'll call you."

"Aunt Tati?"

"Yes."

"Who is this friend of yours? You must have been very close for her to contact you after all these years."

"I met Lily shortly after we arrived in Shanghai, in 1906 or 1907. She was the daughter of your grandfather's business partner. In those days, for a foreigner to operate a business, he had to have a Chinese partner. Your mother, Lily and I went to Saturday morning English classes together. Our teacher was Mrs. Wilkinson, and we used to compare her to Queen Victoria. Anyway, Lily and I sat next to each other, and we became friends. Very close friends."

"Was she connected to that murder Mother was talking about?"

I hesitated. "Yes, she was," I said. "The young man who was killed was her son's piano teacher. Leonard, Lily's son, had shown a lot of musical talent. Daniel was the son of another friend of mine, and I brought them together. Daniel was a brilliant pianist who was becoming quite well known in Shanghai, thanks to Lily and her husband. Lily's family was very well connected in Shanghai. Her father was a friend of Chiang Kai-shek. "

"Did they ever find out who killed him?"

"As far as I know, the case was never solved."

We were sitting at the kitchen table drinking coffee. Ana leaned forward and lowered her voice. "Do you have any idea who did it, Aunt Tati?"

Anastasia seemed fascinated by the murder. I smiled. Should I tell her I had always had my suspicions? There were things that had happened that nobody but I knew about. Things I've never told anyone, not Olga or Lily or Annette. Not even the police. Should I have told them? I've wondered, especially lately. At the time, I was trying to protect Annette, who had fallen into a deep hole of despair over her son's death. I didn't see what purpose would be served by revealing what I knew or suspected. But now I wonder if I deprived Daniel of justice. Did I let his killer, or killers, get away with it?

"There were several possibilities," I told Ana. "Shanghai was a dangerous place in those days. Lots of political intrigue going on. Labour strikes, student demonstrations. He could have been hit by a stray bullet during a street battle. I was almost killed myself, twice. Ask your father. He'll remember."

"I will," said Ana, her eyes wide with interest. She was on the edge of her chair.

"Who knows? Daniel might have been in some kind of trouble we weren't aware of. Maybe he fell in with a bad crowd. Or maybe he had an affair with someone who had a jealous husband. He was very handsome, and I'm sure women often fell in love with him. We were all so shocked when it happened, and he'd been missing for a month before his body was found."

"How horrible for his mother," said Ana, shaking her head.

"Yes. It was terrible," I said. I would never forget Annette's devastated face and the sound of her crying.

~ ~

Although Katarina had pleaded with her to stay after Sergei died, Tatiana had gone back to her rooms on Bubbling Well Road, and she didn't go out for days. Finally, after a week, Annette arrived and knocked on her door.

"*Chérie*," she said, as she continued to knock. "Are you in there?" Reluctantly Tatiana opened the door. "Oh, *chérie*, I've been so worried. Not a word. No one has seen you for weeks. What's happened?"

Tatiana told her about Sergei, and Annette immediately

put her arms around her and hugged her, murmuring soothing words in French and rubbing her back.

"I'm all right," Tatiana said. "I'm all right. Really." But she was crying and couldn't seem to stop.

"You're exhausted," said Annette. "And you probably haven't eaten in days." She looked around at the shambles of Tatiana's apartment. The maid had tried several times to come in and tidy up, but Tatiana had told her to go away. The same air had been confined in her two rooms for a week because she had kept the windows locked and the curtains drawn. She followed Annette's eyes to the brown velvet sofa and chair that sagged in the middle, because the cushions hadn't been plumped, and the dark green carpet that needed a good sweeping. A thin grey layer of dust covered the tables, and little clumps of dust had gathered in the corners of the room. In the bedroom, the sheets were a jumble in the middle of the bed that hadn't been made in a week. "And you've been smoking that damned opium pipe." Annette looked at her with sad and disappointed eyes. "It's so bad," she said.

"I know," Tatiana said, "but don't lecture me now. I'm not in the mood."

Annette went into the little room that served as a kitchen and started making tea, boiling water on the gas burner and rummaging around for the tea. There was no food in the apartment, not even a stale biscuit. When she came back into the main room, Annette flung back the heavy drapes and opened the windows. Suddenly the room was filled with the noise of the street. Tatiana smelled smoke coming from the cooking food below the window and heard the sounds of life as it carried on without her.

Annette handed her the cup of weak tea she had made from the dregs in the canister and told her she was going out to get them something to eat.

"Do you have any cigarettes?" Tatiana asked her. "I've run

out." Annette handed her the silver cigarette case she always carried in her purse. It had been a gift from a German "friend" from before the war. Before she was out the door, Tatiana was inhaling one of the French-made cigarettes as if it were life-saving oxygen.

Annette returned about ten minutes later with several packets of food wrapped in banana leaves and newspaper and tied with string. She found a couple of bowls and some cutlery in the kitchen, and they sat on the floor in front of the low coffee table, from which Tatiana had wiped the dust with a towel from the bathroom. They opened the packets of rice, vegetables and fried pork. Annette pulled the cigarette, Tatiana's third, out of her mouth and said, "Eat." Tatiana started to pick at the rice and Annette said, "Eat, *chérie*, or I shall feed you myself, like a baby." Tatiana forced herself to eat a bit of rice and some of the fried cabbage. Annette handed her a piece of pork. She took it with her fingers and began to chew on it. It was quite tasty, and she found herself spooning more rice and vegetables into her mouth. She was starving.

"It's a good thing I came," said Annette. "What were you going to do? Wait for the neighbours to complain about the smell and send for the undertaker? Eh?"

Tatiana smiled, picked up another piece of greasy pork and stuck it in her mouth. It was delicious.

"You're an angel," she said. "An angel from heaven."

"No, I'm not," Annette replied. "I'm your friend, and I was worried about you. Especially because I knew you couldn't take care of yourself. You're no better than a spoiled little princess," she said, smiling and squeezing Tatiana's arm, "but even spoiled little princesses need friends."

~ ~

I laughed for the first time in weeks and thought how lucky I was at that moment to have such a friend. I had been drowning in my own misery, and Annette had rescued me from myself. Someone had cared enough to come looking for me. I was not alone, as I had thought. I had gradually pushed everyone away, ejected them from the castle and pulled up the drawbridge so they couldn't get in. And why? Maybe I thought they were getting too close to the truth about me. That I was a shallow, worthless human being who had nothing to offer them.

~ ~

"How's Daniel?" she asked Annette after she'd devoured all the food and lit another cigarette. They were finishing off a bottle of Scotch, the last thing in the apartment left to drink.

"He's so happy, I can't tell you. Your friend Lily has been so good to him. He has a concert nearly every week, and she showers him with gifts. Her little boy must be the most precious thing in the world to her. She would do anything for him. He is so lucky," she sighed and took another drink of Scotch. "To have such a mother."

"You're a good mother, too," Tatiana told her. "You've done everything for Daniel. Everything you possibly could."

"Thank you, *chérie*, for saying that." Annette smiled sadly. "But is it enough? Could I have done more? Lily has done more for Daniel in a few months than I could ever do. And I'm grateful," she said hurriedly, "but it should have been me. His own mother. I should have been able to do more."

Should, Tatiana thought. *That awful word again.* All the wishing in the world wasn't going to give Annette what Lily had been born with. "Annette," she said, "you weren't born rich. Lily was. It's just the way things are. She has not had to sacrifice to give her son things the way you have."

Tatiana lit another cigarette and blew smoke at the ceiling. "Is Leonard as talented as Lily thinks he is?"

"Daniel says he's very talented. But he's still a child. Only time will tell if he has the will and the discipline to work as hard as he must."

Will. Discipline. Work. *Three things I seem to know nothing about*, thought Tatiana. She looked at Annette and realized how much she had accomplished in her life, just by raising her son. In spite of all the obstacles fate had thrown in her path.

"I think I need to sleep," Tatiana said, butting out the cigarette. "I'm very tired."

When Olga's baby was born, Tatiana was relieved that it was a boy, although she had no idea why. Too many years in China hearing about "maggots in the rice," she suspected. It was such a difficult birth, they were all afraid the baby would not survive. But Olga and Jean Paul were overjoyed when Nicholas, a big, healthy baby, came into the world, kicking and screaming and fighting for their attention.

Katarina, who by this time was spending most of her days in bed, got up and ate a huge lunch of smoked salmon, salad, roast beef with new potatoes and a piece of sponge cake with peaches and whipped cream for dessert. Finally, something good had happened to them, something they could celebrate. The two months following Sergei's funeral had been grim for all of them. After her father's death, Tatiana had vowed she would try to spend more time with her mother. If Katarina had been sad before Sergei died, her spirit was now almost completely broken. Never one to be demonstrative in her affection, she now hugged her daughter fiercely whenever she visited. She cried and clung to Tatiana with the tenacity of a starving dog that had been thrown a scrap. Tatiana was amazed by the strength of her arms, which were thin as sticks.

"Oh, Tati," she said once, "I'm so lonely. When I think of how badly I treated your father, I wish I could have a second chance to make it up to him."

"Don't talk nonsense," Tatiana said. "You didn't treat Papa badly. It's normal for married people to have arguments, but you always made up in the end. Papa loved you. He was happy."

"But he could have been happier if I had been less involved in my own misery. If I had tried harder to like Shanghai and to embrace our new life. I see that now. But it's too late."

Tatiana wanted to protest again, but she knew that what her mother said was true. Katarina had wasted years of her life sunk in a pool of misery, without even attempting to pull herself out of it. Tatiana was as intolerant as ever of her mother's unwillingness to adapt to Shanghai because, in her own callous way, Tatiana saw it as a choice, one that Katarina had refused to make. She didn't understand how a person could be so overwhelmed by sadness and loss that they could become a prisoner in their own mind.

"You know, Tati, I really did love your father. In the beginning, I wanted only to please him. I thought that to love him would be enough. To have him in my life, then Olushka and you, would completely fulfill me. But when we moved away from Russia, I felt so empty. I felt like an egg whose insides had been drained away. Do you remember, Tati, how at Easter we used to put tiny little pinholes in each end of the eggs, then break the yoke inside with a needle and watch as everything came out that little hole? That's how I felt after we moved here. Like a shell. A hollow shell."

Tatiana never knew what to say when her mother talked about happier times in Russia. She remembered them, too, but it was like looking at a photo album, images frozen in time. The dead were still alive between the pages of the album. Everything was perfectly preserved but static, unchanging. Her father had believed that people, as individuals and as a civilization, died if there wasn't change. As she looked at her mother, Tatiana realized she had been dying a slow and sorrowful death by resisting it.

Painful as these visits were, Tatiana was determined to maintain a connection with her mother. She did not want to make the same mistake she had made with Sergei by abandoning him at the end of his life. Olga had predicted that she would regret it. Besides, with her mother Tatiana could pretend, for a few hours at least, that she wasn't leading a wasteful life. She could pretend that she was better than a taxi dancer or an opium addict. Whether Katarina hid from the facts or had no clue as to the kind of life her daughter was leading, she treated Tatiana as if she were the decent, respectable daughter she had raised. It was as if she, not Tatiana, were addicted to opium. Katarina lived in a hazy dream world, where the past was always fresh and golden and the present was suspended until the pipe was finished. Tatiana was glad, in a way, that her mother had found this place, sad and pathetic as it was. It was her means of escape from crushing loss. The things she had lost—her life in Russia, Sergei—could never be regained, except in memory.

Unlike her visits with Lily, which were a constant reminder of how far she had fallen in life, Tatiana's visits with her mother took her back to a place where she could re-imagine her future. With her mother, she could believe there was such a thing as a second chance in life. With Lily, she knew there was not.

It had been ages since she'd seen any of the old crowd. Ben, she'd heard, had gone back to England. Roger, Leo and Betty were still around. She saw them occasionally at the clubs. Iris was getting married, someone had told her, to an American, and they were going to New York. George still worked for the bank, and the last time she'd seen him, he'd insisted on talking about Russian politics.

"Those bloody Bolsheviks of yours are making a right mess of things," he had said. "Economy's down the toilet. Keep killing each other. Revolutionaries fighting counterrevolutionaries. Nobody knows who anybody is any more. Now Lenin's dead, and that fellow Stalin has taken over and seems to be eliminating all his competition. If they don't start pulling themselves together, there won't be a country left for anybody to run."

"They're not my bloody Bolsheviks," Tatiana reminded him. "I haven't lived there for twenty years. I was a child when we left, so why would I care?"

"Pity. Missed the whole show, didn't you?" said George. He looked at the people sitting at her table. "Maybe you should consider going back to the old country," he suggested. "Might be better for your health." The well-dressed woman on his arm raised her right eyebrow in a cool appraisal of Tatiana and her companions. "Let's go, darling," she said. "We don't want to be late." George smiled and tipped an invisible hat in Tatiana's direction as they left.

Go to hell, she thought.

Chapter Sixteen

Annette told Tatiana how much Lily was doing for Daniel, but she had yet to be invited to one of his concerts. Nor had Tatiana, for that matter. She figured it was probably Wu-ling, Lily's husband, who was pulling all the strings, even though it was most likely Lily who was asking him to do it. It would have been unthinkable for Wu-ling to include the two women in any gathering that was made up of his friends and associates. Wu-ling and Number Two Brother were close, and Number Two Brother knew a lot about the company Annette and Tatiana kept.

Nonetheless, an invitation came in the mail after several months, inviting Tatiana and Annette to an afternoon concert for Lily's "lady" friends. Much to her surprise, Olga also received an invitation.

"I can't possibly go," she told Tatiana. "I'm much too busy with the children."

"Don't be silly," Tatiana told her. "The amah can manage for a couple of hours without you. That's what she's there for. You have an overdeveloped sense of responsibility, Olga. If I tell Jean Paul you refused the invitation, he'll be annoyed with you."

Olga was looking harried, and for no good reason other than that she was trying to do everything herself. She didn't trust anyone to do things as well as she did, and she could work herself into a boiled stew because once she became frenzied, she didn't know how to switch herself off. It annoyed Tatiana more than anything else about her. At those times she became insufferably self-righteous. Nothing was ever good enough.

Nobody worked as hard as she did. "For heaven's sake," Tatiana said more than once, "you have servants. It's not like you're some peasant living in a hovel with sixteen children!" This, of course, would only make things worse.

"Maybe if you took some responsibility for your life and had a proper home, you'd make something of yourself. Look at you. You always look so perfect and you wear expensive clothes and lounge around in clubs all night. What kind of a life is that? You're selfish, Tatiana. Selfish and self-centred." At this point, beads of sweat would appear on Olga's forehead, and she would start wringing her hands.

"Olga! Stop this right now. You're making yourself crazy over nothing." Tatiana knew it did no good to argue with her sister when she was like this, yet she couldn't bring herself to be sympathetic. The words would stick in her throat like a dry pill. "You can't control everything in the world, so don't even try. And you especially can't control me."

They'd had this same conversation in various forms at least once a month. It was one of those discussions that never went anywhere. They were like two old women who had forgotten why they used to like each other.

In the end, Olga went to Daniel's concert with Tatiana and Annette. Lily's lady friends were mostly the wives of Wu-ling's associates, women much like Lily herself. Young mothers who spent their afternoons in each other's company. A few of Lily's cousins and Wu-ling's female relatives were there as well. They assembled in the music room, where chairs had been placed in rows forming a semi-circle around the grand piano. The red upholstered chairs were a fixture in the room, now that "musical evenings", as Lily called them, were a frequent form of entertainment in her home.

Most of the women were dressed in casual afternoon frocks that their dressmakers had made from the latest patterns in Paris. Tatiana and Annette stood out with their elegantly

understated cocktail dresses and beaded evening bags.
Annette's gown was a rich aubergine silk with a scoop neck
and tight sleeves. Tatiana, in midnight blue satin, noticed that
Annette seemed nervous, almost agitated, as she constantly
patted her unruly curls. Annette, who was usually proud of her
thick red hair, seemed to be trying to tame it into submission.

"Stop fidgeting," Tatiana whispered. "You're behaving like a
girl on her first date. Everything will be fine."

Olga, who had worn a sensible black cashmere skirt and
jacket, leaned over and cast a stern look in their direction.

When all the women were comfortably seated, Daniel
entered and walked to the piano. He bowed briefly and sat on
the bench. Silence filled the room, as though all the women had
simultaneously stopped breathing. Tatiana saw that Lily was
sitting on the edge of her chair, leaning forward and watching
Daniel intently.

He played for nearly an hour, barely stopping between
numbers to acknowledge the polite applause that sounded
like rain falling gently onto polished stones. Chopin, Mozart,
Debussy and Mendelssohn, music for ladies on a leisurely
afternoon. Annette became very still once her son began to play.
She sat with her eyes closed, a look of melancholy rapture on
her face. Lily appeared not to move a muscle the whole time, as
though transfixed by a potent magic spell. Tatiana also sat very
still, a calmness coming over her that she could only attribute to
Daniel's mastery of the music.

When Daniel lifted his hands from the keys in a graceful
upward sweep, Leonard, as if on cue, entered the room and
approached the piano. Daniel stood and turned toward him.
He shook the small boy's hand and bowed formally to indicate
that they were equals. Then he picked Leonard up and placed
him on the bench in front of the keyboard. Again the room
fell silent with expectation. Leonard looked up at Daniel and
the teacher nodded to the pupil, who placed his hands on the

keys and began to play. Tatiana felt the room smile as Lily's son gracefully and flawlessly executed a simplified version of Strauss's "Tales from the Vienna Woods."

This time the applause was enthusiastic and prolonged. Lily had tears in her eyes, and her smile threatened to split her face in two. She stood and bowed to the audience in gratitude, bobbing several times to the ladies, to Daniel and to Leonard. Tatiana turned to Annette and saw a look on her face she had never seen before. Her lips had formed a half smile, and her eyes seemed to be gazing into a timeless space. She seemed to be asking the universe a question that could not be answered.

A week after the concert, Tatiana decided to drop in on Lily one afternoon when she knew Daniel would be there. She wanted to see for herself—and to hear from Lily's own lips— how much she was helping Daniel and how much Daniel was helping Leonard.

"Tatiana," she said, when they were in Lily's private sitting room, "he's wonderful, isn't he? I'm so glad you brought Daniel to my attention. He's the perfect teacher for Leonard. So sensitive. So gentle. They're like big brother and little brother. They're so close. And Leonard is playing beautifully. Don't you agree?" She was positively glowing. Every time Lily spoke of Daniel, her face lit up. "I just adore him," she said. "We all do."

"All of you?" Tatiana asked. "Even Wu-ling?"

Lily laughed. "Well, maybe adore is going a bit far. I can't speak for Wu-ling, but Leonard adores Daniel. Like an older brother. And it makes me happy to see Leonard doing so well."

Lily was usually so restrained, especially when it came to talking about her emotions, that Tatiana was surprised by her openness. The success of her afternoon concert had raised her esteem considerably. Her energy was so infectious, Tatiana felt almost giddy. She looked at the large bouquet of round pink peonies in a blue and white jug sitting on the low, black lacquer table in the centre of the room. Their fragrance was intoxicating.

"Lily," she said. "I've never seen you like this. What's going on?"

"I'm happy. That's all," Lily said. "I've never been so happy."

They could hear the sound of the piano in the music room. Leonard was practicing scales. Lily nodded in time to the music, the smile never leaving her face. After a few minutes, the music changed, and so did Lily's expression. She closed her eyes and sat motionless as they heard Chopin being played by someone much more accomplished than Leonard. "Is that...?" Tatiana started to say.

"Shh," said Lily, putting her finger to her lips. "That's Daniel. He always plays something when the lesson is finished. I think it's to inspire Leonard." The music was beautiful, as fine a performance as when he'd played it a week ago. Tatiana wished for a moment that Sergei could have been there to hear it. He had loved Chopin. She closed her eyes too and listened.

A few minutes later, Daniel came into the room. Lily jumped up from her chair and applauded. Feeling embarrassed, as if she were intruding on a private moment, Tatiana put her hands together and clapped. "Bravo," she said. "That was wonderful, Daniel."

"Aunt Tatiana," he said. "How nice to see you." He bent to kiss her cheek, and she noticed he was wearing a new suit, shirt and tie, beautifully cut, very expensively tailored, all in silk. *This is China*, she reminded herself. *Of course he's wearing silk.*

She remembered Annette telling her that Lily always gave Daniel tea at the end of each lesson. It was their habit that Daniel should come to Lily's sitting room and drink tea with her, just as Tatiana was doing. He seemed very comfortable in his surroundings, and Lily started bubbling about what she'd done earlier in the day, what they'd been talking about, what good friends they were, and so on.

She's in love with him, Tatiana thought. *She's infatuated with this boy.* But, of course, he wasn't a boy any longer. He was a young man. A very handsome young man who paid attention to everything Lily said, nodding and laughing when she said something funny and shaking his head when that was the appropriate response. As Tatiana watched them, she tried to tell herself that she was imagining things. Lily was his employer, his patron. He was a polite young man who gave her son piano lessons. It was a situation that made everybody happy. Why shouldn't they be?

But it made Tatiana uncomfortable. Even though she had known Lily most of her life, she felt that she was the intruder, taking up their time together, their private space. Could he be in love with her, she wondered? What was going on? Tatiana suddenly felt like getting up and flinging open the window to let in some fresh air. She was suffocating.

"Excuse me," she heard herself say. "I must be going. I forgot I have an appointment on the Bund. At the bank," she added, unnecessarily. It was ridiculous. What had made her think of such a thing? She never made appointments with the bank. Jean Paul did her banking for her and gave her cash every week according to the terms of her father's will. Her money was safely hidden away in a silk-lined handbag under her mattress.

Daniel looked disappointed that she was leaving, but Lily was unconcerned. "Come again soon, Tatiana," she said. "There's so much to talk about, and I don't see you enough. How is your mother?" she added. "And the new baby?"

"Fine," she said quickly. "Everybody's fine. The baby's growing like a weed, putting on weight every day. He's very handsome," she added. "Just like a movie star." They all laughed, and Tatiana made an exit worthy of a great actress.

On the street in front of Lily's house, Tatiana hailed a rickshaw and gave him the address on Bubbling Well Road.

It seemed to take forever. She kept shaking her head, telling herself she had imagined everything. It was just happiness she had witnessed, nothing more. Happiness. A state of mind Tatiana had become so unfamiliar with that she didn't recognize it when she saw it. *It's none of your business*, she told herself. *So just leave it alone.*

But she couldn't. Her brain kept going over it. Should she say something to Annette, she wondered? But what would that accomplish? Maybe she should have a word with Daniel. But what would she say? Don't get involved with Lily, she's a married woman? He already knew that. And he knew what an important and influential man Lily's husband was. Did he know about Number Two Brother? From everything Tatiana had been hearing, he was a man to be feared. She wondered if Daniel was endangering himself by associating with Lily.

~ ~

I don't think I knew the word "paranoia" at the time, but certainly my thoughts were paranoid. I had never been one to probe too deeply into my own mind, and maybe if I had been, I would have seen that my habits and my lifestyle were starting to play havoc with my imagination. I had worked myself into a terrible state and had no way of pulling myself out of it. I couldn't talk to Annette about it. And I certainly couldn't talk to Lily. What was I to do? My only sources of relief had become my cigarettes, Scotch whiskey and my opium pipe. They calmed me and comforted me and made everything all right.

~ ~

Tatiana was so relieved when she finally reached her apartment that she ran up the stairs and locked herself in. She went straight to the cabinet for the bottle of Scotch and poured two fingers into a glass. Down the hatch and then two more. *That's better*, she thought. She could feel her brain slowing down, her system starting to unwind. She found her paraphernalia and prepared her pipe the way she had done a hundred times, heating the ball of opium paste on the end of a needle over the lamp, then spreading the softened paste in the bowl of the pipe and inverting it over the flame till it vaporized. She inhaled slowly until she could take in no more then exhaled through her nose. That was the good thing about opium; no waiting around for something to happen. Relief was almost immediate. She closed her eyes and felt the blood in her veins go warm, her stomach muscles unclenched and whatever it was that had seemed so important didn't matter any more. Maybe she slept, maybe she didn't. When she came around, she felt calm and relaxed. Her head was clear, and her thoughts of Lily and Daniel were already a fading memory.

She watched the sun go down in a blaze of colour, then she got up and ran a bath. She felt like going out and being with lots of people. She didn't care who they were or whether she even liked them. She wanted to hear the noise of empty conversation and music played by a live orchestra where the musicians wore white dinner jackets and sat on a bandstand watching their leader wave a baton in the air. She wanted to drink very cold champagne and feel the bubbles run down her throat. She wanted to dance with a stranger and put her head on his shoulder, feeling the strength of his arm against her back. She wanted to fling her head back and laugh at his jokes as if he were the funniest man on earth. She wanted to meet his friends and laugh and talk then never see any of them again. She wanted an everlasting night in a ballroom that never closed with an orchestra that never stopped playing. She wanted no pauses for thought, no silent moments to question what she heard or saw, no tears, no regrets, no looking back, and no looking forward. She only wanted now.

Chapter Seventeen

The time for regret has come now, many years later. Now, as I watch the snow fall outside my window, I have too much time to think and to remember. I have begun to fill up the empty spaces in my life with all the things I tried to avoid in my youth. It's as if Time, the ugly monster that rides us all, has been waiting with all the saved-up memories he's been carefully storing. Waiting for me to falter, to pause long enough for him to throw it all back at me, all the things I thought I'd never have to see again. All those memories, piling up like the snow that won't stop falling.

If I could go back, are there things I would do differently? Oh, yes. I would say some of the things I didn't say at the time, and I would take back some of the things I did say. But that's not ever going to be possible. The damage has been done and those to whom it was done are all gone. I'm the only one left— except for Lily—so I get to tell the story my way and live with the consequences. I wonder if the story will change after Lily gets here. Has she her own secrets she's kept all these years?

But who's to say things would have turned out differently? By now I've come to realize that we delude ourselves if we think we have any control over anything, especially other people's lives. But if I had only paid more attention, if I had known my own mind, trusted myself more. If I had bothered to learn the lessons that were all around me. "If." Another word that shouldn't exist. An empty word, like "should", that leads only to false hope.

The fact is, I did all the wrong things, but I did them with the best of intentions, I'm sure of that. Still, you can't sit back for years, ignoring reality or hiding from it, then expect to understand what it is or how it works. I try to remember what it was that made me so uncaring and so careless. Had I been born that way? Had I just given in to my own nature? I ask Olga, "What was I really like? Did I have any character at all? Or was I always a weak, passive individual with no moral compass and no purpose?"

"Tatiana," she says, knowing for once that this is not the time to be honest but the time to be kind. "Don't punish yourself so much. You weren't a bad person. You just went in the wrong direction. You were headstrong and stubborn—like Anastasia, only worse." She laughs, thinking it will lighten the mood to compare me to my niece, who is beautiful, smart and funny. "You fell in with a bad crowd that you thought was glamorous, and you wanted to be like them. You were so young." Not fair, of course, to ask a sister such huge, important questions.

But Olga doesn't know the half of it. She remembers a sister who was a part of her own childhood. She remembers me before the war, before she married Jean Paul, before Anastasia and Nicholas were born. She doesn't know anything about after. Except perhaps for one conversation, a conversation that she has most likely forgotten. A conversation that precipitated an avalanche that destroyed a world. The "should" conversation, as I now call it.

~ ~

Almost a year would go by before Olga and Tatiana had the "should" conversation. She was to discover that Lily was, indeed, in love with Daniel. Lily told her one afternoon when they were having tea by the river at the Astor House. She had insisted they meet there, and Tatiana later wondered if she had purposely chosen this very public place to tell her something so personal.

"I love him," Lily said simply. "I can't help it. It's one of those things that just happens, and you can't do anything about it."

Tatiana was staring out the window at the river, with its filthy brown water that supported so many junks and sailboats and corrugated tin boats that were home to so many people. How many, she wondered? A thousand? Ten thousand? A million? She had no idea. They were the same boats she had seen from the deck of the ship when they'd arrived in Shanghai twenty years before.

"Does that mean you're not going to do anything about it?" She prayed Lily's answer would be yes.

"I don't know," Lily said. The boats on the river rocked gently back and forth, and Tatiana wondered what it would be like to spend your entire life on one. To grow up, have babies and grow old in a tiny, stinking space you shared with so many other people.

"This is awful," Tatiana said. She watched a single tear slip down Lily's cheek and realized this was probably the one situation her friend's upbringing had not prepared her for. There was no rule book on love, except the one that said adultery was grounds for divorce.

"You haven't…" Tatiana tried to say. "You didn't…"

"No," Lily said. "I haven't slept with him, if that's what you're asking." She was staring into her teacup with a look of intense sadness on her face. Then she looked up and smiled, but it was a sad smile. "I love him so much, Tatiana."

"How much?" Tatiana asked. "Enough to ruin your life over him?"

Lily couldn't answer. "Do you know why adultery is the worst sin a Chinese woman can commit?" she asked.

"No. Tell me."

"Because it can undermine the ancestry of her husband's family."

"But I thought a childless couple could adopt a boy from another family as their own."

"Yes," she said, "but only from the husband's bloodline. The most important thing is to maintain the ancestral line through the men in the family. If a married woman commits adultery and has a child that is not her husband's, she brings shame on his family."

"Do you love Wu-ling?"

"Not like this," she said. "But I was fond of him, and he was good to me." She looked out at the dirty river. Tatiana didn't like the fact that her friend was speaking in the past tense. "I would lose everything," she said. "I would lose my son."

"Then do you really have a choice?"

"No. There is no choice. Only suffering."

"What about Daniel?" Tatiana asked. "Does he love you?"

"I believe so," Lily said. She was looking into her teacup again. "I haven't asked him."

"But have you told him how you feel?"

"No, of course not," she said. "That would be foolish. But my heart is his, and I believe his heart is mine, and that may be enough."

"Oh, Lily," Tatiana said, "even I know that's not true."

Tatiana knew she didn't have the imagination to comprehend what Lily was going through, but she believed her friend was suffering and in the grip of an impossible dilemma. Chinese women had killed themselves and often their illegitimate babies because they were left with nothing after a divorce. They could not return to their parents' home because they had been disowned. If Wu-ling chose to divorce Lily, her fate would be no better than that of an unwanted girl baby. She would be shunned and condemned to a living hell that she would not be able to survive. Without her husband and her son, Lily did not exist as a person. Because of them, she had status and some measure of autonomy, at least in the raising of her son. But that was all she had.

And yet, Tatiana wondered, if the moment were right, if Daniel professed undying love, begged her to go away with him, say, to Paris or America, if she saw the possibility, the means, the escape…would she go?

If…if…if…
Since Tatiana had never been able to deal with her own problems, let alone someone else's, she was not much help to Lily. She could only listen and ask questions, but she couldn't give answers. Tatiana didn't see how sacrificing everything for one person could bring happiness. It was a romantic notion, and when it was used by writers and artists, it always led to glorious tragedy where everyone wept copious tears then died at centre stage. In reality, it meant getting up every morning and facing what you no longer had, because what you had gained wasn't enough to make up for losing it. And, although Tatiana didn't say it, she wondered if Daniel's shoulders were broad enough to bear the burden of Lily's loss. He was a young man with an obsession and a talent to play the piano. He needed to be free to pursue his art, wherever it might take him. She was sure that if Lily told him about her love for him, he would be crushed under its weight, unless he was as misguided by passion as she was. Then their mutual blindness could lead anywhere and possibly destroy them both.

But why, Tatiana asked herself, was she only thinking in terms of death and destruction? Why couldn't she find any joy in the possibility of the triumph of love over custom, culture and adversity? Wasn't there a small corner of her heart that wanted Lily and Daniel to explore and live true love? Had her heart turned to stone? Maybe she was misreading the messages that life was sending her. Maybe. But Tatiana was not happy about what Lily had told her. She felt a gloomy sense of unease. Not foreboding, but unease. She didn't think Lily would do anything foolish, but she could see her friend's life stretching before her in one long line of meaningless performance. She would do her duty, fulfill her obligations, as she always had, but now it would be with the knowledge of what might have been, the knowledge that leaves a bitter taste in the mouth and the grip of disappointment around the heart.

Chapter Eighteen

Tatiana said nothing to Annette, but instead waited to see if Annette would tell her that Daniel had confided in her. Lily had said that her heart was Daniel's, and she believed his heart was hers. Had she imagined it, or was she now privy to the language of love, one that was as foreign to Tatiana as Dutch? Would Daniel have confided such a thing to his mother? She realized she didn't know who his friends were or if he even had any. Did a young man tell his friends about true love, or did he just boast about his conquests? She hoped Lily's secret was safe.

Life went on for Tatiana without any changes as 1926 drew to a close. She was not looking forward to the arrival of 1927 because it would bring her thirtieth birthday in June of that year. When she looked in the mirror, she could see the tiny lines forming at the corners of her eyes and around her mouth. But that was only in the harshest daylight. In the evening, with her make-up freshly applied, she could pass for twenty-five. Tatiana was vain enough to think that nobody noticed or cared. She had always been so careful about her appearance. If a dress didn't fit perfectly, she discarded it. Her shoes always looked like she had just bought them. She had custom-made shoetrees for each pair so that they would hold their shape. She always carried an extra pair of silk stockings in her bag in case she snagged one of them. People took note of what she wore and complimented her on her fashion sense, but she knew that one day they would stop noticing. As she looked at the gently drooping faces of the once-beautiful Russian taxi dancers, or even Annette for that matter, she saw that once the slide had begun, it could not be reversed.

"*Chérie*," Annette said to her one night, a little drunkenly, "it's what's inside that counts. What does it matter if you have a few lines on your face? Beauty comes from within. Everybody knows that."

They were sitting in Annette's dim little parlour sipping English sherry, one of her favourite drinks. Tatiana had been to visit her mother that day and was full of helpless despair. Katarina seemed to be fading away before their eyes, and there was nothing they could do about it. All that was left of her life was regret and unhappiness. She was not even sixty years old, but she might as well have been ninety. It made no difference any more. The best of her life had ended decades ago, and Sergei's death had written the penultimate chapter. All that remained now was her own dying.

Tatiana was particularly disheartened and didn't have the energy to tell Annette the real reason for her gloomy mood. She remembered Sergei reading them *The Picture of Dorian Gray* when she and Olga were children, so she told Annette the story of the ever-beautiful Dorian Gray, whose evil and corrupt soul was reflected in the changing face of the portrait he kept hidden in his attic.

"I wish I had such a portrait in my attic," Tatiana told her, "that would age while I stayed young."

Annette laughed. "You would get tired of youth, eventually," she said. "The only thing the young have is their beauty. They have not lived. They have no experience, no memories except childish ones, no stories of great joy or great sadness to tell, no love affairs to fuel the heart and keep them warm on cold nights."

"Precisely."

Annette burst into laughter, as if Tatiana had told the funniest joke in the world. "You are wonderful, *chérie*. I have not laughed like this in ages."

"I don't see what's so funny," Tatiana said. "What's so

wonderful about getting old? Accumulating memories so you can think about the past while your body and your mind decay?"

"Don't say that, *chérie*," Annette said, suddenly becoming serious. "That's so sad. Everybody gets old. You may as well have something good to remember when that's all you're able to do. How tragic to reach the end of your life and think only of regret and unhappiness." She was quiet for a moment and then asked, "What happens at the end of this Dorian Gray story?"

"He tries to destroy the portrait, thinking that he will also be destroying all the terrible things in his conscience, but by slashing the portrait, he kills himself."

"Ah," said Annette, "he thought he could separate his soul from himself. That he could kill one without killing the other."

"Yes, I suppose so."

Annette did not speak for several minutes. Finally she said, "What is it you regret so much that you can't talk about it?"

"Nothing," said Tatiana. "I don't know what you're talking about. It's a story, a book, written a long time ago."

"It's a book, yes, but the story does not stop being written."

Tatiana finished her sherry and stood up. "I have to go," she said.

It was cold as she walked away from Annette's house. The Shanghai winter cold was damp and icy and went right to the marrow of her bones. *I should buy a fur coat*, Tatiana thought, as the piercing sleet blew into her face and felt like sharp little needles against her skin. *This is the real definition of misery*, she told herself. *Not those unhappy love stories that end in tragedy, but this bone-chilling greyness that lasts for weeks and doesn't let up. Hell is not a pit of eternal fire. It's a freezing cold, endless winter without light or heat, without even the faintest memory of warmth.*

She couldn't find a taxi, or even a rickshaw, which was unusual, but, given the slippery film of ice that was accumulating underfoot, it was understandable. People were in a hurry to get home, so cabs were scarce. She turned into a teashop to warm up and found a table near the back. Her tea came when she was halfway through a cigarette, and she gratefully bent her face into the steam and wrapped her hands around the cup.

"Hullo," she heard an English voice say. She looked up. "I guess you don't remember me," he said. "We met about a year and a half ago at the Shanghai Club." Tatiana looked at him blankly. "Name's Ian," he continued. "Ian McCaffrey? You were with a bunch of your pals, and I stopped by to say hello to one of them. You and I spent some time together and got on quite well until that little incident in the taxi. Remember? Bloody student riot in the street? Gunfire and all?"

"Oh, yes," she said, remembering the tall, broad-shouldered man with the pencil moustache, dark blond hair and ruddy face. How could she forget? They'd shared one of the most frightening evenings of her life. "Still living in…Bombay, is it?" she asked.

"Actually, just quit the place. On my way to Malaya. Thought I'd stop off for a few weeks. Bit of a holiday. Visit some friends."

"Ah," she said vaguely, trying not to encourage him. She wasn't in the mood.

"Taken a job as manager. Rubber plantation in Malaya. Contract starts in a month."

"Ah," she said again. She nodded her head and smiled wanly. Tatiana had no desire for conversation, let alone to rekindle a relationship that she considered over.

"Um, mind if I sit down?" he persisted.

"Well, all right, but I'll be leaving in a few minutes."

"Bloody awful out there. I wouldn't be rushing off anywhere if I were you. Might slip and break your leg. Wouldn't want that, now, would we?" He laughed heartily at what he must have thought was a joke.

"No," she said. "We wouldn't."

"So," he said. "I'm uh…sorry, but…I've forgotten your name."

"Tatiana," she said reluctantly.

"Just Tatiana?"

"Just Tatiana."

"Ah yes," he said. "Russian." He was determined to have a conversation. Cold and unfriendly as Tatiana was, it was colder and more unfriendly outside.

"Yes," she said, "Russian."

She saw his eyes shift focus as he tried to find another conversational tactic. "I remember," he said, brightening. "Came here with your family, right? New beginning and all that. Right place at the right time, I always say. Sometimes that's all it takes." She nodded, and he signalled for a pot of tea, holding up two fingers. He was expecting her to stay and chat.

"I really must go," she said, starting to get up.

"Oh, please don't go," he said rather urgently. "Stay and talk for a bit. It's damn miserable out there. Besides, where do you have to go that's so important?"

Tatiana looked out the window. It was dark, and the sleet striking the glass sounded like bullets hitting their mark. "All right," she said. "But just until it stops."

"Good," he said, evidently relieved.

The tea arrived, and they drifted through a conversation about many things. He reminded her that he'd done a stint with the Indian civil service, monitoring goods going through customs at the port of Bombay. "Mostly paperwork. But sometimes it got interesting. Little bit of contraband now and then that somebody thought they could smuggle in. Gets to be a game after a while. Spot the smuggler." He laughed. "It's usually the well-dressed *pukka sahibs* you have to watch, not the oily types who look like criminals. Officials always give them a hard time, but a smart criminal knows it's best not to stand out. Nice and clean, good clothes, quiet, patient manner. Almost invisible they blend in so well. Except," he continued, raising an eyebrow and bending toward her as if he were conveying some top-secret information, "there's always a look in their eyes. Wary-like, if you know what I mean. Always watching. Eyes flicking around the room, never resting. That's how I spotted them every time. Watch the eyes. Dead giveaway." He sat back and hooked his thumbs into his suspenders. "Dead giveaway."

Tatiana remembered how easy it was to have a conversation with Ian McCaffrey. He did all the talking. She just had to decide whether to really listen or merely pretend to. Either way, it took the same amount of energy. But if she only pretended to listen, her mind would drift back into her own thoughts, and she didn't want to go where they led. Ian provided a distraction.

"Decided I'd had enough of India and all the malarkey," he was saying. "So one day I just up and quit. Said, 'I've had enough, chaps. Time to move on.' That's when I came across an ad for this job in Malaya. Nice and quiet, I thought. Away from all this stuff and nonsense."

"I thought you said you enjoyed catching the criminals. That it was a game."

"I did enjoy it," he said. "For a dozen years or so. But a man gets tired of doing the same old thing, year in and year out. Once you can do the job with one eye shut and both hands tied behind your back, you want a bit of a challenge. When this Malaya thing dropped into my lap, I thought, there's the ticket. Manage a rubber plantation. Nice house in the jungle. A couple of servants and a few workers. Be the big boss and make the rules for a change, instead of following them."

The sleet had stopped tapping on the window, and Tatiana picked up her gloves and handbag. Ian reached forward and grabbed her free hand. "Care for a spot of supper?" he asked. "Wouldn't mind a bit of company tonight. And our last date was rather rudely interrupted, if you recall." He smiled. "I still owe you dinner."

She thought it over for a minute or two. She really had no plans for the evening, other than the usual. And frankly, she was getting a bit bored with the usual. Why not? He just wanted to talk, and Tatiana wanted someone to distract her from the things she didn't want to think about. "All right," she said. "But just dinner. Then I'm going home."

"Fair enough," he said and smiled like a drowning man who'd just grabbed onto something that was still floating.

They went to a small place in the French Concession that had pretensions of being Parisian and served a very nice bouillabaisse with crusty bread and real butter. Ian ordered a bottle of champagne, which was easier than picking through a list of unfamiliar wines. Tatiana told him she liked champagne, and he was pleased with himself for having chosen well.

They returned to the topic of the rubber plantation and its remoteness from civilization, which he said he was looking forward to.

"What about your wife?" she ventured. She couldn't remember if he was married or not. "Will she mind the isolation?"

"Ah, there's the problem. Haven't got a wife. Not really the marrying kind."

"Won't you be lonely out there with no one to talk to?"

"Don't know till I try it," he said. "Might go stark raving mad. It happens, they tell me. Chaps go out into the jungle for a few years, and they're never seen again."

"Well," she said, "maybe you should find a wife before you go. Someone to keep you company."

"Are you volunteering?" he said.

Tatiana laughed for the first time in days. "Good heavens, no," she said. "I'm not the marrying kind, either. I'm just giving you some free advice."

"Well, it might work out then. We're two peas in a pod. What say we give it a try? Are you game, then?"

"Not on your life," she said. "You won't catch me going into the jungle. Not for anything in the world. I like Shanghai too much. Besides, I like to go out and dance and have fun."

"Oh, come on," he said, and she could tell he was making a game of it, "don't know till you try. I've got an old phonograph. We could go dancing every night."

"Thanks for the offer," she said, "but I think I'll pass."

"Too bad," he said. "Chance of a lifetime, and you're throwing it away." He shook his head, and Tatiana decided to change the subject.

"How do you like the bouillabaisse?" she asked.

Chapter Nineteen

Tatiana was home by nine o'clock and was just about to run a hot bath when the phone rang. It was one of her nightclubbing friends, Michel, who liked to frequent the cabarets where transvestites and homosexuals hung out. He always said the best floorshow in town was not the one on stage but the one put on by the patrons.

"Darling," he said, in his exaggerated faux English accent. "There's something I think you should see."

"Not tonight, Michel," she said. "I'm too tired. I'm going to take a bath and go to bed."

"No, you're not," said Michel. "You're going to meet me at the Klub Kitty Kat for a drink. Don't disappoint me."

"Michel…" He hung up before she could say any more.

Damn, thought Tatiana. She really didn't want to go out again, but something in Michel's voice told her it was important. If it turned out to be a stupid joke, she'd wring his neck.

She changed her clothes, made sure she had enough cigarettes in her bag and went down to the street to hail a cab. The night was icy clear and cold. The one good thing about winter was that all the puddles froze and the rotten stink of decaying waste and death got trapped under the ice like carp in a frozen pond. Once again, she reminded herself to buy a fur coat. She would not spend another winter in Shanghai without one.

The Kitty Kat was lit up like a carnival midway. The outline of a large cat was strung with flashing white lights on the building's façade. A canopy over the sidewalk emerged from between the cat's front and hind legs, and a red carpet led from the curb to the front door, which was painted to look like leopard skin. The doorman wore a black fur coat, and when he reached out to open the door of the cab, Tatiana saw he was wearing leopard-skin gloves. In any other city in the world, this would have seemed outrageous. In Shanghai, however, it was tastefully understated.

The Klub Kitty Kat was a place where men could be women and women could be men, and they could all come together in an infinite number of combinations. Smoke hung in the air like a gauze curtain behind which the patrons could hide their true identities. Some of the men wore more make-up than the women, and it was startling to see how beautiful they looked. In some cases, it was only the broadness of their shoulders or a telltale Adam's apple that gave them away. The dance floor was crowded with couples clinging tightly to each other, some in tuxedos, some in evening gowns, some barely dressed at all.

Tatiana searched the room for Michel and finally saw him on the other side of the dance floor with a group of young men. As she got closer, she saw they were mostly Chinese and all elegantly dressed in black trousers and white dinner jackets. They all wore make-up, which seemed to render them sexless. Michel, forty if he was a day, also wore make-up but looked like an old hag.

"Darling," he screeched when he saw her. He jumped up and planted phantom kisses on both her cheeks. "You should have worn more make-up," he said, examining her face. "You look positively ill."

"Shut up," she said. "You should have your eyebrows plucked. You look like an old school mistress."

"Oooh," he said, relishing the idea. "Think of the possibilities. 'It's time for class, everybody!'" He cackled like an old witch, and the young men around the table giggled.

"Now," she said, picking up a glass of champagne, "what's this all about? What am I supposed to see?"

Michel turned his head toward a table about thirty feet away, where a group of young men, much like the group surrounding Michel, except that about half of them were Europeans, was laughing and talking. Some of them had paired off, and their arms were flung over each other's shoulders.

"So?" said Tatiana. "More friends of yours? Do you want me to pick one of them up for you?"

"Very funny," he said. "I can do my own picking up, thank you." He pursed his painted lips, arched his bushy, pencilled eyebrows and pretended to be offended. "Look again," he said. "Isn't that Daniel? Annette's son?"

"What?" she snorted, nearly choking on her champagne. "What would Daniel be doing in a place like this?"

"Calm down, darling," Michel said between clenched teeth. "We don't want to upset the clientele and get thrown out."

"Please," she said. "I've been thrown out of better places than this. Have you brought me here just to upset me?"

"No, darling, no," he said soothingly. "I just thought since you and Annette were such good friends, you should be the one to tell her."

"Tell her what?" Tatiana persisted.

"Look, darling. If it isn't Daniel, just say so and go home. But if it is …"

"If it is, what? What am I supposed to do? Spank him and send him home?"

"No, darling. Don't be ridiculous. If there's any spanking to do, I'll do it." He smiled and put his cigarette holder in her mouth. "Now, take a nice deep puff and look again."

She inhaled on the cigarette and looked over Michel's shoulder at the table of young men. One of them was staring intently into the eyes of his partner, a handsome young Chinese man in a tuxedo. Tatiana felt the hairs on her arms stand up. Suddenly the Chinese man leaned forward and kissed Daniel passionately on the lips. She couldn't take her eyes off them, and, after a couple of minutes, Daniel pulled his head back and turned to look right at her. His lips were red, the same colour lipstick his mother wore, and his eyes were rimmed with kohl, giving them a lost, angry look. He kept his gaze on hers, and his fierce expression said only one thing. *Don't. Don't say anything. Don't do anything.* Then she saw something else in his eyes, and she understood that he was begging her. *Please. Go away.* "Oh, God," she whispered.

"It *is* him, isn't it?" Michel sounded excited, as if he'd just discovered a gold mine. "Are you going to tell Annette?"

The Chinese man turned and looked at her. His eyes were cold and hard and shone like ice in moonlight. She looked at Daniel again. He had turned to face the mirrored wall beside him. He was watching her, and his kohl-rimmed eyes were filled with pain. She suddenly felt very tired and very sad. It wasn't Annette she was thinking of. It was Lily.

Chapter Twenty

You should tell her," Olga said. "She should know about this so she can decide what to do."

Tatiana had told Olga everything the next day, because she had no one else to confide in. She hadn't slept a wink, and her heart and head were pounding from anxiety. After she had torn herself away from Michel and the Kitty Kat, Tatiana had taken a cab back to her apartment and smoked three pipes, something she had never done before. *This can't be happening*, she thought. It wasn't that she was upset about Daniel or his behaviour. After all, who was she to talk? But all she could think about was Lily and how Daniel didn't love her the way she thought he did, and that it would break her heart if she found out.

Olga had listened patiently to the whole story without interrupting. Tatiana reminded her of how she herself had introduced Daniel to Lily as a possible tutor for Leonard and how well Leonard was doing with Daniel as his teacher. How Lily and Wu-ling had arranged concerts for Daniel, and how he was becoming better known because of it. How Lily had confessed her love for Daniel, and, finally, how she'd told Tatiana that she believed he loved her, too.

"How can I tell her something that will hurt her more than anything?" she said to Olga. "It would be so cruel." Her sister was embroidering the edges of a tablecloth with dark red thread. It was a favourite pastime of hers, and even Tatiana had to admit that her delicate stitches were never less than perfect.

"It's the truth that matters," Olga said, looking up from her work. "Only the truth matters."

"But why does she have to know? Why can't she just go on living with her fantasy if it makes her happy?"

"If she finally knows the truth, then she can get on with her life and leave this behind. Isn't that better than wasting your life on a fantasy?" Olga was tying the thread in a small knot where the pattern ended.

"I don't know, Olushka. I wish it were that clear to me. But I honestly don't know which is worse."

"Listen," said Olga, putting the tablecloth down, "I would want to know. I wouldn't want my son taking piano lessons from someone who might seduce him."

"What?" Tatiana couldn't believe she was hearing this from her own sister. "Daniel wouldn't do that," she said. "He would never do that."

"How do you know?" Olga countered. "You didn't know about his, his, whatever you want to call it. Why do you think you know anything about him?" She picked up a small pair of scissors and cut the thread close to the knot.

"I've known him since he was a little boy," Tatiana said. "He's a sweet, gentle young man."

"Who happens to like other young men," said Olga. "And how do you know that doesn't include sweet young boys, too?"

"Olga," she said. "That's disgusting. You're making assumptions and judging him guilty of things you know nothing about."

"Listen, Tatiana. I know Annette is your friend. And Lily is your friend. And even Daniel is your friend. And now you know something about one of them that can affect all of them. The best thing you can do for your friends is to tell them the truth."

"I'm not sure I agree with that," said Tatiana. "Why should I tell a truth that is very hurtful and can do a lot of damage? Why do I have to say anything at all? Why is it up to me? It's really none of my business."

"I can't believe you're saying that, Tatiana. You have an obligation. The truth is the truth. What if something terrible happens because you didn't say anything?" Olga had cut a length of green thread and was now passing it expertly through the eye of the needle.

"You're being melodramatic," Tatiana said. "Nothing terrible is going to happen."

"No. *You're* being melodramatic. You're acting as if nothing's changed and things will simply go on as they did before. But they won't."

"But what they don't know won't hurt them."

"Where did you get that idea? Of course it can hurt them. And it can hurt Leonard, who is the most innocent one of all."

"You're just saying that because you're a mother, and you always see disaster, even when it isn't there."

Olga rolled her eyes and took a deep breath. "Look," she said, "of course I'm thinking from a mother's point of view. And so will Lily. Her first concern will be for her son, and that's as it should be."

"Should, should, should," said Tatiana. "I'm sick of should. What gives you the right to dictate who should and shouldn't do what?"

"Tatiana," Olga said sternly, "you asked me. And I told you what I think you should do. If you don't want to take my advice, I can't force you. But, clearly, this episode has upset you, or you wouldn't have told me about it. You're on the horns of a dilemma, and I'm only trying to help."

"I know," Tatiana said, deflated. "I'm sorry. You're right. There's a part of me that thinks I should tell Lily for her own good and a part of me that feels it would be wrong. That I would be interfering or telling tales. What if Daniel was just doing this for the first and only time? What if he was just experimenting or out for a lark with his friends?"

Olga looked at her. "You're joking, of course," she said.

"But if you're not sure, then you should ask him. Tell him you saw him at the Pussy Cat, or whatever it's called, and you want to know what's going on."

"I can't do that. He'd be mortified. He'd think I was spying on him. Then I'd be mortified."

"You can't have it both ways, Tatiana. Either you want to know the truth, or you don't. You can't be squeamish when it comes to the truth."

"What is this 'truth' you keep talking about? You're always talking in absolutes, like the world is black and white. It's not, Olushka. There are many shades of grey."

"Maybe in your world," she said, "but not in mine." Olga began pulling the green thread through the fabric of the tablecloth.

"Well, that's where we're different, then. I'm not sure what's right and what's wrong. Or even if there is a right or wrong."

"That's your problem, Tati." Olga's voice was surprisingly gentle. "You don't know what's right and what's wrong, and you're ruining your life because of it. Don't ruin Lily's life, too."

Tatiana was suddenly angry with her sister for being so certain. Olga was like a brick wall. How could she be so certain about things? She would never budge, not one inch, and she acted like she was judge and jury about everything. What gave her the right? And yet Tatiana had come to her sister. knowing she had always been like that. She had come looking for certainty, and Olga had given it to her. And now she didn't know what to do with it. Was Olga right when she said Tatiana's uncertainty was ruining her life? Would she be ruining Lily's life if she didn't tell her about Daniel? Or would she ruin Lily's life by telling her what she knew? She felt like she was walking on the edge of a knife.

In the end, with Olga's "shoulds" ringing in her ears, Tatiana did tell Lily. And, as she had predicted, her friend was distraught. Tatiana tried as gently as she could to tell her that it was nobody's fault, that Daniel couldn't love her the way she wanted him to. That she, Tatiana, was sure he was very fond of her, and grateful for everything she'd done for him, but that he was homosexual and loved other men. That's just the way it was.

No, Lily kept saying. It's not true. I won't believe it. I know his heart is mine.

"Why, Tatiana? Why are you telling me this? How can you be sure it was Daniel? That man was wearing make-up. How could you recognize him? Daniel would never wear make-up. He would never go to that place."

"Oh, Lily," Tatiana said. "I wish this weren't happening. I wish I had never gone to the Kitty Kat and seen him. Then everything would still be the way it was. You'd still have your dream, and I wouldn't have taken it away from you."

But she had gone back to the Kitty Kat two more times, just to make sure, and both times he avoided her and wouldn't even look at her. But Tatiana knew it was him. She knew by the tilt of his head, by the way he swept back his hair with his beautifully shaped fingers. She had watched him grow up. She knew the line of his jaw, the shape of his nose and his ears, so perfectly flat against the side of his head. She had known that first night when the tremor of recognition had travelled through her body. She had not been mistaken.

~ ~

To this day, I cannot unravel the thought process by which I came to the decision to tell Lily. I agonized over my decision as I had never done before. I wished a hundred times that my father had been alive so I could talk to him about it. Papa would know what advice to give me. As a rebellious young woman, I had destroyed the relationship we'd once had. I used to climb onto his knee and ask him anything, and he would

always take his time and give me an answer that satisfied
me completely. I needed that kind of guidance now, and not
the black-and-white absoluteness of Olga's words. I needed
someone to lead me through the forest of my own thoughts so
I could find out what was in my heart. The fact that I was thirty
years old and had no idea what to do or no one to turn to also
tore me apart. Several times I thought of going to Annette and
telling her, but I didn't know where to begin. If Annette was
as fierce a mother as Olga, she would not stop loving her son.
I was pretty sure of that. But, on the other hand, if her love for
her son was blind to everything outside of their history together,
she might turn against me and hate me for betraying Daniel's
secret. What did she care about Lily and Lily's obsession? Why
should that be her concern?

At the bottom of it all was my fear that, because of my own
ineptness and lack of moral character, I would lose both my
friends. And, in fact, that is what happened. But not in the way I
had expected. Not at all in that way.

Chapter Twenty-One

Tatiana went back to see Lily every afternoon for a week. She was worried, but she also felt a terrible guilt, as if it had all been her fault. True, she had introduced Daniel to Lily as a teacher for Leonard, but how could she have known what it would lead to? She had only the best of intentions, she kept reminding herself, but her father's words rang in her ears: "Hell is paved with good intentions, Tatiana. As the English like to say, actions speak louder than words. You would be wise to remember that." Well, she had acted, hadn't she? And what she had done was threatening to overwhelm all of her so-called good intentions. Tatiana did not understand that her guilt was a result of having acted against her better judgment. By listening to Olga, she had let her sister make the decision for her, thinking it would absolve her of responsibility. But it didn't work that way. In fact, Tatiana was being eaten alive by the monster she had created.

Lily was inconsolable. Tatiana couldn't seem to reach her, no matter what she said. Lily cried every time they were together, and Tatiana could not comprehend the depth of her anguish. It seemed to her like an overreaction, but she had never been in love like that. She didn't know what it was like to lose someone that way. It wasn't just that he didn't love her, it was that she had been so wrong about him—that was the part that cut so deep. Over the course of the next few days, Tatiana watched her friend change from a brokenhearted lover to a tortured soul.

"Don't do this to yourself," Tatiana pleaded. She tried everything to distract Lily from her self-flagellation. "You know how they say that love is blind. Well, you were just blinded by your love for Daniel. It doesn't mean you're stupid or crazy. Just normal. Like everybody else." When platitudes didn't work, she said, "Lily, this is just not like you. You're being so, so…"

"Un-Chinese?" Lily offered.

"Yes," she said. "Un-Chinese. You're frightening me."

"I can't help it. I've never felt like this. I feel as if I betrayed myself. Do you know what that feels like? To betray yourself?"

"Yes," she said. "I think I do."

"No, you don't. You don't know what it feels like. Otherwise, you would be overwhelmed by such a feeling of sadness that you would be suffocating under it. You would be incapable of pulling yourself out of the deep hole I've fallen into. That's what you would feel like."

They were in Lily's sitting room. Lily's amah, always hovering in the background, had built a fire in the small pot-bellied stove. The kindling must have been damp because a light haze of smoke drifted above their heads. The room was too hot but Lily was wrapped in a heavy woollen shawl that reached her knees. Tatiana's eyes stung from the smoky dryness of the air.

"If you can't do this for yourself," Tatiana said, "do it for your son. For Leonard. Don't you owe it to him to pull yourself together?" Tatiana couldn't believe it was her voice that was saying those words. She, who had been unable to pull her life together, was now counselling Lily to do the same.

Talking about Leonard only seemed to make things worse. Lily just shook her head repeatedly, saying, "No, no, no. Not my baby. Not Leonard."

"Lily, please," Tatiana said. "Please. Come back."

If Lily sought the oblivion of some undefined hell, Tatiana looked for relief in the constant chatter of the cabarets, in smoking and drinking until her lungs felt heavy and her head felt light. Years of practice had taught her to close her mind to unpleasant experiences. She could turn herself on and off like a faucet. It was what she did. Years before, she had asked Annette how she could be with so many faceless men and still look in the mirror and see herself.

"*Chérie,*" her friend had said. "It's not so difficult. I just close my eyes and imagine something else. The diamond bracelet I will be wearing tomorrow, or how beautiful I will look in that *jolie* robe I saw in the shop window. Sometimes I imagine Daniel in Paris, giving a concert. It's a small price to pay. Besides, would I rather work in a shop all day? Standing on my feet being polite to fat old women I hate?"

So Tatiana imagined the fur coat she would finally buy that winter. If Annette could escape unpleasantness by living in a fantasy world of her own creation, so could Tatiana. If she couldn't make the unpleasantness go away, she could pretend for a while that it didn't exist.

One night, Tatiana ran into Ian McCaffrey again. She saw him crossing the dance floor of the Majestic to get to her table. "Hullo," he said. "Fancy meeting you here."

Tatiana laughed with a little too much hilarity and greeted him like an old friend. "Ian," she shouted over the din of the music and the jabbering, "how've you been?"

"Fine," he said. "Splendid, in fact. Off to Malaya in a couple of weeks."

"Good, good," she said, as if she meant it.

"Any chance of a bit of lunch tomorrow?" he asked, raising his eyebrows.

"Sure. Why not?"

"Good. Shanghai Club? One o'clock?"

"Yes. See you there." Tatiana wagged two fingers at him and smiled till her face hurt.

She had no particular desire to see Ian the next day, but it was a week for saying yes to everything. She wanted to banish all negative thoughts, and imagined she could do that by agreeing to anything that came her way. It was hard work and took a lot of energy to keep up, but time was flying by. The less time there was to think, the fewer negative thoughts could squeeze into the cracks. Besides, she told herself, Ian wasn't such bad company. A bit boring, but the sort who could keep himself amused if no one else was listening. And it was only lunch.

Ian was already seated at a table by the window when she got there, and he signalled for the waiter as soon as he saw her come in. Tatiana ordered a gin and tonic and let her coat slip off her shoulders onto the back of the chair. The room was large and half empty, a sea of white tablecloths and white-coated waiters with white towels over one arm. She looked up at the white ceiling and shivered.

"Another beastly day," Ian said, looking out the wide, wood-framed window at the grey February sky spilling snowflakes like feathers from a burst pillow. "Seems whenever we meet, the weather's bad."

"That's just because it's winter," she said. "If it were summer…"

He laughed. "It would be beastly, stinking hot. The river would be putrid and we'd be sweating like horses."

"Excuse me," she said in a prissy voice. "Ladies don't sweat. We perspire."

He laughed again. "Quite right," he said. "Quite right. What about spring? Shall we try again in the spring?"

"You'll be in Malaya," Tatiana reminded him. "A long way to go for lunch."

"Might be worth the trip," he said. "You might like it there."

"In the jungle?"

"I guarantee there'd be no snow."

"That's true," she agreed, leaning forward while he lit her cigarette. "Just snakes and frogs and lions and tigers."

"Well, snakes for sure. I'll have to let you know about the rest. Not sure about the lions. Thought they were only in Africa."

They parried and bantered a bit longer and ordered some lunch. He wanted roast beef, he said, and Tatiana chose chicken with cream sauce in a pastry shell. She didn't have the energy to chew on red meat.

She didn't know whether it was the white tablecloths and the snow outside or just the fact that she didn't know another soul in that large dining room and Ian was starting to feel like an old friend, but she began to tell him about her hypothetical friend and her hypothetical problem of being in love with a homosexual man. Once she started talking, it all came spilling out like water down a drainpipe. She couldn't stop it.

"What would you do if you had a friend who was spiralling out of control over some hopeless, lovesick affair of the heart?"

"You mean if I were you?" he asked.

"Yes. I suppose. If you were me."

"Don't know," he said, scratching his chin and looking at a spot just above the top of her head. "Suppose I'd give her a good talking to. Tell her to stop being foolish."

"And if that didn't work?"

He lowered his eyes and looked into hers. "That bad, is it?" he said.

She nodded.

"What about the fellow?" he asked. "Can't he talk to her? Tell her it's just not on?"

"I'm not even sure he knows how in love with him she is."

"You couldn't put in a word, I suppose? Let him know what's going on?"

"No, I couldn't," she said. "I just couldn't."

"Then it's got to be nature taking its course," he said. "Time's the only thing that'll fix it. Time, the great healer and all that."

Time. How much time? And why did she feel there wasn't enough time in the world to bring Lily back?

Tatiana felt only slightly better for having unburdened herself. At least Ian hadn't laughed at her or told her she was being foolish. He'd actually been rather kind and had taken her dilemma seriously. He hadn't talked in absolutes like Olga. He'd let her talk and had appeared sympathetic, as she imagined her father would be. She'd thrown out a line, and he had caught it, briefly, and tied her boat to the dock. She was still bobbing up and down in deep water, but she wasn't being tossed around by huge waves of fear and doubt. She no longer felt like she might drown.

Ian ordered some sort of custard for dessert, and Tatiana asked for a pot of coffee. They lingered over the coffee, smoking cigarettes and watching the snow accumulate outside. Ian started talking about the political situation in China and how he was glad to be leaving. "Bloody labour unions," he said. "Don't know if you noticed, but there was a strike here that lasted for two days. Practically shut down the whole city."

"No, I didn't notice," she said. "I don't go out much in the daytime. Especially to this part of town."

"Well," he said, "you'd be well advised to keep an ear to the ground. The Kuomintang's in bed with the Communists, and Chiang's determined to use them to help wipe out the warlords. But never trust a commie, I say. They're as likely to stab you in the back as anyone. Things are going to heat up around here soon, and it could get ugly. Don't you have someplace you can go until it all blows over?"

"No," she said. "I live here, and so does my family. I'm certainly not going back to Russia, or whatever it's called now."

Ian smiled indulgently. "No, I wouldn't advise going there. I was thinking maybe London or Paris. There's lots of displaced Russian royalty hanging around the Champs Elysées." He pronounced it Shomps Elleezay. "Must be somebody who can put you up." Tatiana thought this was very funny and told him she thought not. She had no desire to hang around with Russians in Paris or anywhere, for that matter. Royalty or otherwise.

"Listen," he said. "I know it's a long shot, but you never know. If you ever do feel like leaving this godforsaken city, or you're passing through Malaya and want to see a bit of jungle, I'll give you my address. Send me a note or a cable, or just come. I'd like to see you again."

"All right," she said. "Why not? I've never been to the jungle."

"There's always a first time," he said.

Down on the Bund, Ian hailed her a cab, and she waved goodbye, wondering if she'd ever see him again but not really caring either way. But in the following days, she caught herself thinking about him and wanting to see him again. He was a decent man, or bloke, as the English said, and she didn't have many decent men friends who were kind and willing to listen to her troubles. But Ian McCaffrey was just passing through her life, she decided, going in the opposite direction. Still, she was grateful to him for letting her talk about her hypothetical friend and her hypothetical problem. He hadn't asked too many questions and hadn't handed her morality on a platter.

The taxi pulled up in front of her apartment building, and she handed the driver the exact change. The snow was already a good four inches deep, and she stepped gingerly from the car, trying not to ruin her leather shoes. There was a canopy over the sidewalk in front of the building, but the snow had drifted into little piles under it. As the cab pulled away, two men in heavy black overcoats approached her from both sides and, taking her elbows in their gloved hands, propelled her to a waiting car and shoved her into the back seat. She barely had time to react before the two men got into the front seat and the car pulled away from the curb. It drove back in the direction she had just come from.

"What's going on?" Tatiana shouted. The men ignored her. She tried opening the door, but it must have been locked from the outside. It was a useless exercise anyway, because the car was moving too fast for her to jump out. It drove back along the Bund into the business and banking district. The road was icy, and the car was going too fast for Tatiana's comfort, swerving between rickshaws and carts and other vehicles. It skidded to a stop in front of a monumental stone building with rows and rows of identical oblong windows. The men got out of the car and one unlocked the door on the street side. Tatiana was pulled from the back seat, again by the elbows, and escorted through the front doors and into a solid brass-fronted elevator. They ascended to the eleventh floor, and the heavy doors slid open without a sound. The two nearly identical men were still holding her by the elbows. During the ride in the elevator, she finally had a chance to see their faces. They were both Chinese, of the tall, heavy-set Northern type, and they looked like they could break her in half without blinking an eye.

They escorted her down a long hall with polished marble floors and equally polished marble walls. Heavy wooden doors, all closed, were evenly spaced along both sides of the hallway. The man on her left opened one of the unmarked doors, and she was half pushed and half pulled into a medium-size antechamber with dark red carpets and sombre leather armchairs. The air was stale and dusty. They continued forward to another door—by this time Tatiana's elbows were starting to hurt—and the man on her right opened it. Her escorts pushed Tatiana into the room, still holding on to her. The man behind the desk nodded, and they let go of her arms, which dropped to her sides like lead weights.

The man behind the desk was Number Two Brother. He was immaculately dressed in a beautifully tailored grey suit and a white shirt whose collar and cuffs were stiffly starched. Each of his gold cufflinks had a blood-red ruby embedded in the centre. Tatiana noticed his manicure, his gold watch, which peeked from under his left cuff, and the brilliantined black hair that was combed straight back from his face, one that she had known since childhood. But now that face was hard and cruel, with sharp angles and thin lips. The eyes that looked at her from beneath their stretched lids were black and unfriendly, like two flat slivers of slate.

The two men in overcoats had receded into the background but two more men, also tall and solid-looking, stood on either side of Number Two Brother's high-backed leather chair. Their expressions were cold and indifferent, as if it didn't matter to them whether she lived or died. The air in the room was warm, but Tatiana felt a chill creep up her spine, and she wished again that she had a fur coat.

"What's this all about?" she asked, although she didn't feel as bold as she sounded. It seemed important to speak first and not to let him think she was afraid.

"You are not to see my sister again," he said.

"What did you say?"

"You heard me. My brother-in-law tells me that she is upset every time you visit. You are to leave her alone."

"She's my best friend," said Tatiana. "I'll see her whenever I want."

"No," he said, firmly. "You will not."

"Don't be ridiculous. You can't stop me from seeing her."

She had irritated him. His eyes flashed in anger, but only briefly. His manicured hands were resting on the desk in front of him and showed no sign of the tension he was likely feeling. He was as still as a block of granite. "Yes, actually, I can stop you from seeing her."

"How?" she demanded.

He smiled. "You don't want to find out," he said, and the smile vanished.

"Are you threatening me?" It occurred to Tatiana that she

was being reckless, but he was Lily's brother, after all. They had grown up together.

"No, Tatiana"—it was the first time he'd said her name—"I'm not threatening you. How could you suggest such a thing? I'm asking you not to see Lily any more. You're upsetting her."

"I don't understand," she said. "I'm her friend."

"Not any more, you're not. That's over."

"Did Lily tell you that?"

He didn't reply. His hard stare made her shiver again. What was going on?

"I mean it," he said. "Don't make me tell you again." He tilted his head to one side in a quick motion of dismissal, and the two henchmen in overcoats stepped out of the shadows. Tatiana jerked her arms from their grasp and wrapped them tightly around her body. "Don't touch me," she shouted. "This is outrageous." She stared hard into Number Two Brother's eyes for a full minute. He didn't blink.

"Tatiana," he said softly. "Prostitutes disappear every day."

She felt a sharp pain in her shoulders as both arms were yanked behind her back, and she was half-lifted off the ground and pulled out the door. She kept her eyes locked on his, turning her head to look over her aching shoulder.

"I am not a prostitute!" she shouted as the door slammed in her face.

Chapter Twenty-Two

Three days later, Annette pounded at Tatiana's door at eight o'clock in the morning. Tatiana was still asleep, her head full of a strange dream about large, terrifying frogs jumping out of trees and hitting the ground with a muffled thumping sound that echoed the pounding of her racing heart. She woke up with a gasp but could still hear her heart hammering in her ears. The apartment was freezing, so she grabbed the silk comforter and wrapped it around her. Her mouth was dry, and her eyes burned. She looked around for a cigarette and realized, finally, that someone was banging on the door.

"I'm coming," she said as she stumbled through the sitting room in her bare feet. It was not usually this cold in the apartment. Something must have happened to the boiler.

Annette fell through the door when Tatiana opened it and threw her arms around her. "Thank God you're here, *chérie*," she said. "I'm frantically worried. Have you seen Daniel? He hasn't come home for three days."

"Three days?" she said. Her brain was trying desperately to catch up. "What do you mean, three days?"

"Three days. Three nights. I don't know," Annette said, impatiently. "He hasn't been home. Occasionally he stays away for a night, so I didn't really think anything of it. He's a young man, after all. Then, after two nights, I began to wonder, and now I'm so worried, I'm sick to my stomach."

Tatiana was shocked. She opened and closed her mouth stupidly, like a fish in a shallow pond, but no words came out.

Daniel? She searched her brain. When had she last seen him? It had been well over a week ago, before she had gone to Lily and told her about him. She had not seen him since.

"I haven't seen him," she told Annette, who was pacing the room. She grabbed Annette's arms. "Sit," she said. "Sit down. Try to calm yourself. I'll make some tea." Her instinct was to do something normal, as if that would put everything right. She put the water on the gas burner and went into the bedroom to get some warm clothes.

"It's freezing in here," said Annette when she came out again.

"I know. Something must be wrong with the boiler." She made the tea and brought out the pot and two cups on a tray. "There," she said, handing Annette a cup. "This will help." They wrapped their chilled fingers around their cups and blew at the steam rising from the top. For a few seconds, everything was normal, grounded in the ritual of drinking tea.

"What should I do?" Annette asked. "I can't even think straight. Should I go to the police?"

The police? They couldn't go to the police. If they went to the police, Tatiana thought, that would make it official. It would mean that Daniel was really missing. They couldn't do that.

Annette was looking at her, watching her, expecting her to decide what they should do.

"Maybe he's staying with a friend," Tatiana said weakly.

Annette's face fell. "He would tell me," she said.

"Of course he would." She desperately wanted him not to be missing. "Have you called Lily?" she asked then instantly regretted mentioning her.

"Yes, I called this morning. They—somebody—told me she wasn't in but that Daniel hadn't been there since Friday. I forgot it was the weekend, and he doesn't teach Leonard on the weekend."

"Oh," said Tatania. "Yes, of course. The weekend." Why couldn't she think? Why didn't she know what to do? Annette was depending on her, and she was letting her friend down.

"What day is it?" Tatiana asked.

"Today?" Annette asked, as if she hadn't understood.

"Yes. What day is it today?"

"Monday."

"And you're sure he didn't tell you he was going somewhere for the weekend? With friends? Are you sure?"

"No, no, *chérie*. I'm sure."

"Maybe he forgot." Tatiana was desperately dreaming up a scenario. "He'll come back today. He'll say he forgot to tell you he was going away for the weekend." She was momentarily comforted by this possibility. It made perfect sense.

"No, *chérie*," said Annette. There was a look of such desolation on her face that it made Tatiana think she believed he must be dead. "That wouldn't happen."

"Annette," she said, "there's an explanation. I'm sure of it. By the end of the day, we'll be laughing at ourselves for being so foolish."

But by the end of the day, they weren't laughing. There was still no sign of Daniel. And in the days to come, they would not hear from him. She and Annette had gone to the police station on Monday afternoon and reported him missing. Because Annette lived in the French Concession, the police, who were French, were very sympathetic. She was one of their own, and they would do everything possible to find her son. Who were his friends? Where did he usually go during the day? During the evening? Did he go to the cabarets? If so, which ones? From her answers, Tatiana could tell that Annette knew nothing of Daniel's other life. She said he didn't usually go to the cabarets, because he needed to spend a lot of time practicing for his concerts, which were usually in the evenings. Tatiana wondered if he had told her he had a concert on the nights he went to the Kitty Kat. Should she say something? Tatiana wondered if she should come back and talk to the police when

Annette wasn't there. It was the "should" dilemma again.

In the days following Daniel's disappearance, Tatiana and Annette lived in the netherworld between life and death. Where was Daniel? Tatiana kept inventing more imaginary scenarios, because she didn't dare imagine the final one. He was ill somewhere, delirious from fever and couldn't remember his name. Some family had found him wandering in the street and was looking after him, nursing him back to health. Or he was in a hospital somewhere with a broken leg, and he couldn't get to a phone to let his mother know. They'd find him soon. Then she thought he must have found a lover, a young man he didn't want his mother to know about. So he had done the cowardly thing and run off with his lover. Soon he'd realize his mistake, and he'd call.

Tatiana exhausted herself dreaming up these scenarios. The whole time, she couldn't get the memory of the young Chinese man with the icy eyes out of her mind. Had he had anything to do with Daniel's disappearance? She had never been so worried in her life, and couldn't even begin to imagine what Annette was going through. Her friend had begun to look haunted, condemned to never knowing the truth, forced to live in a suspended state of constant, gnawing fear. Her fear was devouring her, and each day of Daniel's absence she grew thinner. Like Katarina, Annette was disappearing before Tatiana's eyes. And she, who had never had to look after anything or anybody, made feeble attempts to nurture her friend so she would not collapse before her son came home.

Where was the justice? You have a beautiful child who is the crowning achievement of your life. You care for him and love him without condition. You do not ask him to be perfect, because you know that he is. Your entire *raison d'être* is to give him life and to protect that life. You would lay down your own for him, because he is all that matters. And now that he is grown, you are made to suffer in a way you could never imagine because you can no longer protect him. Why? It was all so unnecessary. Why couldn't they all just go back to the time before all of this had happened? But as the days turned into a week then into another week, it was clear that Daniel was not coming back. Annette had begun taking laudanum to help her sleep. Tatiana knew she was drinking heavily as well, and that frightened her. As the weeks passed, Annette gradually receded into a kind of stupor. At times she was convinced that Daniel was dead, and she would never see him again. But it was not knowing for certain that was killing her. The tiny glimmer of hope—because he had not been found, so he could be anywhere—kept flickering and leaping up like a flame in a pile of dying embers. She was now inventing scenarios the way Tatiana had done on the first day. In her hazy reasoning, she saw him running off to Paris and becoming famous as a concert pianist. "But he doesn't want to tell me until it's certain," she would say. "Then he'll surprise me and send me a ticket. He'll shower me with gifts and present me to *tout le monde*." Her eyes shone as she stared into her vision. Tatiana tried not to cry in front of her when she hallucinated, but every night she wept into her pillow and cursed fate.

Tatiana felt the kind of anger that only the truly helpless feel. Because she had let things happen all her life, and had never taken a stand on anything, she could not even rely on the illusion of control. She started doing mundane things that she had never done before, like cleaning her flat, even though the maid came every day, re-washing the floors and re-polishing the furniture. She no sooner drank a cup of tea than she rinsed out the cup and dried it until it shone. She became obsessive about washing her stockings and underclothes. She bathed and washed her hair two or three times a day. Tatiana's skin shone from being scrubbed, and her hair fell in lank hunks around her face. She could no longer stand all those creams and lotions and lacquers touching her body. They made her feel dirty, and their scent irritated her nostrils.

Olga was shocked when she saw her sister. She thought Tatiana must be ill, and in a way she was. Sick of life and the cruelty of fate that caused so much human suffering. It seemed that all Tatiana could see any more was suffering. She was no longer party to joy. She couldn't remember what happiness felt like and had no memory of the satisfaction that comes from doing something well. She took no pleasure from food and smoked her opium pipe only from habit and because it allowed her to sleep briefly without dreaming.

"What has happened to you?" Olga asked when Tatiana came to visit their mother one Sunday. Katarina had moved in with Olga and Jean Paul because she rarely left her bed any more. She ate only crackers, occasionally with butter, and drank black tea constantly. Tatiana hated visiting her now; she was another reminder of death. Katarina had become a ghost who floated in some sort of ether that the rest of them couldn't breathe.

"They still haven't found Daniel," Tatiana said. "I don't have time for such foolish things as going to the hairdresser and putting on make-up. What kind of a person do you think I am?"

"I'm sorry," said Olga. "I'm just worried about you. That's all. I know you're under a terrible strain. I don't want you to fall ill."

"I didn't mean to snap at you," Tatiana said wearily. "I'm just terribly tired. And worried."

"Of course you are. And what about poor Annette? How is she doing?"

Olga had never liked Annette, but Tatiana knew her concern was sincere. It was the compassion of one parent for another, knowing that children never really grow up and the fear of harm never goes away.

"She's not coping very well. I want her to go to the doctor, but she's afraid to leave her house in case Daniel comes home. It's terrible." Olga nodded her head sympathetically. "How is Mother?" Tatiana asked.

"The same. I've started leaving a cup of consommé by her bed every morning, and sometimes, by the end of the day, she drinks half of it. It's a start."

A start. How like Olga to think in terms of beginnings, even when all the evidence pointed only to endings. Her views on life and human nature had always been much harsher than Tatiana's, but she knew that the sun came up every day, and it was their responsibility to make each day a stepping-stone to the next. In this she was like their father. He had believed you built a life, and it gave you back what you put into it. Tatiana was only beginning to understand what that meant.

Chapter Twenty-Three

Tatiana had not forgotten about Lily during this time, even though her first concern was for Annette. Lily had been unreachable for over a week. Rather than go in person, Tatiana sent a messenger frequently to her house. He always returned with the same reply. "Lily is away and unavailable for the present." Did that mean she didn't know Daniel was missing? Where was "away"? Was she visiting relatives somewhere? And what about Leonard's piano lessons?

Despite Number Two Brother's warning, Tatiana was determined to see her friend. She knew that going in the daytime would be useless. She was sure the servants had been instructed to send her away if she came, so she waited till the evening, when Wu-ling would be there. She was determined to speak to someone.

Tatiana stood at the front gate of Lily's home and told the servant she would not leave until she saw either Lily or Wu-ling. He shuffled away, and when he didn't return in five minutes, she rang the bell again. She did this five more times before the servant opened the gate and let her into the compound. She was relieved because it had started to rain, and she hadn't brought an umbrella.

He led her to a part of the house she had never been in before, Wu-ling's private quarters. He had his own sitting room, as did Lily, and Tatiana knew he was never to be disturbed there. Lily and Wu-ling had a very formal living arrangement. Tatiana knew they ate meals together with Leonard and that

Wu-ling's parents and several other relatives lived in the large compound, but she realized now that she didn't even know if Lily and Wu-ling shared the same bedroom.

Wu-ling's sitting room was furnished in a mixture of Chinese and Western styles. The chairs and sofas were plush and comfortable, unlike traditional Chinese furniture, but the tables and cabinets were lacquered and elaborately ornamented with hand-painted scenes and ornate brass handles. Combined with the thick carpets and heavy drapes, the effect was one of nineteenth-century extravagance. Tatiana could not imagine who had decorated this room. For all she knew, Lily might have had a hand in it. Lily rarely said much about such things. Yet it was so unlike her own very feminine sitting room where all was light colours and fresh flowers.

Wu-ling was sitting in an armchair and did not get up when Tatiana was shown into the room. He gestured to an identical chair placed on the other side of a table that had a lamp and a pile of books on it. He had apparently been reading.

"You are persistent," he said when she had sat down.

"I'm fine, thank you, Wu-ling. And how are you?" Tatiana wasn't sure why he was being rude to her. Their relationship had always been distant but courteous. Unless it had something to do with his brother-in-law, Lily's Number Two Brother. Were they both conspiring against her seeing Lily?

"If you wish to see Lily," he said, "I'm afraid that's impossible."

"Why is it impossible? Where is she?"

"I have sent my family to stay with relatives west of the city," Wu-ling said, examining the fingernails of his right hand so he could avoid looking in her eyes. "As you may or may not know," he said, looking up, "the political situation in Shanghai is heating up. The labour unions are causing problems, disrupting business, and the National Revolutionary Army is on the march, dealing with local warlords who are trying to prevent democracy in this country. Chiang Kai-shek himself will be in Shanghai at the end of the month. I thought it better if my family were out of harm's way, in case there is fighting in the streets. Perhaps you should consider leaving, too."

She remembered something Ian had said to her a month earlier, when they'd had lunch, something about things heating up in Shanghai and her going to London or Paris.

"Politics doesn't interest me," she said.

Wu-ling half-raised his eyebrows and shrugged his shoulders. "Do as you wish," he said.

"If you give me Lily's address, I can write to her."

"I think not," said Wu-ling. "I would prefer if she had no contact with you for the time being."

"The time being?" she said. "What's that supposed to mean?"

Wu-ling began examining the nails on his other hand. "My wife was quite upset the last time you visited her. I have no idea what you said to her, but I don't wish her to be upset by you again." He looked up and straight into her eyes. "I trust I make myself clear."

Tatiana was pretty sure this had something to do with Number Two Brother and nothing to do with politics in Shanghai. She hadn't been able to shake off the horrible feeling of being called a prostitute by Lily's brother. It had disturbed and frightened her. She'd told herself he had said it to shock and hurt her, a heavy-handed but effective tactic. She believed he had also meant it as a kind of warning. But what kind of warning? Surely he hadn't meant that he would kill her. For years she had been hearing about his connection to gangs, and especially the notorious and savage Green Gang, but she hadn't really believed it. Number Two Brother had always been a show-off, and he liked to throw his weight around. He hadn't changed.

Number Two Brother knew that she went out nearly every night to the clubs. He'd seen her there on occasion. He knew about her lifestyle. But what did he know about her relationships with the men she saw? Those things were private. The episode in his office had all been a show, a cruel display of power that had something to do with her friendship with Lily.

For some reason, neither of these two men wanted Tatiana to see her. Did they think she was a bad influence? That she might persuade Lily to go drinking and dancing with her, corrupt her and turn her into a drug addict? It was ridiculous. Unless Lily had told them, which Tatiana doubted, they knew nothing about Daniel and her feelings for him. But she couldn't rule out the possibility of servants spying on them and reporting their conversations. Who was being punished here, she wondered?

She could hear the rain beating against the windows and felt the dampness seeping into the room. It was March, another ugly month in Shanghai, when the weather was unpredictable and unpleasant. She had no desire to prolong her visit with Wu-ling, but she wasn't keen on going out into the rain, either. Which, she asked herself, was the less disagreeable option?

"Why won't you tell me what's really going on?" she asked, making one more attempt to get at the truth. "This can't be about Lily being upset. Everybody has ups and downs. I'm her friend. I can help her get over whatever's bothering her. That's what friends do."

Wu-ling shook his head. "You are very foolish," he said. "You cannot see that you are the problem and not the solution. Now, please go away and don't come here again."

He might just as well have slapped her. Wu-ling was putting up a wall between her and Lily and making absolutely sure there were no cracks in it. Obviously, he felt he didn't owe her an explanation. It had been decided, and now it would be carried out. Maybe he'd discovered that Lily had fallen in love with Daniel, and he was punishing her.

Then, for one wild moment, she wondered if Lily and Daniel had run away together, and Wu-ling and her brother had been shamed by it. It would be an enormous loss of face for both of their families. Was it possible? Could Lily ever have done such a thing? Tatiana was tempted to fling Wu-ling's insulting behaviour back in his face and ask him, but the words stuck in her throat. *Say it*, she told herself. *Ask him.*

He was already opening the door for her to leave. The servant was waiting on the other side to make sure she left. *Say it*, a voice said. *Say it now.* She took a deep breath.

"Has Lily run away?"

He looked at her with what she could only consider hatred. "Don't be ridiculous," he said harshly. The door closed in her face exactly as it had after her visit with Number Two Brother.

It was pouring by the time Tatiana reached the street. There were no taxis available, and she was drenched to the skin when she finally caught one at the corner. She was shaking as she sat in the back of the cab, shaking from the cold and the clamminess of her wet clothes against her skin but also from the emotions her encounter with Wu-ling had aroused. It had been very impersonal and yet, in a way, it had been very personal. She had felt his disapproval and seen the dislike in his eyes. But why should he hate her so much? Was it because he thought she was a loose woman? What did that mean? Loose woman. Loose. She knew it meant a woman of loose morals, but what were morals anyway, except a collection of social rules? This was the twentieth century. Surely every individual had the right to decide what rules to live by. She was a single woman. She didn't run around behind her husband's back or steal from people. Who was she hurting except herself? In Shanghai, lots of people smoked opium. Did they have loose morals? If that was the case, almost everyone she knew had loose morals, except Olga. And Lily.

It was silly to judge people on those terms. It was immoral to kill people in a war, but surely not to smoke cigarettes and drink alcohol. It was immoral to throw girl babies on the garbage heap, but not to sleep with men without marrying them. It was immoral to torture people and murder them. It wasn't immoral to smoke an opium pipe once or twice a day. People had no perspective on these things. They measured everything with the same yardstick. It was too black and white. She wasn't like Olga, and she wasn't like Lily. She wasn't even like Annette. She was herself, and she could decide what kind of morality she would follow.

Oh, she was tired, so tired as she climbed the stairs to her apartment. The rainstorm had caused a power failure, and the elevator wasn't working. She let herself into her dark apartment and peeled off her wet overcoat. She took off the rest of her clothes and crawled into bed under the silk comforter. It was all so ridiculous. Who was she trying to fool? She had never thought about morality in her life. She hadn't "chosen" anything, she had merely let things happen, and she had been a passive receiver of experience. A receptacle. She hadn't questioned her actions or her feelings. If anything, she had avoided facing the question of morality. Her indignation was a sham. She had been careless with her life and had ignored any chance she'd had to become a person with a purpose in life. But what was the point? None of it mattered in the end anyway. In the end, you were dead, whether you had a purpose or not. Who would know or care anything about her in a hundred years?

I've become an empty, soulless person, she thought, *who has destroyed the lives of her two best friends.*

Chapter Twenty-Four

A month after Daniel disappeared, the police came to see Tatiana. First they introduced themselves, then they said they had something to tell her, and it would be better if she were sitting down. At first she thought it might be about Lily—she hadn't heard a word from her friend—but there was something in the gravity of their manner that produced a feeling of horror. She knew that something terrible had happened. The police would not come to her with bad news about Lily. It had to be Daniel.

They asked her if she would identify his body.

~ ~

It's hard to describe the mix of feelings that surfaced when they told me they believed they had discovered Daniel's body washed up several miles downriver from the Bund. Somehow I knew it was true, and yet, because they were asking me to identify him, there might be the slightest possibility it wasn't him. The uncertainty of the last few weeks had been almost unbearable, and the certainty of knowing the worst would be a relief when it came. With each day, of course, our hopes had worn thinner, even as Annette had dreamed up crazy scenarios that I knew were impossible. These hallucinatory imaginings were giving her a sense of false hope that the world wasn't coming to an end. But it was.

~ ~

Why did they think it was Daniel? she asked. They showed her the small gold medallion he had worn around his neck ever since he had won first prize at the Shanghai Conservatory of Music piano competition. Her heart felt like it was collapsing. "Why do you want me to identify him if you already know?" she asked.

"It's just a formality," replied the more senior of the two officers, Inspector Malbon. "And the mother does not seem able to do it. She asked if we would speak to you." Malbon was a man whom life had made weary. His entire face seemed to droop, as though gravity were pulling his flesh toward the ground. He reminded Tatiana of a Bassett hound with his sad, heavy eyelids and his jowly jaw. His skin was the same colour as his shabby trench coat, somewhere between flat beige and flat grey. But his moist brown eyes were kind.

Annette knows then, she thought. *They've already told her.*

"I have to go to her," Tatiana said. "She can't be alone right now. She'll be devastated." She was frantically looking around for her shoes, her handbag, her coat.

"It's all right," Inspector Malbon said. "There is someone with her, and a doctor is coming to give her an injection. The sooner we confirm her son's identity, the sooner she will be able to begin the process of grieving."

"She's been grieving for a month," said Tatiana, impatience putting an edge on her words. "His disappearance has torn her apart. We've both been fearing the worst."

"Please, *mademoiselle*. Let us conclude this business so you can go to your friend."

In the car on the way to the morgue, Inspector Malbon tried to prepare Tatiana for what she would see. He explained that the body had been in very cold water for a month, so it had not completely decomposed. He said that it would not really look like Daniel. It was bloated from being in the water so long, and she must try to recognize him by some distinguishing feature.

"*Mademoiselle*," he said, "I will not try and fool you. This will be difficult and unpleasant. We are almost certain it is the young man but, if there is anything to cast doubt on his identity, we must know it. Your first impression may be your best, but, if you are not sure, you must say so."

~ ~

I won't try to describe what I saw lying on the table in the morgue, even though I remember every detail clearly. The image has never gone away. Sometimes when I can't sleep and I close my eyes just to rest them, it's what I see. At the worst times in my life it haunts me, flashing onto the blackness of my closed eyelids like a piece of film in a darkened movie theatre. I have never been able to erase it, even though I spent less than a minute looking at it.

In the end, it was his beautiful, delicate ears and his long, finely formed fingers, wrinkled and without nails but unmistakable, that told me for certain that it was Daniel and that he was truly dead. I sobbed as the inspector led me away, and I felt the contents of my stomach turn into bile and force their way up my throat. I retched into a basin and smelled death all around me. It was in my mouth and my nose, and in my hair and my clothes as well. I thought I was used to the stench of death, living in Shanghai, but this was something worse than the rot and decay of the streets. This smell was mixed with the odour of all the chemicals that were used to mask death and its putrid presence. It burned my nostrils every time I inhaled and tore at the back of my throat every time I swallowed. When I stepped out into the street, I tore off my overcoat, even though it was freezing, and took a deep breath through my nose then another through my mouth. I began to shiver in my thin silk dress, but I didn't care. I wanted to feel the cold. Maybe I hoped it would freeze me into a block of ice and put an end to all the horrible things I was feeling.

~ ~

Inspector Malbon picked up Tatiana's coat and put it over her shoulders. He led her to the car and gestured for her to get in. "We will go now to see his mother. I will tell her, and you will try to comfort her." He spoke from long, hard experience. She could see it in his sad, drooping eyes. He had done this too many times before.

The doctor had arrived before them, but he had held off giving Annette a sedative until the Inspector could speak to her. Tatiana was relieved, because she thought he should know that Annette had been taking laudanum, in what quantities Tatiana didn't know, and she was also drinking heavily.

"Then I cannot do much for her," the doctor told Tatiana. "It would be unwise and even dangerous to try and sedate her." He was tall and thin, and the fingers that rummaged in his black leather bag were long and bony, like the knobby twigs of a tree that had shed its leaves. "I can give her some powders that may help to calm her, but she probably will not be able to sleep. Someone will need to stay with her." Tatiana could smell Annette's despair in the room. It penetrated the furniture and the carpets, trapped like the air in a tomb.

She nodded at the doctor's words and thought how unprepared she was to look after anyone. Suddenly she wanted Olga to be there, with her solidness and her no-nonsense approach to everything. She would know what to do. She would roll up her sleeves and take charge. While Tatiana would do what? Crawl under the carpet like a bug and disappear?

She felt ashamed and ineffectual. She understood the worthlessness of her own existence. Why was Daniel, someone so full of talent and promise, lying dead in the morgue, while she was allowed to continue her stupid and frivolous life? Wasn't there something terribly wrong with a world that played itself out this way? Tatiana had never done anything for anyone, had never sacrificed anything, never struggled for anything, or even tried to help someone else along the way. How Olga must despise her. Because she *was* despicable. She hated herself at that moment and thought she had surely reached rock bottom, that she could not hate herself more nor feel worse.

They buried Daniel a week later. The police had needed to do an autopsy and would not release the body until they were done. It had been the hardest seven days of Tatiana's life. She had gone back to her apartment while Annette was sleeping and packed a bag so she could stay with her day and night. There was no food in Annette's house, so she had gone to the market and bought tea and coffee and eggs, some milk and butter, a loaf of bread and some biscuits. Luckily, in Shanghai, food was always available cheaply from street vendors. If she or Annette got hungry, which seemed unlikely, she could find something quickly and bring it back while it was still hot.

On the day of the funeral, which they had arranged with the help of one of Annette's neighbours who knew what to do, Tatiana made strong tea and fried eggs and buttered thick pieces of bread so they could get through the day. She could not bring Annette out of her self-induced stupor, but she was able to help her dress and put on some lipstick. The food and the strong tea seemed to bring Annette around, but she could only look at Tatiana with such intense sadness that all Tatiana wanted to do was tuck her back into bed and let her pull the covers over her head. She knew it was necessary, however, for Annette to go through the ritual of a burial, so that maybe she could also bury some of her past with her son.

Olga and Jean Paul attended the brief service and came to the cemetery, for which Tatiana was grateful. For it was not just Annette who was grieving, but Daniel's Russian piano teacher, now a very old man, and the neighbours who had watched him grow up. They needed to be there for each other so they could say that this was a life that, however brief, had a purpose. People had cared about Daniel and he had touched their lives. They could not allow him to disappear without acknowledging his brief journey. These rituals, Tatiana realized, helped them to believe, in the end, that his life had some meaning.

Inspector Malbon was also at the cemetery, but Lily was not there, nor was Wu-ling. After the service, Tatiana went up to the inspector and invited him back to the house. Olga and the neighbours had arranged for food to be served, and he was welcome to join them.

"*Merci, mademoiselle*," he said, "but I must return to work. Unfortunately, crime does not stop for funerals." His use of the word crime surprised her. She remembered that there had been an autopsy to determine the cause of Daniel's death. It was something she had not allowed herself to think about. It was enough that he was dead, so why prolong the pain by thinking about why or how? But now she realized she needed to know.

"Do you know what happened to Daniel?" she asked.

He looked at her for a moment as if assessing whether he should tell her or not. "I have just received the report this morning," he said. "I am sorry to say, mademoiselle, that there were two bullets in the young man's chest. Small calibre, but deadly nonetheless."

"You mean he was shot?" she asked incredulously.

"Yes. He was shot. He did not drown. His body must have been thrown into the river after death to conceal the crime."

The crime. Daniel's death had been a crime. Not an accident. Not suicide. He'd been shot, then thrown into the river.

"Do you know who did this?" she asked. She had reached out and taken hold of the Inspector's arm because, for a moment, she thought she might faint.

"No, mademoiselle. The investigation will begin today." He put his hand over hers. "Do you have any idea how this could have happened?"

"Me?" she said. "No, of course not. Everybody loved Daniel. He was such a wonderful young man. With so much talent and a future. Why would anybody do this?" She couldn't bring herself to tell the inspector about Daniel's other life. She didn't know who his friends were or whether they had anything to do with his death, but she knew that Annette was in no shape to hear any of it.

"I have no idea why these things happen," said Malbon. "I have been a policeman for thirty years and can only tell you that nothing surprises me any more."

Chapter Twenty-Five

Who could have shot Daniel? It seemed inconceivable that such a gentle young man should meet such a violent end. Daniel's body had been pulled from the river. It had probably been there for weeks, which meant he might have died soon after Annette had said he'd gone missing. Had Tatiana really thought his death was an accident? That he had somehow fallen into the river—slipped on some ice, perhaps—and drowned. The thought of suicide had briefly entered her mind—maybe his lover had broken his heart—but she didn't want to think that Daniel had taken his own life. Now there was no denying that he had met a horrible and brutal end.

Shanghai had become an increasingly violent city. There were sporadic outbreaks of gunfire, especially during the frequent labour strikes, and the political situation that Tatiana had been warned about was volatile. Was it possible that Daniel had been in the wrong place at the wrong time? Could his death have been anonymous, stray political bullets on a darkened street?

Tatiana couldn't erase the memory of Daniel and his Chinese companion at the Klub Kitty Kat. She decided to go one more time and confront the man, if she could find him. She had her hair done for the first time in weeks, had a manicure to repair her neglected fingernails, and dressed with particular care. Her nerves were on edge, maybe because she feared what she would find out. Or was it simply because she found the once familiar ritual of dressing for an evening on the town something she no longer cared about.

She arrived at the Kitty Kat in a taxi, and the leopard-skin-gloved hand of the doorman reached into the cab to help her out. The flashing lights that emerged from between the cat's legs hurt her eyes and made her feel tired. The costumed crowd eager for a night of surprises no longer amused her. What had once seemed effortless fun now seemed like something that required too much exertion. She forced a smile to her lips and looked around for Michel's familiar face. It hadn't occurred to her he might not be here. But she needn't have worried. She spotted him on the dance floor surrounded by four of his fancy boys, who took turns grabbing each others' buttocks and striding about the floor in an elaborately suggestive tango.

Tatiana waited until the music stopped, then raised her gloved hands and applauded as Michel and his troupe walked toward her and the empty table behind her.

"Darling," crooned Michel, his voice embracing every note of the musical scale. He blew her a kiss. "Long time no see."

"Hello, Michel," she said. "You hardly look a year older than the last time I saw you. When was it? Two months ago?"

"Ha, bloody ha," he said, his eyes frosting over like sleet covering a paved road. "Shouldn't you be sleeping? You look like you've been up for days."

"I have been," she said. "I need to talk to you, Michel." She looked at the little group of dance partners that fluttered on either side of him, like a bodyguard of ballerinas in tuxedos. "Alone."

"Order some champagne," Michel said to the boy on his right. "I'll be right back."

They walked across the carpet that ringed the dance floor and found a couple of upholstered armchairs in a quiet corner. "Now what's this all about?" Michel said. "You look so serious, and it's unbecoming."

"I *am* serious, Michel," she said. "Haven't you heard?"

"Heard what?"

"About Daniel. Annette's son. He was murdered."

"Oh, that," he said, dismissing the topic with a wave of his hand. "That's very old news, darling."

"Not to me, it isn't. And not to his mother. We've been going through hell. And the police haven't been able to tell us anything except that he was shot and his body was thrown in the river."

Michel took a white silk handkerchief out of his pocket and waved it in front of his face. "Please, darling. Enough. I don't need to hear all the sordid details. Why are you telling me this?"

"I want to know if you've heard anything that the police don't know. You know Daniel was coming here, and that he had liaisons. Have there been any rumours? People must have been talking."

"They talked very little about it, my dear. You know these Chinese are very superstitious." Michel kept glancing over at his table to see if the champagne had arrived. "It was probably just some stupid, senseless thing. Somebody made a mistake and shot the wrong person."

"That's no comfort, Michel." Tatiana stuck another cigarette in the long ivory holder she liked to use when she went out at night. She thought it was elegant. A white-jacketed waiter leaned over and lit the cigarette before she could even turn to look for someone. "What about that mean-looking Chinese boy he was with that first night, when you called me? Where is he?" She waved the smoke away and looked around the room.

"Long gone, darling. Long gone."

"Gone?"

"Yes, Tatiana," he said, hitting the t's as if he were hammering tiny nails into a wall. "Gone. Not here. Do I have to spell it out for you? G-o-n-e."

She chose to ignore the nastiness in his tone. "That looks suspicious, don't you think?"

"This is Shanghai." He shrugged. "People come and go. They get used up very quickly in this town. You should know that, darling."

"Ha, bloody ha," she said.

~ ~

Now, many years later, I realize how deeply I had buried my fears. I wanted to believe anything but that Daniel's death had been personal. I couldn't allow myself to think that someone might have wanted him dead. It was so much easier to believe in the myth of accidents. But a deliberate act of murder was unthinkable. If I had allowed myself to go down that road, there would have been no return. What had happened to my silly, inconsequential life of drinking, dancing and laughing with strangers? How had it so quickly been consumed by death?

~ ~

Jean Paul sent a taxi one night, ten days after Daniel's funeral, to bring Tatiana to the house for dinner. He and Olga had something important to discuss with her. They had decided to move to Canada. They'd had enough of Shanghai and saw no future for their children there.

"Look what's happening, Tati," Jean Paul said. "Every fourth person on the street is a soldier. There are warships in the harbour. Labour strikes are paralyzing the city, and the Communists—backed by Stalin—are threatening to take over. It's only Chiang Kai-shek who holds it all together, but he is being opposed by both the warlords and the Green Gang, who control most of the Chinese business interests and want the Communists out of the Kuomintang. It's a mess, a frightening, dangerous mess."

"How do you know all this?" Tatiana asked.

"I'm a businessman," he replied. "The foreign interests in Shanghai amount to millions and millions of dollars and pounds and francs. The Chamber of Commerce has had secret meetings with Chiang and also with the Green Gang. We can't afford to have labour unrest and labour unions disrupting business every day. We need a strong, anti-communist government that will protect our interests, or everything will be lost."

Olga had been upstairs putting the children to bed. She came down and sat across from Tatiana at the dining room table where she and Jean Paul had been drinking their after-dinner coffee.

"So that's why you've decided to go to Canada?" she asked, looking from one to the other.

"Yes," said Olga. "We are afraid for the children, but we are also afraid that we will lose everything we have. If the Communists are in control of the Kuomintang, then everything will change. We know that the Russians are backing them and that their goal is based on an ideology of political domination by the workers. If that happens here, people like us will be thrown in prison. Or worse."

"You must be exaggerating," Tatiana said. "Surely it wouldn't come to that."

"Oh, no?" said Olga. "Do you have any idea what's happening in Russia? Stalin disposes of his enemies in ways you cannot imagine. People are executed without any kind of trial. They are not allowed to defend themselves. Their families aren't even allowed to bury their bodies. We've had letters, Tati. We know."

"But don't you remember? Papa said China was the future. Russia was the past. It's different here."

"Not any more," said Jean Paul. "Outside of Shanghai, China is a country of peasant farmers, just like Russia. There is too much money concentrated in the hands of too few, and so much of the wealth is controlled by foreigners, like us. It was only a matter of time before they began to rise up and protest. It's possible that Chiang's army can hold them back, but it's just as possible that they can't. Who will win in the end? Millions of angry peasants and workers? Or a few thousand soldiers with guns? We cannot afford to be optimistic. We have to consider our children."

"What about Mother?" Tatiana asked. "What will happen to her?"

"Of course we will take her with us," said Jean Paul. "She is weak, but we will try to make it as easy as possible for her. There is no choice. She can't stay here without us."

"I could take care of her," Tatiana said, grasping for some kind of future for herself without Olga and Jean Paul. Olga looked at her, and Tatiana knew what she was thinking. She wasn't capable of looking after Mother. She wasn't even capable of looking after herself.

"Come with us, Tati," Olga said. "Come to Canada. We can still be a family. It's a big place, like Russia. We can find another future there. We can be safe."

"Canada? What would I do in Canada?"

"You could find a job," said Olga. "There's lots of work there. We can all find jobs. We'll buy a house, and the children will go to school. We already speak English, Tati. They speak English in Canada."

A job, thought Tatiana. Olga wanted her to get a job. But what was she good for? Working in a laundry? Scrubbing floors? She didn't want that kind of a job. All she could think of were the White Russian taxi dancers who had flooded into Shanghai after the Revolution. They couldn't get jobs, because they had no skills or connections. They only had their beauty and their desperation. Tatiana didn't want to be a desperate thirty-year-old Russian woman in Canada.

She told them she would think about it, but in her heart she knew she was not going to Canada. They tried to persuade her, but she couldn't see a future for herself there. Better a dismal future in a place she knew than a dismal future in a strange country.

Jean Paul wanted her to spend the night, but she refused, saying she needed to go to check on Annette, but that was a lie. She was worried about Annette, that was true, but she really needed to be by herself. She was being suffocated by all the demands on her. On the one side was Annette, who needed her company desperately to stave off the demons that would not let her rest. They were quieter, she said, when Tatiana was there. She could ignore them for a while, but as soon as Tatiana left, the screeching began, and she couldn't bear it. On the other hand were the demands of Tatiana's family, who claimed they were concerned for her safety, but she believed they were more concerned for their own peace of mind. They wanted her constantly in sight where they could watch over her. Sometimes she couldn't breathe for all their concern about her. *Leave me alone*, she wanted to say. *Don't get too close.* It was so much easier to be with strangers. They didn't care, and that meant she owed them nothing. It was a good exchange, and it suited her.

Out on the street in front of Olga's house, Tatiana could hear gunfire, or was it cannon fire in the distance? Occasionally, she could see puffs of smoke in the sky after a particularly loud explosion. She had no idea that this was the night the Green Gang, acting under the guise of the Society for Common Progress, was planning to launch a series of attacks against the city's union headquarters. Many people would die in the next few days and weeks, either in the fighting or in the executions that followed the fighting. The labour unions would be declared illegal, and there would be no more strikes, but it would not be the end of China's troubles.

Tatiana walked for blocks looking for a taxi. Had she been listening more closely to Jean Paul, had she understood what he was trying to tell her, she might have been afraid for her life. Instead, she was merely annoyed at the inconvenience. She hadn't worn walking shoes, and the thin soles of her pumps were little protection against the loose stones and broken pavement. The fighting sounded far away, but it was much closer than she realized. It wasn't until she turned a corner onto Avenue Joffre, where she knew there was a taxi stand, that

Tatiana came face to face with the war that was happening on the streets of Shanghai.

She heard them before she saw them, but she had enough sense to duck into the shelter of a doorway where she couldn't be seen. She watched as three soldiers beat a man then, one by one, put a bullet each into his head. Tatiana didn't know a word large enough to describe the horror she felt. She thought of Daniel, with two bullets in his chest, and wondered if this was what had happened to him. She pressed her back against the bricks of the entranceway and willed herself to be invisible. How close had she come to being in the wrong place at the wrong time? If she were discovered, would they kill her? Of course they would.

Tatiana heard the soldiers say something in Chinese, and she held her breath, praying they would not discover her. Luckily, they headed in the opposite direction, but she waited a full five minutes before emerging from her hiding place. The man they had beaten and shot lay in the middle of the street, like a sack stuffed with body parts, his arms and legs askew in the uncomfortable position of death. She started to run, keeping close to the darkened shops and ducking into doorways along the way. She had never known this kind of terror. It was the animal fear of the hunted, the cringing fear of the weak and undefended. She ran for blocks, listening to the sound of gunfire in the distance, trying to determine if it was coming closer or moving away. Even though she didn't see another living soul, she still felt that at any moment an army could descend on her from nowhere.

Tatiana didn't stop running until she saw the traffic on Bubbling Well Road. Apparently the fighting hadn't reached there yet. She was so relieved, she almost cried. She raised her hand to hail a taxi to take her the last few blocks. The driver was shocked by her wild-eyed and breathless appearance. He said something to her in Chinese that she didn't understand. She just nodded and waved her hand to signal that he should drive on.

When she reached the safety of her apartment, she went straight to the bathroom and turned on the faucets to run a bath. She peeled off her clothes with shaking fingers and discovered, to her horror, that she had wet her pants.

Chapter Twenty-Six

Tatiana was afraid to leave her apartment and stayed cooped up for days with the curtains drawn. Occasionally she would crouch down and pull back the edge of the curtain to take a quick peek out the window. She was terrified that there might be a sniper waiting to shoot anything that moved. She told herself she was behaving irrationally, and there was no fighting on Bubbling Well Road, but she could still hear the sound of shots from time to time in the city. This was a civil war, with Chinese fighting Chinese, but how did she know she wouldn't become a target? The person holding the gun would decide who the enemy was. What was there to stop some half-crazed boy soldier from shooting her? She didn't trust anybody.

Finally, after three days, Jean Paul came and rescued her. He was shocked by her appearance and insisted she pack a bag and come back to the house with him. "It's all right, Tati," he said. "The fighting is north of here. You don't have to be afraid. It's very localized. The army has succeeded in breaking the unions. The leaders have been arrested, and many of them have been executed."

She was so grateful, she didn't even ask Jean Paul why he had come. In the cab on the way over to the house, he told her there had been a report in the paper that Wu-ling had been killed in the fighting. "That's Lily's husband, isn't it? Tang Wu-ling?"

"Yes, that's him," she said, shocked. "What happened?"

"Well, they're suggesting that he may have been ambushed by leftist elements in the Kuomintang. It's well known that he was extremely anti-communist and had been funding the

Green Gang in the war to oust the leftists from the party. He was playing a dangerous game. I think Lily's family was also involved in the movement."

"I'm sure her brother was, Number Two Brother. I thought he just liked playing the gangster, but now I'm pretty sure he was one of the leaders of the Gang." She told Jean Paul she had seen Lily's brother out on the town occasionally with a well-dressed entourage of thugs that were probably his bodyguards. She didn't tell him about her frightening visit to his office at the invitation of a couple of these thugs.

"Now that Wu-ling is dead," she said, thinking out loud, "I wonder what will happen to Lily."

"Have you seen her lately?" asked Jean Paul.

"No. I've tried, but they keep telling me she's away. Wu-ling told me he'd sent her and Leonard to stay with relatives somewhere west of Shanghai so they'd be safe. He warned me there was going to be trouble."

"Then I doubt very much if she'll be back," Jean Paul said.

"Why not?"

"China is all about families and clans. If she's been sent to stay with relatives of Wu-ling's, she'll probably be absorbed into that wing of the family. I wouldn't be surprised if it was one of Wu-ling's brothers."

"But that means I might never see her again. I never even got to say goodbye to her."

"Maybe she'll get in touch with you. She knows where you are, even if you don't know where she is."

Tatiana moved in with Olga and Jean Paul. She started to feel less like a hunted animal, but she couldn't shake off the heavy fist of sadness clutching her heart. Every so often she would start to cry, and the tears seemed to come from out of nowhere, as if they had a life of their own.

But gradually she began to find herself again, the real Tatiana, the one that had been buried for a decade under layers of stubbornness and unhappiness, contrariness and rebelliousness. Watching Olga and Jean Paul with their children, she realized how much she and Olga had meant to their parents and how carelessly she had flung their love back in their faces. They had done everything for their children, always putting them first, just as Olga and Jean Paul were putting the future of Ana and Nicholas before everything else. Tatiana understood how she had broken her father's heart with her selfish and self-destructive behaviour. He had gone to his grave knowing he had lost her, yet he had never given up on her. She realized he had loved her in spite of everything, just as she would always love Ana and Nicholas as if they were her own children. They were a part of her.

"I've made a decision," she told Olga and Jean Paul one night. The children were in bed, and Katarina was already asleep. Tatiana had made a pot of tea and sliced some poppy-seed cake, Olga's favourite. "I've given it a lot of thought, and I don't want any arguments. I want you to go to Canada with the children and leave Mother here with me. I'll take care of her. I promise. It's my turn."

The both stared at her for a long minute, and finally Olga spoke. "Tatiana. Do you know what you're saying?"

"Yes," she said. "It's time for me to do my share. You've been carrying the whole family on your shoulders for too long, Olushka, you and Jean Paul. You need to do what you think is best for the children. Mother and I will be fine. Honestly."

"But why don't you come with us, Tati?"

"We've been through all this, Olga. I'm just not ready to go to Canada. And Mother's too weak. It's better this way." Tatiana could tell by the look in her eyes that Olga knew she meant it. She was very calm. In the weeks since Daniel's funeral, she had gradually weaned herself off opium. It had been a frightening and painful withdrawal. She had spent several nights sweating through nausea and vomiting or shaking with chills and fever, but she knew it was necessary, and she had done it. Once she had gone beyond her limit of two pipes a day, Tatiana feared the day would come when three or even four pipes would not be enough.

Olga knew her well enough to see that Tatiana had turned a corner in her life and needed to be allowed to atone. Being Olga, however, she wasn't entirely convinced her sister could do it. That was all right, Tatiana told herself. Actions would speak louder than words.

Even though she was preoccupied by so many things— Daniel's death and its affect on Annette, Wu-ling's death and what would happen to Lily and Leonard, Olga and Jean Paul going to Canada and taking everything she knew and loved with them—Tatiana gave her mother as much love and attention as she could during those final weeks. She read to her or rubbed her back until Katarina fell asleep; she held her mother's hand and talked to her about the happier times in their life. She made sure Katarina saw as much as possible of Ana and Nicholas. She and the children played games in Katarina's room while she sat up in bed, her skin almost as white as the pillows. Olga and Jean Paul were busy packing, deciding what to take and what not to take, tying up all the loose ends that are part of leaving a place forever. Jean Paul often looked in on Tatiana and the children as they entertained Katarina and got to know each other.

They were wonderful children, and Tatiana had almost missed knowing them. Ana was nearly five and a regular chatterbox. She was tall for her age and looked a lot like Tatiana, with her honey-blonde hair and blue-grey eyes. She had a stubborn streak, too, and was determined to figure everything out for herself. If someone tried to help her, she pushed them away and said, "No. I want to do it myself." But for all her petulance, she was a sunny child who laughed easily and loved to make her baby brother laugh. Nicholas, almost a year old, was a curious, patient child who watched everything people did as if they were presenting a theatrical production just for him. He sat among his pillows like an Ottoman potentate, laughing and clapping while they performed.

Tatiana was sad that they would be leaving and she might not see them grow up, but the thought of Canada, about which she knew almost nothing except that it was almost as big as Russia and a lot emptier, did not appeal to her. She pictured vast, unpopulated expanses of flat, snowy fields, with the odd tree here and there and the occasional mountain or lake breaking up the landscape. She had grown up in a noisy, intensely exciting city. She was used to the people and the street markets, the smells and the sounds, the shapes of the buildings and the trees. Shanghai was home for her. It was not a beautiful place—in fact, many things about it were ugly, dirty and even repulsive—but it was a place that vibrated with life and possibility. She wasn't ready to leave it yet.

In the middle of the noisy chaos of Shanghai during that spring of 1927, Katarina died a very quiet death. She simply went to sleep one night and did not wake up. It was as though she had finally faded out of life. Tatiana's last conversation with her was about Sergei. Katarina had been preoccupied with him much of the time and spoke about him as if he were in the room with them.

"Papa says, 'Don't look so sad, Tati. Everything will be fine. You'll see.'"

"Papa was usually right," said Tatiana.

"Yes, he was."

"I miss him a lot."

"But he's right here, Tati. Can't you see him? He's smiling at us."

"Yes, I see him, Mother." She was brushing her mother's

long, silky hair, an activity that seemed to soothe and relax her.
"What else is he saying?"

"He says, 'Remember the time we went to the lake for a
picnic? And it was a perfect day, except Tati lost her shoes? Do
you remember?'" She lifted her hand and pointed her finger at
something on the other side of the room.

"Of course I remember," Tatiana said.

"I was convinced you'd thrown them in the lake because
you hated them."

"I did. They were ugly shoes. And they pinched my feet."

Katarina laughed. "I knew it," she said. "But you would
never admit it. You told me you left them by a tree, and a
blackbird stole them. Remember?"

"Yes, I do. I thought it was a brilliant lie. I was furious when
you didn't believe me."

"Papa says he believed you. But then, he would. He always
saw the best in people. He's laughing now, Tati. He knows
now. He says you're right. It was a brilliant lie."

They buried Katarina on a beautiful day at the beginning of
May, five weeks before Tatiana's thirtieth birthday. Olga and
Jean Paul hadn't left yet, and she was glad they were still
a family. The sun shone in a cloudless blue sky, and spring
flowers bloomed in explosions of colour. The peonies were in
bud and full of promise. In the past, it would have been a day
for a picnic or a trip to the zoo. A day to feel the sun touch
your bare arms and let the wind play havoc with your hair.
A day to run barefoot through the newly green grass. Tatiana
cried more for the loss of those simple pleasures than she did
for her mother because, in a way, Katarina had been gone
for a long time. A part of her had died when they'd come to
China then, bit by bit, other parts of her had withered and died
from neglect. Tatiana told herself they had done everything

they could to help her. *Surely we must have*, she thought. She remembered how angry she used to be with her mother for not pulling herself out of what must have been the depths of despair, and how Sergei had tried to explain how difficult it was for some people to change. Tatiana was angry, because her mother had taken something away from her. She had deprived her daughter of her childish joy and replaced it with her own adult sadness, and Tatiana had resented her for stealing her innocence. But now, finally, she understood. Katarina had not done anything to her except prove that she was human. Tatiana had been threatened by her mother's fragility because it had suggested that she might not be perfect, and if her mother wasn't perfect, then maybe she wasn't, either.

Chapter Twenty-Seven

Olga, Jean Paul and the children left for Canada at the end of July. Tatiana's thirtieth birthday had come and gone with only a brief acknowledgement.

"You're officially a spinster today," said Olga.

"Are you trying to cheer me up?" Tatiana was neatly folding the wrapping paper from her gift. Olga had given her a silver-framed picture of Ana and Nicholas. In the photograph, the children were smiling straight into the camera, but it looked as if they were smiling at her.

"A woman of thirty, Tati. You know what they say."

"No. I don't know what they say. And who are 'they', anyway?"

Olga chose to ignore her sister's sarcasm. "A woman of thirty, they say, cannot be choosy. She should say 'yes' to the first man who asks her to marry him."

"You know very well if I had wanted to be married, I would have been by now. I prefer being a single woman. It suits me."

Olga rolled her eyes as she did every time they had this conversation. "You'll be sorry some day," she said. "You'll be all alone with nobody to look after you."

"Is that any way to talk to me on my birthday? You're supposed to shower me with good wishes and celebrate my life. Not tell me I'll be a lonely old woman some day. Besides," she said. "Ana and Nicholas will look after me. At least they love me, if nobody else does."

"Yes," Olga conceded, "they do love you. And they're going

to miss you terribly. Why don't you reconsider, Tati, and come to Canada with us?"

Tatiana sighed heavily. "Olga, we've been over this a million times. I don't want to go to Canada. I would be like a fish out of water there. I think I would hate it."

"You don't know unless you try," she persisted. "They say it's a very nice place, and the people are nice, too."

"They, again. Who are 'they'? You keep talking about them as if they were a group of experts who knew everything about everything. They, they, they."

"Okay, okay," said Olga. She knew once the note of exasperation crept into Tatiana's voice, there was no point in discussing it any longer. "You can always come later if you change your mind."

The investigation into Daniel's murder had so far shown no results. There were no witnesses. There was no murder weapon. Nobody had confessed, and there were no suspects. Tatiana had paid one last visit to Inspector Malbon to see if the police were any closer to solving the case. He could only confirm that the bullets found in Daniel's chest were small calibre, probably from a woman's gun.

"Why do you think the gun belonged to a woman?" she asked.

"Because usually women carry such small guns. It fits nicely into a handbag and is enough for self-defence. You would not need large hands or strong arms to use it. What I'm saying is, it was definitely a lady's gun that killed the young man, not a soldier's or a gangster's."

"But that doesn't necessarily mean that a woman killed him," said Tatiana.

"That's true, mademoiselle. There are absolutely no clues. I'm sure of one thing, though. There was a man involved."

"Why do you think that?"

"Because a woman does not throw a dead body into the river." In Shanghai, he said, these crimes were rarely solved. Too many secrets.

Tatiana didn't know any women who had a gun or, at least, not any that had told her, but when she thought about the kind of people Daniel had associated with at the Klub Kitty Kat, it seemed plausible that one of them might carry a "lady's" gun. It would be easier to conceal in a pocket or an evening bag. If that were true, it provided a long list of suspects. She was forgetting, of course, about motive. But who knew? Maybe one of Daniel's friends had a jealous lover. Should she tell Malbon about the Kitty Kat? If she did, would the police go down there and round up all the patrons? Including her friend Michel? Tatiana decided to say nothing.

Annette was managing, one day at a time, but each day took the toll of two, and she was sinking further into a bottomless abyss of despondency. Tatiana had slowly begun to realize that she might never come out of it. Early on she had asked Inspector Malbon not to tell Annette that Daniel had been shot. She was so fragile, Tatiana was afraid it might finally push her over the edge. She didn't expect Annette to recover from Daniel's death the way a person recovered from a bad cold or a broken bone, but she had hoped that at some point her friend would begin to re-establish some of the day-to-day routine of her life. But that didn't seem to be happening.

Maybe it would take more time. Everyone grieved in their own way, and grieving the death of a child was the hardest of all. It could take years. But it was as if Annette had no shred of self-preservation in her. Her behaviour became more self-destructive every day, as if she needed to punish herself for outliving her child. It was terrible and heartbreaking to watch.

Tatiana had long ago given up pleading with her to leave the house. She wouldn't even go to the market. It was an effort to persuade her to take a bath and change her clothes.

"*Chérie*," she said, "what difference does it make whether my clothes are clean or dirty? I don't feel any better wearing clean clothes, and it's so much trouble."

"I'll help you," Tatiana said. "You have to try, Annette. You can't just give up."

"Why can't I give up?" she said angrily. "I have nothing to live for. Every day is the same as the last, and they're all empty. Do me a favour, *chérie*. Buy a gun and shoot me. If you want to make me happy, do that." She grabbed hold of Tatiana's hand and held onto it with a surprising amount of strength. Her eyes were already half dead.

In August, Tatiana began to sell off some of her trinkets. They meant nothing to her now and they only took up space, in her apartment and in her mind. Jean Paul had given her money before they'd left, and it was enough for her to live on comfortably for several years. He had promised to send more money once they were settled in Canada and had jobs, but Tatiana didn't want to be dependent on him and Olga. Besides, things might not go as easily as they were hoping, and they might need to be frugal with the money they had. Jean Paul had sold Sergei's bicycle business for a small profit but, because of the unstable political climate in Shanghai, he had not made as much as he should have. It was still a thriving concern, but the purchasers knew he was anxious to leave China, and they drove a hard bargain. He and Olga estimated that the money from the business would keep them going in Canada for a couple of years. Olga felt that Tatiana should get a share of it, even though she had never had anything to do with the business, that it should be part of her inheritance. Now that both of their parents were gone, it was only fair that she get something.

Tatiana had also lost interest in going out at night. A kind of ugliness had crept into the Shanghai nightlife that hadn't been there before. It didn't seem as elegant any more, but she wondered if maybe it was she who had become ugly and less elegant, not Shanghai. Things looked different to her. The smiles on people's faces stretched a little too wide, and sometimes the laughter seemed a little crazed. Maybe it had always been like that, and she just hadn't seen it before. Was it her, or had the entire tableau become perverted? Was the whole world spinning out of control, or just the part Tatiana was looking at?

With Olga and Jean Paul gone and Annette in a depressed stupor, she realized she had no one to talk to any more. She received letters from Ian telling her about his rubber plantation in the jungle and inviting her to visit. She had no desire to go to Malaya, but she continued answering his letters, because the connection mattered to her. She felt he was one of the few friends she had made who had seen her as the person she was, not the person she appeared to be. She wouldn't have minded seeing him again in Shanghai and having a "spot" of lunch or a drink. For the first time in her life, Tatiana was lonely. Sometimes, on her way home from the market, she would ask the taxi driver to pass by Lily's house, just in case she was there. Jean Paul had said she and Leonard would most likely be absorbed into another part of Wu-ling's family, probably by one of his brothers, who would take over the responsibility of caring for them. Lily had almost no options in life. She was now a burden on her husband's family, but Tatiana believed that because of Leonard, she would be taken care of and treated with some respect for the rest of her life. Her son was a direct link to his father's ancestors, and nothing was more important to a Chinese family.

Then, one day in late October, when she had almost given up, Tatiana saw a light in one of the houses of the Tang family compound. Could it be, she wondered? She was almost afraid to find out. Maybe it was just a servant sent to clean out one of the rooms. Or maybe it was a cruel trick of the light, the setting sun reflecting on the glass of one of the upstairs windows.

Tatiana told the driver to stop, and she went up to the gate and rang the bell. In a few minutes, an old woman with a bent back came shuffling over to see who was there. Tatiana recognized her immediately, Lily's amah, the servant who had been with her all her life. She had slept in the same bed with her charge when Lily was a child, had been there, in the background, sewing and mending, picking up after her every time they were together, the family retainer who was closer to her and possibly even loved Lily more than her own mother did. She squinted at Tatiana in the fading light, and suddenly a toothless smile lit up her face. She nodded several times and continued nodding as she opened the gate and let her in.

"Is Lily here?" Tatiana asked, sure the amah would say no.

"Yes, yes, missee have got, have got. Topside. You see." Lily was upstairs. It had not been a trick of the light.

Chapter Twenty-Eight

The house had the dusty smell of abandonment about it. Tatiana was struck by the absence of what should have been there, the faint odour of boiled rice and fried garlic; the smell of human presence, of soap and dirty socks; the scent of perfume and hair oil that lingered long after the wearer had gone; the dampness that hung in the air from bath water and wet laundry. Lily's amah led her through the empty house, up stairs and down hallways to what had been Lily's sitting room, the room where they'd shared tea and talk for nearly a decade.

Lily was sitting on a slipper chair that she had moved to beside the window. She was staring vacantly into the courtyard below, once the hub of the household and now so silent and devoid of activity. She turned her head slightly when they entered the room, as if she'd heard a faint sound, like a fly buzzing or a tap dripping in a bathroom down the hall.

"Lily," Tatiana said, rushing to her side. "Lily. I'm so glad to see you. You've been away for so long."

It took Lily a few seconds to recognize her. She must have been miles away in thought. "Tatiana?" She focused her eyes on her friend's face. "Tatiana? Is it really you?"

"Yes, it's me." she said. The air in the room was very still, as if all the energy had been sucked out of it and the windows sealed shut. "Aren't you happy to see me?"

"Why didn't you come last spring? Why didn't you come to say goodbye?"

"What are you talking about? I tried several times to see

you, but they kept telling me you weren't in. They wouldn't let me see you."

"Who wouldn't let you see me?"

"Your brother and Wu-ling. They told me you didn't want to see me."

It was as if a light had come on in the room. "They did?" Lily said.

"Yes." Tatiana was getting annoyed. What was the matter with her? Lily seemed to take forever to register what she was saying. She wondered if her friend was on some medication that kept her in a kind of fog. "Are you all right? Has something happened?"

"Yes," Lily said. "A lot has happened. Daniel is dead. My husband is dead. I have lost my son, and I have become a ghost wandering through my own life."

"Yes, of course," said Tatiana, regretting her anger and taking hold of Lily's hand. "I'm so sorry about Wu-ling. It must have been terrible. How is Leonard? Does he understand what happened?"

Suddenly Lily covered her face with her hands and began to sob. "Oh, Tati," she cried. "They've taken him away from me. They've taken my son."

"They've taken Leonard? Who's taken him?"

"Wu-ling's Number One Brother and his wife. They have no children, and when Wu-ling died, they said it would be better if they adopted Leonard and raised him as their own son." Lily's face was twisted in agony, and she made no attempt to wipe away her tears.

"But they can't do that," said Tatiana. "He's your son. You're his mother."

"No," Lily said, shaking her head, "he's Wu-ling's son. He belongs to Wu-ling's family. I'm a widow now, and they can decide my future. Without a husband, I am like a ghost."

"What do you mean, a ghost? You're not a ghost. I can see you."

Lily smiled, but it was a small, bitter smile. "In China," she said, "a single woman is subject to her father and her brothers, and a married woman is subject to her husband and her mother-in-law. If my son were a grown man, he could protect me, but he is still a boy. Wu-ling's parents and his brother have decided I am not able to raise Leonard properly, and I do not have the right to contradict them."

"This is the twentieth century, Lily. There are courts and lawyers. You can fight them."

"You don't understand, Tati. I have no money. I no longer exist." Lily had stopped crying, and Tatiana saw how thin she had become. There were dark circles under her eyes, and she had hollows under her cheekbones that hadn't been there before.

"How is Annette?" Lily asked, suddenly changing the subject.

"Not very well at all," Tatiana replied. "She's having a terrible time over Daniel's death. You know what happened, don't you?"

"Yes. I read about it in the newspaper."

"Did you know he was shot and his body thrown in the river?"

"Yes," Lily said, looking at her hands, which were clasped tightly together in her lap. "I know all about it." The newspaper had only reported that Daniel's body was found in the river. The police had not released any other information. Tatiana didn't ask how Lily knew he had been shot. Someone must have told her.

Lily asked if she would take her to see Annette some time. Tatiana said Annette had bad days and worse days, but she would tell her that Lily wanted to see her. "She doesn't know about you and Daniel," Tatiana said, "and she doesn't know that Daniel was murdered." Lily flinched at the word "murder", and Tatiana regretted having used it. "I'm sorry," she said. "I wasn't thinking. I asked the police not to tell her because I was afraid it would be too much for her. She's so close to having a complete breakdown. I didn't know what else to do."

"I see," said Lily. "Then it's probably best that she doesn't know."

The amah brought them tea, and they began to talk about other things. Lily asked how Tatiana had been, and Tatiana told her of the many changes in her life. Lily was surprised to hear that Katarina had died and that Olga and Jean Paul had gone to Canada.

"But now you're all alone," she said. "How terrible for you."

"Yes," said Tatiana. "I didn't realize until they had gone that I had nobody left I could talk to. That's why I kept checking to see if you'd come back. Nobody would tell me where you were, and I had no way of finding you."

"After Daniel…" Lily hesitated, "…disappeared, I was completely beside myself. Wu-ling had the doctor come and give me something—I think it may have been morphine—to help me sleep. I lost track of the days, and the next thing I knew, Leonard and I were staying with Wu-ling's eldest brother, and I had no way of communicating with anybody. They watched me constantly. I wasn't free to come and go, and I was only allowed to see my son when they permitted it. I was treated like an invalid, or a criminal." She began to cry again. "Oh, Tati," she said, "you have no idea what it's been like. I'm so ashamed. Sometimes I just want to die."

"Don't say that. You can't die, Lily. You're all I have left." Tatiana couldn't bear to hear her talk that way. Everything and everybody she cared about had either left her or, like Annette and Lily, were drifting away, and she had no way of preventing it.

Tatiana's life during the next two months was that of a visiting nurse with two patients. She spent most of her time going back and forth between Annette and Lily, performing the tasks neither of them seemed capable of. She brought them food, filled their doctors' prescriptions, took their dirty clothing and linen to the laundry and delivered it back to them when it was cleaned. It was as though she were performing some kind of penance, and, in some part of her unexamined soul, Tatiana believed that she deserved it. It was right that she should be taking care of these two women whose misfortune she had had a hand in creating. Had she not, however inadvertently, initiated a series of events that had left both Lily and Annette bereft? If she hadn't brought Daniel to Lily in the first place, none of it would have happened. She had interfered with the natural course of events and now she was being punished.

Lily hadn't asked again to see Annette, but Tatiana kept looking for an opportunity to bring them together. She thought perhaps they might be able to comfort each other in a way that she could not comfort either of them herself. Finally, near the end of December, with Shanghai plunging into another nasty bout of winter weather, Tatiana suggested to Lily that they call on Annette. She was on her way over there with some groceries, and it seemed like an opportunity. She thought that Lily hesitated for a moment, but then she told herself she had imagined it. Maybe Lily was just trying to decide whether she should change her clothes or go in what she was wearing.

Lily went and got her fur coat, and Tatiana realized that she would probably never buy one for herself. She pulled her cloth coat a little more tightly around her and went out to the street to hail a cab. Lily didn't speak at all on the way over. She was like an actress silently rehearsing her part before going on stage. She seemed to be concentrating very hard on whatever was in her mind. Tatiana thought it best to leave her alone. Lily had become more and more withdrawn over the past two months, which was worrying. Lily rarely left the house, and then only if Tatiana put her foot down and insisted. It was hard enough watching Annette disintegrate; she didn't want the same thing to happen to Lily. She knew Lily needed time to grieve, as did Annette. In fact, all three of them were grieving and needed occasionally to sink into their own sadness, but Tatiana kept one eye on an invisible clock in a futile attempt to pull both of her friends back.

Lily and Annette greeted each other tentatively. Tatiana had told Annette that she would be bringing Lily for a visit at her request. Annette accepted it, as she accepted most things Tatiana said, with a noncommittal shrug. She was no longer capable of saying yes or no to anything. Life had become a slow-moving panorama that she watched through a thick pane of glass. Nothing seemed to touch her or move her. The glass wall was there twenty-four hours a day, a permanent installation. Who was left to smash it down?

Annette and Lily had never been friends, but they had shared Tatiana between them for so many years that they had become a kind of strange threesome. Now they had more in common with each other than Tatiana had with either of them. She watched as Lily approached Annette, who had not risen from her chair. Tatiana noticed that Annette's ankles were swollen from inactivity, and there was a network of blue veins working their way around them like threads unravelling from the hem of a dress. Lily knelt down in front of Annette and took her hand.

"I'm so sorry," she whispered. "I'm so very sorry for what has happened."

Annette looked at her and nodded. "It is a nightmare," she said, "from which I will never awake."

"I know," said Lily.

Then Annette started to talk to her in a way she had not spoken to Tatiana or anybody since Daniel's death. She told Lily that everything about her had died with Daniel except her body. It still walked around the house, ate and slept, bathed and changed clothes, but it was a meaningless existence. Like a machine that you put fuel into so the wheels would go round. It had no heart, no soul, no feeling.

Tatiana left them to their conversation and went into the kitchen to make tea. She hadn't expected this reaction from Annette, but she felt a surge of hope that maybe this would be the impetus for change. Maybe Annette had just been waiting for the right person to tell, or the right time to tell someone, but Tatiana should have learned by then how cruel the fates can be.

Lily stayed for a couple of hours. She told Annette what it had been like for her since Wu-ling's death, and the decision of his family to take Leonard away from her. "But he is still alive," Annette reminded her. "You must never give up hope. He will always know who his real mother is." Tatiana thought Lily seemed to take heart from this, but maybe it was just her imagining they were comforting one another. Maybe Tatiana wanted it so badly she believed it was really happening.

On the way back to her house, Lily didn't speak. She had said she did not want to be alone and asked Tatiana to come back with her. She suggested they could have something to eat together. She would send her amah out to get some food. Tatiana realized Lily had not been comforted by the visit and was agitated and more distressed than before. She didn't know what to say, so she said nothing.

They got back to the compound and, as soon as they entered the house, Lily asked her to wait in the main sitting room. She said she had something she needed to do. But first she would find the amah and tell her to go out and get some food for them. Tatiana went into the sitting room and turned on one of the lamps. It was cold in the big room, and she wondered why Lily had asked her to wait there instead of letting her come upstairs with her. They had never used this room before. It was formal, and the furniture was uncomfortable. Tatiana sat down on the edge of one of the wooden chairs and waited. She kept her coat on and stuffed her gloved hands into her pockets to keep warm.

After several minutes, the amah came down the stairs and went out the front door. Tatiana waited, expecting Lily to follow, but still she did not come. Tatiana tried to think of a reason why Lily would keep her waiting in this unheated room and finally decided it was because she had wanted to have a good cry. The visit with Annette must have been more upsetting for her than Tatiana thought. They had spoken to each other from the heart, as mothers, but for Lily it must have been especially painful, because she had a secret she could never divulge to Annette. She had been in love with Annette's son, and he had broken her heart. Tatiana thought about her part in Lily's imagined love affair and asked herself again if it would have been better if she had said nothing about seeing Daniel at the Kitty Kat with his homosexual friends. Every time she asked herself that question, she came up with a different answer. Olga's words always rang in her ears: "It's the truth that matters. Only the truth matters." How would things have been different if she had not told Lily the truth? If she had said nothing or told her a kind lie? Or if she had let her find out some other way that her love was impossible. Maybe Lily would have come, in time, to realize on her own that it had been a girlish infatuation, and they could have laughed about it. But Daniel was dead, and there would have been no time for Lily's infatuation to fade. It had ended so abruptly.

She heard the front door open, and the amah come in carrying the food. At the same time, she heard Lily coming down the stairs. Tatiana got up and walked into the hallway. Lily was carrying two suitcases, and Tatiana could see she *had* been crying. Lily put the suitcases by the door and said, "Come. Let's eat."

They went into the dining room, and the amah started unpacking the food and setting out bowls and chopsticks. Then she went into the kitchen to make some tea. Tatiana wasn't very hungry, but Lily dished some food onto the plates, and they began to eat. Rice. Steamed chicken in broth. Fried pork and vegetables. Street-vendor food.

"I've decided to go back," said Lily. "I will live with my shame so I can be near my son."

"I understand," Tatiana said. She knew Lily had no other choice.

"When I left my brother-in-law's house," Lily said, "it was with the intention of never going back. I was treated no better than a servant and was only allowed to watch my son from a distance. I couldn't bear to see him with his new parents." She said this with much bitterness. Tatiana also heard anger and hurt in her voice. "I thought a life of solitude would be preferable, but now I realize I was wrong," Lily continued. "As Annette said, at least my son is alive. Even watching him grow up as someone else's son will be better than not seeing him at all."

"Oh, Lily," Tatiana said. "I'm so sorry."

"Please," she said, "don't pity me. When I look at Annette, I realize that I am the lucky one."

They had their tea, and Lily went back upstairs to pack a few more things. Tatiana went with her and the amah to the station and stood in line with Lily while she bought the tickets. She helped them find their seats then stood on the platform and watched as the train slowly pulled out of the station.

Toronto, Canada
1957

Chapter Twenty-Eight

Today, after thirty years, I will go to Union Station in Toronto to meet Lily's train. It's a day I never thought I'd see. I have cleaned up the apartment and prepared the bed in the spare room. Anastasia took me shopping yesterday, and we filled the refrigerator with food. I'm not sure how long Lily will be staying with me. There's so much to talk about.

Toronto has a good public transportation system, so I take the streetcar to Yonge Street then switch to the new subway train that goes underground to Union Station. We will take a taxi back, but there's no point in spending money needlessly when I can use the transit. I enjoy riding in the new red streetcars. The city has gradually been replacing the old wooden trams with these "red rockets". Actually, I will miss the old trams. They remind me of Shanghai, where a wooden trolley ran up and down Nanking Road. Olga and I used to ride it, pretending we were "travelling ladies". Now I sometimes just get on the streetcar and go for an outing. I still like sitting by the window and watching the buildings and the people go by. I see something different every time. The streetcar moves slowly, so I can see the details I might miss riding in a car or even walking. I feel like a tourist. The subway is modern and fast, but there isn't much to look at except the advertising posters and expressionless people reading newspapers.

Union Station is a magnificent edifice with a domed ceiling like a cathedral. Sounds echo off the marble walls, and it's filled with the excitement of people on the move. Lily's train, which is coming from Vancouver, is the one that goes across Canada to Montreal. Her ticket allows her to get off the train wherever she wants and get back on and continue her journey whenever she chooses. But she has come direct, without stopping. It has taken two nights and three days for the trip. Her brother has paid for a sleeper, so she doesn't have to sit up the whole way.

I have arrived in plenty of time so I won't miss her. I'm not sure what she looks like after all these years, but I'm sure I'll recognize her. I sit on a hard marble bench for a while, then get up and pace back and forth before the arthritis in my hips starts to ache. The train's arrival is announced over the loudspeaker, and those of us who are waiting turn our heads expectantly toward the gate. We're not allowed onto the platform, so I have no idea whether Lily has gotten off the train first or last. People start to appear, looking weary and dragging their luggage. Some are accompanied by porters, or redcaps as they're called because of the flat red caps they wear, their luggage piled onto carts. I watch for a Chinese face, heart-shaped with a fringe of black hair cut straight over the eyes. A few Chinese women come through the gate, accompanied by husbands, children, grandparents. But none of them looks like the Lily I am expecting.

Then one of the grandmothers separates herself from a family and walks toward me. She is short and stocky and walks stiffly, dragging a canvas bag. She's wearing a shapeless, ill-fitting dark blue outfit of pants and jacket and carrying a puffy, quilted black coat. Her hair is cut short like a boy's and streaked with grey. There are deep lines in her face, especially around the mouth, which is set in a straight line, as if she never smiles.

"Tatiana?" she says, and I hear an old woman's voice. It can't be her.

"Lily?" She sees the look of shock on my face and smiles. The lines on her face and around her eyes turn up. Her cheeks puff out like apples.

She drops the handles of her bag and throws her arms around me. It's the first time in our lives we've hugged each other. I'm amazed at her strength and remember my mother's desperate hugs from so long ago.

"I can't believe I'm here, looking at you," she says when she has released me. "You look the same."

I throw back my head and laugh. "I do not," I say. "I'm an old woman now."

"So am I," she says. "Look at me. I'm fat. You're still so thin and so smartly dressed."

"I worked in a dress shop for years after I came here," I tell her. "Employee discount. They wanted us to be attractive for the customers."

"You always wore good clothes," says Lily. "So did I, for that matter." She sighed. "So many changes. We have a lot to tell each other."

When we get back to the apartment, Lily takes a bath while I make lunch and a pot of tea. I have bought the best black tea I can find. Anastasia took me to Eaton's department store, to the section where they sell imported biscuits, chocolate and tea. I have made homemade chicken soup with noodles I bought in a shop in Chinatown. I got the chicken from a butcher on Queen Street, and I have carefully removed the cooked meat from the bones. There are also two chicken hearts in the soup, one for Lily and one for me. Lily used to tell me I didn't eat enough vegetables, but there are plenty of vegetables in the soup— carrots, onions, celery and parsnip.

When Lily comes into the kitchen she's wearing clean clothes, black pants and a white long-sleeved blouse. Her hair is damp and her skin shines from being scrubbed with soap. She looks relaxed, but she is probably just tired. I know she's tense about going to live with her brother. She told me in the taxi she didn't know if she had the energy to look after small children. The years under the Communists have been hard. Food has been scarce, and she has had to work without days off or holidays.

Where do we begin? She solves the problem by asking me when I came to Canada.

"In 1936," I say. "Olga and Jean Paul managed to make it through the Great Depression after the stock market crashed in 1929. They had started a dry cleaning business. Olga was such a good seamstress, she had a full-time job mending and making alterations to the clothing their customers brought in. When I arrived in Toronto, they gave me a job at the counter that paid my room and board."

"It must have been hard for you. Did you work there many years?" Lily asks.

"No. After a year, I found a job in a dress shop where I was on my feet eight hours a day. It was much harder, but I was more independent. It was a good shop, right downtown near Yonge and Queen, and it catered to a stylish crowd. The owner had hired me because she saw I had good fashion sense and was well groomed. She thought my Russian accent gave me a European authority, and she told the customers I was from France. They didn't know the difference. After twenty years, she laid me off, saying they wanted to attract a younger clientele. Fortunately, I had saved my money carefully and could manage. When things are really busy in the shop, I sometimes work part-time to help out."

We've finished the soup and are drinking the strong tea and eating chocolate biscuits. "So decadent," Lily says, taking another. "But what about in between?" she asks. "After I left Shanghai, what did you do?"

"I got married," I say.

Lily is genuinely shocked. "No. Not you, Tatiana. You said you would never get married."

"I know. But I was so lonely after you left. I turned my back on the life I had been living in Shanghai, but I had nothing to replace it."

I learned what Lily meant when she said she had become a ghost walking through her own life. I felt completely used up in those days after Lily left Shanghai. If someone had stuck a pin in my arm, I doubt I would have noticed.

"During the month of February," I tell her, "I must have smoked a thousand cigarettes. After a week I stopped drinking; my stomach felt like it was full of razor blades. Food didn't interest me either, and I was subsisting on one bowl of rice and a bowl of soup a day." On the first of March, in an act of desperation, I had sent a telegram to Ian in Malaya.

Russian spinster seeks marriage to plantation manager stop Does offer still stand stop

"Ian sent me a ticket within a week," I continue. "I arranged for someone to check on Annette and buy her groceries. Part of me knew I was abandoning her to her despair, but another part of me knew I had to leave Shanghai. I had nothing left to give Annette. What she needed nobody could give her. She needed her son back." Lily is nodding, staring at the chocolate biscuit that is slowly melting in her fingers.

As I stood on the deck of the ship and watched the Bund recede into the distance, it was as if I were watching a film going backwards. Twenty-two years earlier, I had stood and watched with anticipation as our ship had moved closer and closer to Shanghai, a city so full of possibilities. I had spent two thirds of my life in China, and now I was leaving to start again in another country. What should have been a great adventure in my life was just another act of self-preservation, not much different from eating a bowl of hot soup every day. I knew it wasn't fair to unload my miserable self on Ian, but I told myself I had changed, and we would make a go of it. Besides, what choice did I have? I could have gone to Canada with Olga and Jean Paul, I reminded myself, but it seemed the more difficult option. I preferred the path of least resistance.

I felt a kind of relief when I saw Ian standing on the dock at Singapore. He represented something solid that I could hold on to. Maybe he would give me the stability I needed. I knew I wasn't in love with him, and I hoped I wouldn't ruin his life. He was a kind man who treated me well, and he was easy to get along with. I thought that might be enough to make a marriage work. We had both declared that we were not the marrying kind, but loneliness has a way of redrawing the boundaries that we're prepared to cross.

Much to my surprise, we managed to stick it out for eight years. They were healing years for me. Or maybe they were hiding years. I had worn myself out trying to understand what had happened and blaming myself for all of it. In Malaya, I tried to let it go. I tried to forget. Ian was away most days, leaving early in the morning and returning after dark for a late supper. I read a lot of books and magazines, planted a garden of sorts and learned to drive. We both drank more than we should have, but there wasn't much else to do in the middle of the jungle. Ian had a phonograph and, as he'd promised, we "went dancing" several nights a week. The first few years passed surprisingly quickly. But I had built my marriage on a foundation of sand, and it was doomed to fail eventually.

When it did, I had only one option left. Canada.

"But why did your marriage fail?" Lily asks. "It sounds like you got on well enough."

"We did, at first. But I think I got bored. We had no

neighbours, so I rarely saw other people, except the planters and the servants. There was no one to talk to. No place to go. The closest town was thirty miles away over a bad road. Even though I had learned to drive, it took almost two hours to get there, and when you did get there, it was nothing but a weekly market and a few shops. You couldn't even get a decent cup of tea." I take a deep breath and brush some crumbs off my lap. We're drinking tea and eating more chocolate biscuits. I've never talked to anyone about my marriage before. It gives me no pleasure to remember it now.

"The best thing about Malaya was the weather. It never got cold. But sometimes it was so hot, you couldn't do anything for days. And when it rained, it came down in torrents. You could drown in the mud, it was so deep. I got irritable and started blaming Ian for my empty days. Sometimes I picked a fight with him just to make something happen. It wasn't his fault."

Lily sighs and shakes her head. "Poor Tatiana," she says. "You were so beautiful, so glamorous, and you knew so many people. But you never fell in love."

It's true. "I never worked hard enough for love," I tell Lily. "I wanted only the highs, and I wasn't prepared to weather the lows."

"And so now you sit here in your apartment and think about the things you did and didn't do," says Lily.

"Yes, I suppose that's what I do."

"And is it enough?"

"I've learned to like my own company—as long as I can get out once in a while and see what's happening. You know how I always liked doing things my own way. I always hated it when somebody tried to tell me what to do." Lily nods her head knowingly. "I'm content, I guess. What right have I to ask for more? Olga and Jean Paul have been so good to me. And Anastasia and Nicholas have been better than I could have imagined. They're my family. Ian sends me a bit of money every month. He's a good man. I think he would have carried on forever the way we were, but it was too lonely for me. It was different for him. He had his work. All in all, though, I can't complain."

Lily smiles, and we both reach for another chocolate biscuit. "And what about you, Lily? Tell me about your life."

But Lily isn't ready to talk yet. She says she's tired, and would I mind if she took a nap. There's time. Her brother isn't expecting her until the weekend. She can tell me about her life later.

Chapter Twenty-Nine

I take Lily out to dinner at a little restaurant I often go to on Coxwell Avenue. It's a family restaurant, run by an Italian husband and wife, Gino and Maria, who've been in Canada for a few years. Gino is a short, round man with a heart as big as his belly. Maria is even shorter and wears clothes that are two sizes too big so it looks like she's lost a lot of weight. I guess she doesn't eat her own cooking. I like the food here. It's always fresh, and Maria bakes bread every day. It's less than a ten-minute walk, but I notice that Lily is breathing a bit heavily by the time we arrive.

"Are you all right?" I ask.

"Yes," she says. "I'm fine. My coat is heavy, that's all."

We find a table, and I introduce Lily to Gino, who brings us water and takes our order. I recommend the spaghetti with tomato sauce. It has little pork spareribs and meatballs in it, and I think Lily will like it. I order ravioli and a salad. Gino brings us a basket of fresh, crusty bread and a little dish of butter. While we wait for our dinner, I ask Lily about Annette. She takes a sip of water.

"So heartbreaking," she says. "Annette died a long time ago. Maybe twenty-five years." The news makes me sad, but I'm not surprised. Annette had lost the will to live after Daniel died. It would have taken a miracle to bring her back. Her behaviour had become increasingly self-destructive.

"How did you find out?" I ask Lily.

"I didn't find out until a few years ago. Someone from Annette's neighbourhood was sent to our village to work in the orphanage. She told me that one morning Annette just didn't wake up. They suspected she had taken too much laudanum and alcohol together. She drank a lot and ate very little. It's no wonder her body gave up."

Gino brings our food, and we begin to eat. The ravioli is so tender it melts on my tongue. Maria's tomato sauce is smooth and delicious as always. It's the kind of food that provides comfort. It delights the taste buds and warms the stomach. I try not to think about what Annette had become in those last months I spent in Shanghai.

I want to ask Lily about Leonard, but I'm hoping she'll talk about him of her own volition. I also want to talk about Daniel, but these will be painful conversations, and I dare not rush into them.

We eat, making small talk, then go home. That night Lily goes to bed early. She says she's so used to getting up at five o'clock in the morning that by eight or nine at night, she's ready for bed. I show her where the tea is and tell her to make herself at home and eat and drink whatever she wants in the morning. When I get up at eight, I tell her, we'll have a proper breakfast.

"I know," she says. "You have always been a night owl. Why should you change now?"

"Exactly," I say. "I'll see you tomorrow."

The next day, we take a walk around the neighbourhood for some fresh air. It's the first of March, but there's no sign that spring is around the corner. Snowflakes flutter and swirl around us and leave a light dusting on the sidewalk that puffs around our feet when we step on it. I am not the fittest person in the world, but I am not winded by our short walk. Lily is, on the other hand, and I wonder if she is well. Life couldn't have been easy for a middle-aged woman in China during the years when the Communists were establishing themselves.

"I want you to tell me about life in China after I left," I say to her when we get back to the apartment. She has taken the stairs slowly, stopping after every two or three to catch her breath. I make her sit in the armchair and put her feet up. "I'll make some tea," I say, "and then you can tell me. I only know what I read in the papers, and I'm sure most of it's propaganda. I want to hear your version."

She begins slowly, trying to put it all together into a story. The 1930s and '40s in China were tumultuous and hard. First there was the Japanese attack on Manchuria in 1931 then, later, all-out war with Japan. Chiang Kai-shek was trying to bring about economic reforms to strengthen his hold on government while, at the same time, Mao Tse-tung was building the Communist Party in the countryside and developing his People's Liberation Army into a guerrilla force. When the Americans declared war on Japan in 1941, Chiang's Kuomintang was recognized as China's official government. But, by the end of the war in 1945, the Kuomintang was seriously weakened by infighting and inflation. By 1949, Chiang had retreated to the island of Formosa, and Mao entered Peking and established the People's Republic of China.

"Because our families were so closely associated with Chiang Kai-shek, our land and houses were confiscated for redistribution to the peasants. Wu-ling's brother tried to fool the Communists into believing we were much poorer than we were, but it didn't work. The family was too well known. We were forced to join reform groups and read the works of Chairman Mao. I was sent up north to work in an orphanage and, by a miracle, re-established contact with my eldest brother. I had lost track of my family a few years after I went to live with Wu-ling's brother. They stopped writing to me, or their letters never got to me. I don't know which." Lily keeps looking at her hands while she talks, rubbing each of her fingers with her thumb, first the right hand, then the left hand, over and over again. "Finally, one of my letters reached him, and he wrote back," she continues. "He told me that he was the only one left. I knew my mother and father had died some years earlier, but he told me that Number Two Brother had been executed—that's the word he used—by the Communists for his association with the Kuomintang. Number Three Brother, though, had immigrated to Canada in 1936, the same year you came here Tatiana, but I didn't know that." I nod my head. "If you remember, he was in the army. He had been wounded in Manchuria and retired. I wrote to my brother in Canada, and he started the procedure to bring me here. I was lucky," she says. "Not many people can get out." I don't see how luck has been on Lily's side. So far it seems only bad things have happened to her.

"You haven't said anything about Leonard," I say gently. "What happened to him?"

This is the part of the story she doesn't want to tell. She bows her head for a minute as if to compose herself, then looks up at me, her eyes shiny with tears.

"Leonard's new parents," she says, referring to Wu-ling's elder brother and his wife, "did not see fit to continue Leonard's piano lessons, even though I pleaded with them. They said there was no future in it. Instead, they sent him to military college after his eleventh birthday." She pauses for a minute to give me time to think about what she has just said. Leonard, her beautiful, talented son, still a child at eleven, had been sent away from his family to become a soldier. To live a life of rigorous discipline, to learn to fight and kill. I can't imagine the sensitive boy I'd known wearing a military uniform and carrying a gun.

"It broke my heart," says Lily. "As if my heart had not already been broken ten times over." I can think of nothing to say to her. There are no words to comfort her. "But that was not the worst. When he graduated from military college and was sent to fight the Japanese in Manchuria, he deserted and joined

Mao Tse-tung's army. After Chairman Mao's victory, he was regarded as a hero and rewarded with an important position in the People's Republic. He was the one who arranged for me to leave China and come to Canada. Otherwise, I would not be here."

Lily is exhausted, and she has gone to her room to have a nap. I sit in my armchair thinking about what she has told me. As far as I can tell, very few of Lily's or Wu-ling's family survived the change of government, except Number Three Brother, who had got out in time and was in Toronto, less than five miles away from my apartment. And Leonard, who had, either by good fortune or good judgment, managed to acquire a place in the new Communist regime for himself. How long would he remain secure, I wonder? Would Mao be better able than Lenin and Stalin to keep his party together, or would it split into factions and be destroyed by political infighting? Would Leonard be lucky twice and choose the right side again? At least he had done one last thing for his mother. He had gotten her out of China and into Canada, where she would be looked after. But at what price? In all likelihood, Lily would never see her son again. She must have known that when she got on the ship. The first time he had been taken from her, she had comforted herself with the fact that at least he was still alive. Would that be enough to see her through this second, and final, separation?

When she wakes up, I ask Lily if she wants to go to Chinatown for dinner and meet her brother. She shakes her head.

"No," she says. "I'm not ready yet. I will have to meet his whole family, and they will ask me so many questions. I don't have the energy. Just a few more days, if you don't mind. I'll try not to be a burden."

I laugh. "You're hardly a burden, Lily. I'm *honoured*," I say, emphasizing the word, "that you chose to stay with me first. You can stay as long as you want."

I tell her Olga has invited us the next night for dinner and that Ana and Nicholas and their families will be there. "Do you think you can handle it?" I ask. "They're very excited about seeing you."

She smiles. "I'll be fine," she says. "But I'll have to rest during the day."

"That's okay. I'm going to the hairdresser tomorrow, so you'll have a few hours of peace and quiet."

We go to Gino's again for dinner. We both order minestrone soup and share an order of ravioli stuffed with spinach.

"This is delicious," says Lily. "I haven't had Italian food for many, many years. Since I was in Switzerland as a student. I remember thinking it wasn't so different from Chinese food— except not fried. Lots of noodles and dumplings."

"And cheese," I remind her.

"And cheese," she says and laughs. "Too much cheese."

"You'll be shocked when you see what passes for Chinese food here. It's nothing like what you're used to. Mostly bean sprouts and thick, gluey sauces. Much heavier than I remember. But I'm sure your brother will give you the real stuff. I can't imagine Chinese people eating sweet and sour chicken balls."

"Sweet and sour what?" she says.

"Don't ask," I tell her. "But if someone tries to serve you something covered in a thick, bright red sauce, say no."

She laughs again, and I can almost imagine the last forty years haven't happened. Given time, maybe we'll be able to recapture some of the easy camaraderie we had once enjoyed.

Chapter Thirty

The next day we spend the morning chatting. I tell Lily about Olga's children and grandchildren and show her the photographs they've sent me after every birthday party and Christmas. Lily seems relaxed, and I don't want to upset her by talking about Daniel, the one topic we haven't yet discussed. Like the elephant in the room, I know we won't be able to ignore it forever, but I want her to enjoy the family dinner at Olga's. For that matter, I want to enjoy it, too.

"How did you find me," I ask, "if you didn't know I'd come to Canada?"

"It wasn't so difficult," she says. "When I wrote to my brother, I asked him to see if Olga and Jean Paul were living in the city. I knew they were also in Canada. He looked in the phone book and found their number. When he called, somebody with an English accent answered and she told him where you were living. Good detective work," she said.

It must have been Olga's cleaning woman who had answered the phone. She's the only one I can think of who has an English accent.

Jean Paul comes and picks us up at half past four in his new car. It has an automatic transmission that he says is much easier to drive with a wooden leg than a car with a clutch. "Life is good in Canada," he says. What he means is, life is good now. In the beginning, during the Depression, life had not been so good. Especially compared to Shanghai, where he and Olga had plenty of money and servants. But they had made the right choice. Life in Shanghai had become very difficult indeed for those who stayed, especially the foreigners. Now their dry cleaning business is prosperous, and Olga and Jean Paul have moved to a roomy bungalow in the west end of the city not far from the shop. They have employees to do the work, but Jean Paul still likes to go in most days.

Olga's house is comfortably furnished and neat as a pin. She's still a meticulous housekeeper, and her cleaning woman comes once a week to help her. Together they turn the house upside down then set it right again. Dust is not allowed to settle in Olga's house. Even in the summer, when the windows are open, I never see a speck of dust. Mind you, my eyes are so well trained in the art of not noticing dust that I may not have seen what was there.

When we arrive, the house is full of cooking smells. Roast chicken with garlic and baked potatoes that I know will be served with sour cream and chives. I can smell red cabbage, which is one of my favourites and, in amongst all the savoury smells, I detect the rich, warm scent of chocolate. Olga has outdone herself. She has prepared a feast in honour of Lily's arrival. Ana and Nicholas don't remember Lily, but they have heard all about her from both Olga and me. Nicholas, who so resembles his father I sometimes call him Jean Paul, is a history teacher. He's interested in the politics of China, which Lily patiently discusses, trying to answer his many questions. I notice that she refers to Mao as Chairman Mao and, occasionally, Fearless Leader, which Nicholas is too polite to comment on. He doesn't ask what her politics are; they speak in much larger terms. The children are amazingly well-behaved, and Lily seems to enjoy watching and listening to them. When Nicholas's wife, Susan, a small, pretty woman with round blue eyes and curly blonde hair, tires of all the political talk, she asks if Lily would like to hold their six-month-old baby girl, Katherine. I see that Lily is both relieved and delighted.

Dinner is easy and convivial. Ana helps Olga put out the two large roasted chickens with stuffing, and Jean Paul carves and serves the meat. There is mushroom gravy and green beans, too. Much more food than we can eat.

"Nobody ever leaves my house hungry," says Olga. "Isn't that right, Tatiana?"

"Absolutely," I say. "It's the Russian way."

After we eat our dessert, large slabs of chocolate cake, we sit around the dining room table drinking tea. Nicholas and Susan say they have to go. Nicholas still has exam papers to mark, and the baby is beginning to fuss. Ana and Keith and the children stay a bit longer but, by eight o'clock, they're gone as well.

I can see Lily is tired, and I am just about to ask Jean Paul to drive us home when, out of nowhere, Olga says, "Did they ever find out who murdered that young man? You know, Annette's son, Daniel?"

I could strangle her. I have been so careful not to mention Daniel until I thought Lily was ready to talk about him. In fact, I had been planning to tackle the subject the next day. I look daggers at Olga but she doesn't seem to notice. Lily doesn't answer at first. She's staring at a gravy stain on the white tablecloth. Then she looks at Olga.

"No," she says quietly. "They didn't."

Olga shakes her head and is about to say something when I interject.

"We really should go, Olga. Lily's usually in bed by nine o'clock and up with the birds. Aren't you, Lily?" She nods.

I thank Olga, perhaps a little too effusively, for the dinner. I don't want the evening to end on a sour note. There will be plenty of time to chew Olga out about her insensitivity. Not that she would care. She was never one to dwell on the past. She probably thought that Lily had put the whole thing behind her long ago. I didn't think so.

When we get back to the apartment, Lily doesn't say anything except that she's had a wonderful time. "You are so lucky," she says, "to have your family. Never take anything for granted, Tatiana. I think life has taught us both that."

"Goodnight, Lily," I say. "We'll talk more tomorrow."

It's Friday and our last day together. I want to ask her about Daniel before she leaves to begin her new life. It seems important that we do it now. We might never again have the chance to speak openly about the tragedy that changed everything. Once she begins taking care of her brother's grandchildren, she might not be in the right frame of mind. Olga has sent us home with leftovers, so we have no need to go anywhere; nothing else is demanding our attention.

"Was it true what you told Olga last night? That they never solved Daniel's murder?" We both have our feet up on the coffee table, drinking coffee after a light breakfast of fruit and toast. We're still stuffed from Olga's dinner.

"Yes, it's true," she replies. "They never found out who did it."

"Were there any rumours? New clues? Anything?"

"I don't know, Tatiana. I left Shanghai."

"Did you ever have any suspicions?" I ask.

She looks at me. "Did you?"

"A few," I say. "But nothing I could back up. Inspector Malbon told me that Daniel was shot with a small-calibre gun. A lady's gun, he called it. So it was unlikely that he was accidentally killed by soldiers during the street fighting, which is what I had originally thought might have happened. But the inspector told me that if a woman had killed Daniel, she would have had help from a man. He said a woman wouldn't be able to dump the body in the river. I always wondered about the people he was with at the Kitty Kat. I never really knew any of them, but a few of them made me uncomfortable. One in particular, I remember. He had very cold eyes. He might have used a small gun, and he would have been strong enough to lift a body."

I can see this distresses her. Maybe I've said too much.

"You never told Wu-ling?" I ask.

"No," she says. Her voice is a hoarse whisper. "Never."

"I just wondered," I say. "He was very protective of you. As was your middle brother. Neither of them liked me much, and they told me to stay away from you. But I told you that, didn't I?"

"You told me they wouldn't let you see me. Not that they said to stay away from me."

"What's the difference?"

"One is protective, the other is very aggressive."

"They said that I had upset you. Which I had."

"Yes. I couldn't hide my unhappiness from Wu-ling. When you told me about Daniel, I couldn't stop crying. I wouldn't tell him what was the matter, so he blamed you. I'm sorry for that, Tatiana. It wasn't fair, but I had no way to change his mind."

"And things happened very quickly after that," I say. "Daniel disappeared. You were sent to your brother-in-law's. Daniel's body was found. Then Wu-ling was killed. You must have been in a terrible state."

"I was," she says. "I don't think I've ever gotten over it. Any of it."

"Even after all these years," I say, "it would be good to know. How can there be justice for Daniel if his killer isn't punished?"

"Yes. It would be good to know."

Lily falls quiet after that, and I go into the kitchen to make myself a chicken sandwich. Lily says she isn't hungry. I turn on the television, and we watch the soap operas, three in a row. I'm hooked on them. The characters' lives are so complicated, it makes me feel better about my own life. At least I'm not dealing with a cheating husband and a pregnant teenage daughter.

"Do you ever wish I hadn't told you?" I ask Lily when I turn off the television. "About Daniel?"

She thinks about it for a minute. "Honestly?" she says.

"Yes, of course."

"Yes," she says, and I am stung. I have spent thirty years blaming myself for everything, and she has just confirmed my worst fears. I guess I had been hoping she would absolve me by telling me she would always be grateful that I had told her Daniel wasn't in love with her. "Everything might have been different," she says.

"How?" I ask. "You could never be together."

"Yes, but I could still tell myself that Daniel loved me."

"Do you really believe that?"

She smiles, a sad half-smile. "Maybe not," she says.

The next morning, when Lily is packing her things to go, I ask her if she's ready.

"Yes," she says. "I'm ready. It will be fine." It makes me think of her wedding day, when she'd told me she wasn't afraid.

I take Lily on the streetcar to Dundas Street in Chinatown where her brother has his restaurant. She seems weary, but I tell myself that maybe she hasn't recovered from the trip yet. She's been in Canada a little more than a week, and there have been a lot of changes to get used to. When we arrive at the restaurant, I'm surprised at how large it is. It's still early so there are no customers, which makes it look even larger. The dining room is decorated with red embossed wallpaper and wall-to-wall red carpeting. Black-lacquered chairs and tables with white tablecloths dot the room. It has a quiet, refined air about it, the kind of place where businessmen come for lunch and which middle-aged couples choose for dinner.

As soon as we walk in, a young Chinese woman sees us and speaks to Lily in Chinese. I think she says Lily's name, her Chinese name, which I have forgotten. She is Number Three Brother's daughter-in-law, and she takes us back into the kitchen, where I see several people preparing little dumplings for dim sum, a favourite with the Chinese at lunchtime. We go up a flight of stairs to the second floor. Luckily the daughter-in-law has taken Lily's canvas suitcase; otherwise I don't think she would have made it without stopping at every step. I can see that Lily is nervous. She speaks animatedly to the daughter-in-law but also bows to her in a rather obsequious gesture that surprises me. I realize that Lily will probably be regarded as a servant, since she will be looking after this woman's children.

The daughter-in-law calls out a name at the top of the stairs, and I see a man, clearly older than Lily and me, with white hair and round, black-rimmed glasses. When he smiles, I recognize Number Three Brother. He has the same playful look in his eyes that he had when we were young. He also uses Lily's Chinese name and greets her formally in Chinese, probably welcoming her to his home. Then he turns to me. "Tatiana," he says, "how good to see you after all these years. I had no idea you were living in Toronto until my sister asked me to look up your family."

"I didn't know you were here, either. I've passed your restaurant hundreds of times without realizing."

He ushers us into a sitting room at the front of the apartment and asks his daughter-in-law, in English, to make us some tea. "This is Jenny," he says. "She is married to my son, Charlie. All English names. Can you believe they call me Sam here?"

I laugh. He seems genuinely glad to see us. I remember he was always the most easygoing of Lily's brothers. His years in the military are apparent in his bearing. He stands very straight, with no hint of an old man's stoop. He's impeccably groomed, wearing a white shirt buttoned to the collar and black trousers with a sharp crease down the centre. On his feet he wears soft leather slippers.

"My wife has gone to Eaton's to do some shopping," he says, "but she should be back any minute. I hope you'll stay for lunch, Tatiana."

I thank him but think it would probably be better if I don't stay. He and Lily have a lot to catch up on. She will be meeting the children and answering a lot of questions, just as she'd said. The children are out with their father but will be back for lunch. When we finish our tea, I get up to leave. At that moment, Lily's sister-in-law returns, and we are introduced. I have never met her before. Alice is elegantly dressed, and her hair is neatly coiffed in the short, head-hugging style that's popular. She's very attractive and reminds me in a way of Lily's mother.

Lily thanks me for letting her stay at my place to "rest up", as she puts it. I tell her it's been wonderful to see her after all these years. "I'm just down the road, you know. We can visit each other any time. Come whenever you feel like Italian food. I'm one of Gino's favourite customers." Her brother extends me an invitation to bring my family to the restaurant any time as his guests. I thank him and make my way back downstairs and out the front of the restaurant. A few patrons have begun to arrive for lunch, and I can smell the dim sum steaming in the kitchen.

Chapter Thirty-One

Iwonder how long it will be before I see Lily again. She'll have her hands full looking after three young children, but surely they'll give her some days off. I know that running a restaurant is almost a round-the-clock occupation, so I don't count on seeing her any time soon.

In fact, it's a month before I see Lily again. She doesn't phone, just arrives on my doorstep one Saturday morning. She rings the bell at the bottom of the stairs, and I come down and let her in. The hardware store is still open but will be closing at one o'clock. I'm surprised to see she has a small overnight bag with her. I take the bag, and we walk up the stairs together, stopping at every third step so Lily can catch her breath. I make a mental note to ask her if she's seen a doctor yet.

Once upstairs, I make her sit down, and I go into the kitchen to put the kettle on.

"Coffee or tea?" I ask.

"Tea, please, if that's all right."

"Of course it is," I say.

"And can I have a glass of water, please? I'm so thirsty."

"Coming right up."

I bring her the glass of water and sit down to wait for the kettle to boil. "How are you?" I ask.

"I'm fine," she says.

"You look tired. Are you sure you're all right?"

"I'm just tired," she sighs. "Three children. I can't keep up." She looks at the overnight bag, which I've left by the door. "I was wondering if I could spend the night," she says, hesitantly. "My nephew and his family are away until tomorrow night. I thought it would be like a holiday for me." She smiles.

"Of course," I say. "I'm glad you came. It'll be a holiday for both of us."

"I'm sorry I didn't call. No notice."

"Not a problem. My life isn't that busy."

"Thank you, Tatiana," she says, as if I've given her a gift.

She tells me that, although her duty is mainly to look after the children, two boys and a girl aged three to seven, she's also expected to do laundry and ironing, some dusting and general tidying up. "Everybody else works in the restaurant," she says, sipping some water. She puts her hand on her chest as if still trying to catch her breath. "Which means they're busy from mid-morning until late at night. They do have break times when they come upstairs with food from the restaurant. That's when they run errands, get groceries and do all the other things a busy family does." Lily sits back and closes her eyes. Then she tells me she has a small bedroom beside the kitchen at the back of the apartment. "A single bed, a chest of drawers, a wardrobe and a chair. It is enough. I just need a place to lie down and go to sleep." The more she talks, the more I realize how exhausted she is.

I heat up some soup, and we eat it with soda crackers. I wasn't expecting her, so I haven't stocked up on food like the first time. Never mind, I think. We'll go to Gino's for dinner. I can pick up a few things for tomorrow while Lily has a nap.

We go to Gino's early, before the dinner rush. I want to order something special, but Lily doesn't seem interested in the food. Since her nap, she's been listless and uncommunicative. I put it down to her fatigue and decide not to say anything. I order something nice for both of us—filet of sole with pan-fried potatoes—and hope she'll perk up a bit. She probably hasn't slept well and is feeling groggy.

She becomes more animated as the evening progresses, and I'm relieved. It makes me uneasy to see her so lethargic. I'm going to insist that she see a doctor, but not right now. I don't want to spoil her holiday.

Lily goes to bed about nine o'clock, and I pour myself a gin and tonic and turn the television on. As usual on a Saturday night, there's a hockey game on. I turn to an American channel from across the lake in Buffalo and watch a western about a bounty hunter. Then I watch an old movie with Joan Crawford, one of my favourite actresses. It's after midnight when I go to bed. Lily has closed her door, so I don't bother looking in. Maybe tomorrow I'll tackle the doctor question. I can start by telling her about my own aches and pains then recommend she go to my doctor for a check-up.

Lily doesn't wake up early the next morning, and she still isn't up when I go into the bathroom around eight, so I let her sleep. I make myself coffee and toast and sit at the kitchen table reading my book. By ten o'clock, I'm a little concerned, so I walk down the hall and listen at her door. I can't hear anything, so I open the door partway and look in. The curtains are drawn, so the room is gloomy but not dark. Lily's asleep on her side with her back to me, the covers pulled up to her neck. I'll give her one more hour, I think. This is probably the first chance she's had in a month to sleep in.

Olga phones at about ten thirty, and I'm sure the noise of the telephone ringing will wake Lily. I have set the ringer on high so I can hear the phone anywhere in the apartment. I chat with Olga for about ten minutes, fully expecting a bleary-eyed Lily to come wandering in, but she doesn't. Now I'm genuinely worried. After I say goodbye to Olga and hang up the phone, I go to Lily's room and open the door wide. She hasn't moved. *No*, I think. *She couldn't be.* I walk over to the bed and touch her shoulder. Then I

shake her. *Oh, God, Lily. Please don't be dead.* But I know she is.
I go to the phone and call my doctor's emergency number.
He's been my doctor for fifteen years, and he knows me well.
"What is it, Tatiana?" he asks. "Are you all right?"
"I'm fine," I say. "But I have a friend staying with me, and I
think she might have passed away in her sleep. I can't wake her
up."
"I'll be right over," he says.
I go back into the bedroom to sit with Lily, half hoping
she'll surprise me and wake up. I berate myself for not having
said something sooner to her about going to the doctor. I should
have guessed she had a bad heart. Then I see the envelope.
She has propped it up on the night table beside the bed,
between a glass of water and the lamp. She's written TATIANA
on the front in clear, block letters. I'm afraid to open it. I look
at the motionless figure on the bed. *What have you done, Lily?*
She's sealed the envelope, and I'm reluctant to tear it open. I go
into the front room and open the drawer in the desk where I pay
my bills. I pick up my letter opener. It seems important to do
everything with a great deal of care and attention to detail. I slit
open the envelope and pull out the folded sheet of paper. "Dear
Tatiana," it begins.

*Forgive me for what I have done. I could not think of
another way. I could not do it in my brother's house
because of the children, in case it brought them bad luck.*
*I did a terrible thing, and there can be no forgiveness.
I took another woman's child from her and ended her life
also. It was my gun that killed Daniel, and my hand that
pulled the trigger. I told myself I did it to protect my own
son from what I feared Daniel might do to him. But now
I believe that was not true. I did it in anger. My heart
was filled with jealousy and thoughts of revenge. My own
heart poisoned me, and I could not think properly. I can*

*blame only myself. I loved Daniel unwisely, with a passion
that was eating me like a disease. I punished him for
not loving me, but I told myself that I was like a woman
warrior protecting my family from some terrible evil.*

*The police inspector was right. My husband and
Number Two Brother put Daniel's body in the river. Wu-
ling tried to protect me for the honour of the family, but
after he was gone, I became a ghost. First they took my
son away and made me a servant in their home. Now I am
a servant to my brother's family.*

*You spoke of justice for Daniel. I have not paid for
my crime, but I have spent every day since his death in a
prison of suffering. There is nothing left for me except to
die. I am very tired. Do not pity me, and try not to hate me.*

Lily

The doctor arrives with his black bag. The first thing he does
is check Lily's pulse. Then he pulls back her eyelids and looks
at her eyes.

"Did she have access to morphine?" he asks.

"I don't know. She left China a couple of months ago.
Maybe she brought some with her."

"It's illegal, you know."

"No one would suspect Lily. She had one suitcase. They
probably didn't even search her."

He looks around the room, sees the glass of water on the
bedside table and opens the drawer. An empty white paper
packet lies folded on the bottom. He picks it up, runs his finger
over it and tastes the white powder residue.

"Did she leave a note?" he asks.

"Yes." He doesn't ask to see it.

"How long have you known her?"

"Since we were children in Shanghai together. I guess you
could say she was my best friend."

"Does she have family here?"

"Yes. A brother."

"You'll need to call him about arranging to have her body picked up by a funeral home. I'll write up the death certificate. If you call the police, there'll be a lot of commotion, and nothing will be achieved." He pulls a form out of his bag and fills in the details as I give them to him. Under cause of death he writes: Heart Attack.

"Thank you," I say. "I'm very grateful."

After they take Lily's body away, I feel more alone than ever. Now I sit for hours, looking out the window at how the winter is finally turning into spring. My mind keeps wandering back and asking the questions I've never been able to answer. I still can't answer them. I can only go over the events again and again, looking for some reason, some meaning. I think I'm looking for absolution. I want to believe I wasn't to blame for what happened, but I keep coming back to the relationship between cause and effect, action and reaction. If I had not introduced Daniel to Lily, if I had not told her about seeing him at the Kitty Kat, if I had been a better person…if…if…if…

I think about the nuns at Les Soeurs de Notre Dame where I went to school. They were so sure of where to draw the lines in an uncertain world. So clear about when to punish and when to praise. Maybe that's when I turned my back on the conviction they tried so hard to instil in us. I could not be so easily convinced, as Olga was, that there was a God in Heaven who had all the answers and who watched over us. Have faith, they said, but there was no room for that kind of faith in a mind that wanted to discover possibilities. I wanted to find out what life was like on the high wire, without a net. I never contemplated the consequences of a fall.

Unlike Annette, I did not keep telling "*l'histoire de ma vie*." I did not add flourishes so it would be more memorable. I preferred not to remember. Then Lily came, and I discovered there is no such thing as forgetting.